ABIDE WITH ME

ABIDE WITH ME

JANE WILLAN

PROLOGUE

The seagull caught a gust of wind and left the high cliff behind. It circled wide, soaring above the choppy waves of the Irish Sea before swooping down onto the frozen beach. After a few investigative hops, the scavenging bird began to peck at the girl's red hair which lay in tangled icicles on the sand. Face down, one leg bent, she offered no protest. Nor did she notice the seawater and foam that filled her wellingtons and soaked the edge of her anorak. The persistent gull next attacked the girl's mobile lying next to her, snatched it up in its black beak and glided down the beach before dropping it on the rocks. With a lonely cry, the gull flew off.

The morning sun crested the cliff and a few miles to the south, the bell in the Pryderi village clock tower, constructed a few years after the landing of William of Orange, chimed the early hour. The inhabitants of Pryderi awoke to the wintry morning, only nine days since Christmas and three days left before the Feast of Epiphany.

The Buttered Crust Tea Shop opened its doors to a line of eager customers while Father Selwyn, the much beloved vicar at St. Anselm Church, tossed back the last swallow of coffee brought in a thermos from the rectory kitchen and stepped into the pulpit to greet his usual morning crowd of six faithful worshipers. And less than a mile away, atop the steep winding climb of Church Lane, the Anglican Sisters at Gwenafwy Abbey pushed back their chairs from the long refectory table to begin the day's work. They wondered why their young guest, Claire MacDonagh, had missed one of Sister Gwenydd's hearty Welsh breakfasts.

The village and the Abbey stirred to life. But for the young woman lying on the beach, there would be no bustling day of work and laughter. For her, the end had come.

CHAPTER 1

"It isn't that I don't *want* to accompany Claire into the village to introduce her to the Archbishop," Sister Agatha said, pulling out a chair and taking a seat at the long farm table across from Reverend Mother. She breathed deeply. The Abbey kitchen offered its early morning aromas of sugar, cinnamon, and baking bread. Sitting at the farm table always brought her a sense of contentment.

"Former Archbishop," Reverend Mother corrected her. Reginald Thurston, retired Archbishop of Wales, had recently located to Pryderi and moved into the Castle View Retirement Condominiums on the renovated estate of Lord Ednyfed. He said he wanted to throw himself into village life after the relentless demands of the archdiocese in Cardiff. And indeed, Sister Agatha often saw him, swathed in his overcoat, muffler, and mittens, stopping by the Buttered Crust Tea Shop, or filling a basket of groceries at Lettuce-Eat-Vegan, or attending the lecture series at the Public Library.

"It's just that today is Tuesday," Sister Agatha continued. "You *know* it's my day to write at the Buttered Crust." Every Tuesday, immediately following Matins, Sister Agatha hurried to the

Buttered Crust Tea Shop where she ensconced herself in the back booth, ordered a pot of tea and a Welsh cake; and then, with her dogeared copy of *Strunk and White* at the ready, she plunged into her own private world of murder and mayhem. Today would be especially crucial. She had left off last Tuesday mired in a plot more convoluted at every page turn. Dead bodies had stacked up while Bates Melanchthon, her protagonist and gumshoe detective, fell hard under the romantic charms of a woman lieutenant at Scotland Yard. Bates-in-love was not something that she had planned. Yet without her bidding, a passionate romance had just poured itself onto the page.

"And anyway," she said. "Why does Claire need to talk to Reggie? Isn't she here to interview all of us at the Abbey?"

"I know and I'm sorry," Reverend Mother said, choosing a scone from the basket in the center of the table. "Claire hopes to get a quote from Reggie concerning the new nuns. I want her to have a proper introduction instead of just barging in on him. Reggie is warm and friendly most of the time, but I have noticed, he doesn't like surprises."

Claire MacDonagh, an eager young reporter from *The Church Times*, was spending a week at the Abbey writing a feature article about the sisters from Los Angeles. Ten nuns-- all in their early 20's-- had arrived at Gwenafwy Abbey only a few weeks earlier. They had said farewell to the Sisters of Transfiguration Convent in Los Angeles and traveled to Gwenafwy Abbey in the North of Wales bringing with them a certain lively festiveness, as well as a mountain of electronic equipment.

Sister Agatha never said so, but she took a dim view of Americans. And she did wish the new sisters had arrived with a translator to interpret their millennial slang. But she had to admit, she loved the laughter and energy that swept into the room every time a group of the young nuns breezed through the door.

She picked up the teapot and topped off Reverend Mother's cup and then her own. The fragrant aromas of the Abbey kitchen mingled with the soft contralto of Sister Gwenydd, the convent's resident chef, singing as she kneaded bread dough on the sideboard. Sister Agatha couldn't make out the words to the song, but she thought one line might have been "who let the dogs out?" Maybe Sister Callwen was right and she did need to get her hearing checked.

She weighed her options as she sipped her tea. A brisk walk down Church Lane and into the village on a winter day might be just the ticket to get the muse back. Perhaps even figure out the path that Bates Melanchthon's romance should take. *Head over heels? Heartthrob? Or an upcoming walk down the aisle?*

"Not a problem, Reverend Mother," she said, pulling her woolly hat out of her jumper pocket and squishing it over her short gray hair. "I'll be happy to take Claire into Pryderi to meet Reggie. A walk will do me good. Clear my head."

"Splendid," Reverend Mother said, slouching a bit as she stood. Reverend Mother, an inch over six feet tall, had been a star basketball player at St. David's before she left it all to take orders at Gwenafwy. "Now if you will excuse me, I have a pile of paperwork and a call to the bank all awaiting me in my office."

"Don't you want a woolly hat or a scarf?" Sister Agatha asked, her voice muffled behind her own scarf. "It's brass monkeys out here."

Claire's red hair blew wildly, her cheeks and nose bright pink. "I'm fine," she replied. "I like an invigorating walk."

Sister Agatha opened the latch to the Abbey's wrought iron front gate with her red-mittened hand. The latch gave a rasping clank. She should ask Ben Holden, the Abbey caretaker, to hit it with a spot of oil.

"Suit yourself," she said. Sister Agatha wore her woolly hat with matching jumper and mittens from November to March. "I think you might fancy one of Sister Winifred's hats. They're not just warm, they're stylish." Sister Winifred not only ran the business side of the Abbey's cheese production, she knitted obsessively and kept the entire convent outfitted in winter wear.

"Did she knit that one?" Claire asked, nodding towards Sister Agatha's woolly hat. She swung a small green rucksack over her back.

"Indeed." Sister Agatha pulled the ear flaps down with a tug. "With wool from our own sheep."

"Well, you do look...warm."

As they started down the steep hill towards Pryderi, stepping carefully over the frozen ruts of the graveled road, Sister Agatha breathed in, filling her lungs with the sharp biting air. She couldn't imagine living anywhere but North Wales. Even now with the sun barely breaking through the clouds, the Welsh countryside held its charms. Brown fields bordered by ancient stone walls formed squares like an unfurled quilt. Clumps of purple heather and flocks of white sheep meandered up to the edges of gray stone crofts whose chimneys plumed smoke into the morning sky. "Are your parents in Dublin?" she asked, turning to Claire.

"When they're home, they live in Dublin. Right now they are the hiking in the Himalayas."

"Oh my, how adventurous." Sister Agatha occasionally wondered if she needed to get out of Wales more often. A little more adventure in her life would be grist for the mill when it came to her writing.

"They're very-crunchy-granola people, if you know what I mean."

"Of course." She didn't have a clue what Claire meant, but she would ask Sister Gwenydd who kept her finger on the pulse of all things contemporary.

"And so they're off the grid."

"Off the grid sounds good to me," Sister Agatha replied. "We should all take a step back from screens." Sister Agatha paused and stood for a moment looking down into the valley. She could just see the spire of St. Anselm Church, built in 1454 by the Normans, as it rose above the slate rooftops of the village houses. The tower of Pryderi Castle to the east cast its long shadow, while the River Pwy, which formed the western boundary of the village, glinted in the winter sunlight like a ribbon set on fire.

"Is it hard having your parents so far away?" she asked, continuing their walk down Church Hill.

"A little. I'm close with my cousin, Peter. He might visit while I'm at the Abbey. He loves Wales and everything Welsh."

"Sounds like my kind of person."

"It isn't so much that I *miss* my parents, I only wish they didn't insist on such exotic hobbies. Like mountain climbing." Clare laughed. "It's not easy when your parents are the fun ones and you're the boring one who stays at home."

"There is something to be said for living life to the fullest."

The two women, young and old, fell into a companionable silence as they strode along, heads down, into the brisk wind. She knew that Claire was a recent graduate of the journalism school at Trinity College. Although Sister Agatha would never give up fiction for journalism, she admired a journalist's ability to write quickly under deadline. Claire's articles read with a straightforward, almost cheeky prose that Sister Agatha found refreshing. She wondered how the young writer would portray the Abbey in her article, especially the new sisters who had left their modern convent in Los Angeles because they desired a more traditional community-- where they could wear the conventional long habit, participate in the celebration of Hours, and serve the poor.

"Tell me about the former Archbishop. Reggie, as you call him," Claire said. "I'm hoping to round out my article with some quotes by people in the church hierarchy. Stuff like the future of the church or what religious orders can bring to the world today."

"He served as Archbishop of Wales for nearly 20 years. Did a terrific job according to Father Selwyn." Father Selwyn had been Sister Agatha's closest friend since primary school. There were those in the village who thought the two had been more than friends when they were young, but then at the age of twenty, Sister Agatha surprised everyone by taking orders at Gwenafwy Abbey. That same year, Father Selwyn had headed to seminary. "Although Reggie is a bit of a politician, if you ask me."

"Like how?"

"Oh nothing negative. Just a bit *smooth*. Always has an answer to make everyone happy. But I guess you have to be that way if you want to be an Archbishop these days."

"You don't like him?" Claire asked.

"Of course I like him! Reginald Thurston is a stand-up chap. Old Wales. Or how people in Wales used to be. He got his start at Trinity College, in fact. Just like you." Sister Agatha paused to admire three Welsh Mountain sheep huddled together in front of a stone croft.

"He went to Trinity?" Claire stopped, and looked back at her.

"Indeed." Sister Agatha loved lambing time at the Abbey. All the sisters did. "Undergrad there and then on to St. John's for seminary."

"How old is he?"

"Not sure. Not that old. Seventy, if he's a day." No doubt *old* in Claire's estimate. For the first time in her life, Sister Agatha had grown conscious of her age. Something about turning sixty-two perhaps.

"So he was at Trinity about fifty years ago. Which meant he was there back when the Old Library was open to anyone. When you could hang out in the stacks with all those ancient books, pull them off the shelves, flip through them. Can you imagine?"

"I can't. It must have been thrilling. Though, not at all nice for the books." Sister Agatha was the Abbey librarian and she loved all libraries--the quiet turn of a page, the faint scent of book binding and parchment. But there was no library as magnificent as the Old Library at Trinity College in Dublin. "What an inspiring place to write."

"Yeah," Claire said absently. "So what year did Reggie graduate from Trinity?"

"Early 1960's I would guess. Why?"

"Just curious. My grandfather was at Trinity around then."

"Was he a writer?"

"Barrister."

"Ah." She stumbled on a rut in the road and caught herself just before pitching headlong. "Are you finding enough material for your article about the Abbey? Because you're welcome to use the Abbey library if it would help."

"Mostly I want to get to know all of the nuns. Immerse myself in the culture."

"Any surprises? While immersed, that is?"

"Lots actually. I expected a group of Anglican nuns to be, well, you know, sedate. Instead, you're all so… interesting."

They rounded the final bend in Church Lane and crossed the footbridge over the River Pkwy --more babbling brook than raging river.

"Of course we're *interesting*." Sister Agatha shook her head. *Youth.*

Soon they were headed down Main Street and stopped to peer into the shop windows along the brick cobbled street: Just-for-You Florist, Between-the-Covers-Bookstore, Lettuce-Eat-Vegan, The Fatted Calf. They stopped at the window of the Buttered Crust Teashop. The teashop was doing a fast trade in scones and Welsh cakes and Sister Agatha cast a lingering eye. The far booth at the back was exactly where she wanted to be right now--her laptop open and an endless supply of tea and cakes. She imagined herself typing with great purpose. Bates Melanchthon might exhume a decaying corpse, or discover poison in an unsuspecting victim, maybe interrogate a suspect with just the hint of intimidation, or preferably end the romance with his new love--the Scotland Yard lieutenant. Gruff, abrupt, but heartbroken all the same. *The job comes first,* he would say, letting her down easy.

"Come on." Claire turned abruptly from the window and began to walk rapidly down the sidewalk.

"Why? What is it?" Sister Agatha said. She scanned the dining room. A tall, lithe young man leaned back in his chair perusing a menu. He had a shock of blond hair that flopped into his eyes, he wore a navy jumper and khaki pants. Even at a glance, he gave off a handsome yet unconscious demeanor. She wondered if the long silver auto, an Austin Healey Vantage, parked in front of The Buttered Crust belonged to him. Father Selwyn had tutored her in British cars. He drove a BMW Mini himself. She trotted after Claire. "What upset you? Do you know that tall boy at the middle table?"

"No. Forget it." Claire picked up her pace.

"Forget what exactly?" Sister Agatha broke into a trot to keep up.

"It was no one. *Please.*"

"Slow down." She grabbed Claire's sleeve and pulled her to a halt. She turned the young woman around to face her. Claire's eyes snapped and her face was red. "My goodness," Sister Agatha said. "Who did you see? And why is that person having such an effect on you?"

"An ex-boyfriend. Didn't expect to see him. That's all."

"What's he doing in Pryderi? Is he from Dublin?"

"I've no idea why he's here." Claire turned around and this time power-walked down the street. "And yes, he's from Dublin."

"Ex-boyfriend? You seem awfully upset if he's an ex." Inexperienced in the boyfriend business, she at least knew that 'ex-boyfriend' was a loosely-used term. "Is he an ex that you still have feelings for?" She could hear Sister Callwen's voice in her head telling her that it was none of her business.

"No!" Claire sighed and slowed her pace. Her face had flushed all the way to the roots of her red hair. The young woman suddenly unzipped her coat and shoved her hands in her pockets. She flipped her hair back. "Forget it. Seriously." They turned the corner by the library and headed towards Castle View Retirement Condominiums.

She gave Claire a sidelong glance. The wall of silence the young woman had put up could have served as a fortress against the Norman invasion. So much for a pleasant walk to the village to clear her head and summon the muse. Oh well. *Maybe the Archbishop would have cake.*

CHAPTER 2

"Would you like cake?" the former Archbishop of Wales asked. Reggie stood in the doorway of a small front room. He wore his usual frayed wool jumper pulled over his rounded shoulders set off by a tab collar. Pear-shaped and short, he always put Sister Agatha in mind of a turtle emerging from its shell. His wrinkled corduroys might have been purchased the year of the Queen's Coronation, along with his worn brown leather slippers. His shock of white hair, surprisingly thick, was perpetually tousled. Sister Agatha thought his brown eyes held an expectant curiosity as if entertaining the two of them for morning tea promised intrigue and had the potential to lead anywhere. Reggie had served as a kind and gracious Bishop, courtly in the old fashioned manner that Sister Agatha admired, and beloved by the Church in Wales. He might not have been as adept at spreadsheets, budgets, and membership numbers as the present bishop, The Right Reverend Suzanne Bainton, but he exuded boundless goodwill, coupled with a generosity of spirit which compensated for any administrative shortcomings. At least that's what the clergy always told themselves when they tried to make sense of his jumbled diocesan spending.

Sister Agatha, relieved to be out of the biting wind, settled into a tattered but sturdy sofa. The small front room emanated warmth and welcome. And it lacked a television. She liked that. Screens now dominated life, and the less of them, the better, she always claimed--although she was never more than a hands-reach from her own mobile. End tables stood at either side of the couch one holding a large tiffany lamp and the other, a towering stack of theological journals. Reggie's long-haired Persian cat, Esmeralda, lay curled in front of a cheery fire that burned in a fireplace grate.

The front room was dominated however, by something far more captivating than Esmeralda. A miniature cathedral, designed and constructed by Reggie himself and the size of a substantial dollhouse, sat atop a table in front of the bay window. Velvet drapes, deep purple and luxurious were pulled shut behind, giving the cathedral a dramatic backdrop. She recognized it as the Cathedral of St. Asaph. The roof was open, so you could see inside and Sister Agatha, who had sat in the real St. Asaph cathedral dozens of times, noticed the stunning accuracy and minute detail of this miniature St. Asaph. Endless hours of painstaking and meticulous workmanship had obviously gone into its creation. She glanced around. While the apartment held a casual, studied sloppiness, the miniature stood out for its detail and perfection. Maybe Reggie put all his energy into his hobby-- the creation of perfect miniatures--and didn't bring such compulsiveness into his everyday life.

"I believe my housekeeper has left a tin with something that looks suspiciously like her famous almond cake. Give me a moment and we shall all have a proper tea." As Reggie bounced from the room, Claire shrugged off her coat and stood, peering into the miniature cathedral.

"He built this?" She looked at Sister Agatha, her eyes wide.

"Yes. It's been his hobby for years," she said, without looking up from her mobile. She resisted sighing. The morning half gone and not a word written on her novel. Reggie was probably thinking they were settling in for a long cozy chat. That was always the problem with retired priests. They had nowhere to go and they thought the entire world shared their leisure. "I'm sure he'll be thrilled to tell you all about it."

Claire continued to examine the miniature cathedral and then pulled out her mobile and snapped a few photos. When she turned around and took a selfie, Sister Agatha tried not to roll her eyes. What was it with the young and selfies?

"This is really amazing," Claire said, turning back to the model and leaning in again. "That's interesting..." she murmured.

"What's interesting?" Sister Agatha twisted in the couch and glanced impatiently into the kitchen.

"Nothing. Well, the whole thing really. The whole thing is interesting." She took another photo.

At that moment, Reggie pushed in backwards through the door from the kitchen carrying a tray with several slices of almond cake, three mugs, a teapot, sugar, and milk.

"Here we are," he said, his smile exuberant. When he saw Claire holding up her mobile to take another photo, his smile disappeared, and he clattered the tray onto the table. "Young lady, if you don't mind, I prefer that you not photograph the model cathedral."

"Sorry," Claire said brightly, slipping her phone into her pocket. "Can you tell me about the tiny bible inside."

"Not much to tell. A bible has sat on the Saint Asaph pulpit for centuries. So I created an exact replica."

"How?"

"Paper, ink, paint. Lots of tiny lettering and painting. It was great fun, actually."

"It's like an antique," Claire said.

"Well, that's the idea, isn't it? To appear authentic. The real cathedral itself is five hundred years old."

"Could I take a closer look at the bible? Take it out and photograph it? I would love to do a story on how you made it. The artwork, what you modeled it after. You know, a human interest story but with an historical bent."

"I'm sure it would make a wonderful addition to your newspaper, but I must ask you to not touch anything in the cathedral. It is not a doll's house to be played with. And the little bible is a replica I fashioned so many years ago that I fear if you handle it, it will fall apart." As he poured tea into each cup, Sister Agatha noticed that his hand trembled slightly. Father Selwyn hadn't mentioned a health problem with Reggie, but maybe his sudden retirement wasn't such a mystery. "Now," he said, smiling again and setting the teapot on the tray. "I understand, Miss MacDonagh, you are writing a story for *The Church Times*?" He took a seat in the recliner, his voice once again affable and relaxed. "Wonderful newspaper, don't you agree, Sister Agatha? Such a pity they are going to online subscriptions only. I detest the loss of the hard copy."

Sister Agatha sat back and enjoyed her almond cake and listened to Claire explain to Reggie that although she was writing a story on the nuns at Gwenafwy Abbey, she really hoped to discuss the future of the Church. Sister Agatha took another piece of almond cake off the platter. The future of the Church was definitely a two-pieces-of-cake question. She wanted to roll her eyes as Reggie began to wax eloquent about fighting the good fight as Sister Agatha and her sisters were. He spoke a bit too glowingly, in her mind, about the vitality and influence of the Church on the future of the world. Well, she thought, maybe he is right. *A little faith, that's all that's needed.*

They finally stood to leave. Claire's eyes strayed again to the miniature cathedral. "I would love to interview you about your hobby. You know, making miniatures," she said.

"Delighted to chat sometime," Reggie said, as he opened the door to a gust of wind. "My next project is going to be the cathedral at Cadeirlan Bangor."

"Will it also have a bible on the pulpit?" Claire asked, standing on the front stoop.

"Well, as most churches do keep a bible on the altar then, yes. Of course."

"Wait," Claire said. "I've left my rucksack."

"I'll get it," Reggie offered. They heard him say, "Esmeralda, *off!* You fat feline!" Sister Agatha heard a thump and imagined that Esmeralda wasn't easy to move. "Here's your bag, dear," Reggie said, reappearing on the doorstep, brushing cat hairs off his pants.

Sister Agatha wrapped her scarf around her neck and watched as Claire rummaged through the rucksack. "Something missing?"

"Just checking for my keys. Do you know that Sister Elfrida charges a fee if you lose your key?"

"Do I know? We could pay off the loan on the new barn roof with her system of fee collection." They headed back towards Church Lane and the Abbey, this time the wind at their backs. "So what did you think of our Archbishop?"

"Interesting. Charming." Claire said. "But I find his understanding of the future of the church a bit naive. Old school, at least. Don't you?"

"Perhaps. Some say that the Church needs to reinvent itself."

"How?"

"No clue. But the idea is all the rage among the clergy."

Claire shoved her hands in her pockets, and they walked without speaking for a few minutes. Sister Agatha wondered about the boyfriend-who-wasn't-a-boyfriend sitting at the Buttered Crust Teashop.

"I'd like to ask him about that miniature cathedral," she said as they started up the hill to the Abbey. "For one thing, how did he make the bible look so authentic?"

"Every trade has its tricks, I suppose."

"You'd have to be an artist to make the colors look so...so...medieval."

"Reggie has lots of talents. He may be an accomplished artist, for all I know." Sister Agatha said, breathing a bit hard on the steep hill. She really needed to get back to the Silver Sneakers program with Father Selwyn at the Pryderi Gym. "You're very observant. You would have been a good detective,"

Claire grinned, the wind whipping her red hair. "A journalist *is* a detective. At least if you want to uncover a really good story."

CHAPTER 3

"Eighty gallons of milk will yield approximately sixty-six pounds of cheese," Sister Callwen said, projecting her voice above the quiet chatter of the young sisters who stood in small groups, taking notes. Sister Agatha leaned against the back wall of the cheese barn and looked around. Times had certainly changed at the Abbey, she thought. And no doubt for the better, she reminded herself.

The older nuns clustered together by the drying racks ready to contribute to the tutorial if needed. Sister Agatha noticed that not everyone was present. She remembered that Reverend Mother had excused Sister Gwenydd from all cheese making since work in the kitchen consumed her time and energy. Sister Harriet wasn't there either. Sister Harriet was knocking it out on her graphic novel sequestered away in her art studio. Sister Harriet had a pressing deadline with her publisher. Sister Agatha, although envious, rejoiced with Sister Harriet for her literary success. And looked forward to the day when she had a pressing deadline with a publisher.

"Remember to smooth out the cheesecloth before you pour in the milk. And never, never disturb the heating milk, other than with very gentle stirring." Sister Callwen shot a glance at Sister Agatha who raised her eyebrows in return. Sister Agatha had been known to use a heavy hand with the cheese and was now relegated to tasks that took a little less finesse. It wasn't that she didn't support the cheese making process, or the much-needed income from the sales from their award-winning cheese, *Heavenly Gouda*. It was simply that hers was a vocation of print, ink, and paper. She would much rather be tucked away in the attic library, writing her own book, or cataloging and shelving the books of others.

A few of the new nuns appeared to be naturals at cheese making. Sister Juniper readily measured and weighed with a deft hand as she chatted with Sister Theodora who watched the thermometer like a hawk. Sister Samantha, on the other hand, slouched, her head bent over her phone. Reverend Mother had shared with her senior staff that she was a bit perplexed about what to do with the young nuns and their mobiles. Although even the senior nuns and Reverend Mother herself often checked their mobiles, the new sisters were positively glued to them. Reverend Mother hesitated to ban mobiles--Sister Agatha knew it was most likely because Reverend Mother would miss her own too much. But there had to be some reasonable compromise. She had declared that no phones could be in the chapel and or at meals. Except Sister Elfrida, the Gwenafwy Abbey business manager whose job it was to be at the ready twenty-four seven to check on cheese orders from the online ordering site.

"And please take care," Sister Callwen continued, "As you begin to strain out the whey. *Do not get in a hurry.* The curds will slowly surface as the whey drips out and you will be left with a wonderful pool of whey at the base of your cheesecloth." She demonstrated by holding up a sack of dripping whey. The young women cheered. Sister Agatha didn't share in the excitement but was glad someone did.

Across the room, Claire stood against the far wall, rapidly

writing. Sister Agatha was reminded of the moment at the window of The Buttered Crust.

She watched as Sister Callwen divided the new nuns into small groups each with an older sister to walk through the steps of cheese making one more time. Sister Agatha was paired with Sister Samantha and Sister Theodora. They chose a quiet spot near the aging room and the two young nuns immediately sat on the floor; habit skirts tucked around crossed legs. Sister Theodora looked up. "Sorry Sister Agatha. But we've been standing all day. Mind if we sit? Criss-cross-applesauce?"

"I beg your pardon?" Sister Agatha said, looking down as Sister Theodora pointed to her crossed legs. "Oh right. I always called it...never mind." She lowered herself slowly to the floor hoping her knees did not creak audibly. As the three sat facing each other, Claire joined them. Sister Agatha noticed with a slight annoyance how easily she dropped to the floor. *Criss-cross applesauce indeed.*

"Don't mind me," Claire said. "I'm only here to listen and take notes."

Sister Agatha turned when she heard a quiet snort from Sister Samantha. She looked at her and raised her eyebrows. "Is there a problem Sister?" she asked. Sister Theodora looked away as Claire glanced up from her notes.

"No," Sister Samantha said. "Of course not."

"So let's start at the beginning," Sister Agatha said. "What is the first task that begins every cheese day?"

"Thoroughly wipe down the cheese room equipment with a bleach and water mix," Sister Theodora said.

"Right," Sister Agatha responded. "Then..."

"Wait a sec," Claire cut in. "Before you launch into the whole thing, could I just get a quote from each of you and then I can go? I don't need to be here the whole time."

"Of course," Sister Agatha said. *The impatience of youth.* "Sister Theodora, why don't you start us off?"

"Well, I would like to say...that I am really enjoying learning something new," she responded, her voice bright. "And I love the idea of making one's own food. You know, being self-sufficient. Farm-to-table if you will. I also like the fact that the Abbey has such a cool way to earn money." Sister Theodora sat back and leaning to the side, snapped a selfie with Sister Agatha, the racks of Heavenly Gouda in the background.

"Cool, indeed." Sister Agatha thought to herself. The never-ending quest for the perfect selfie. What would Jesus have done? *Okay guys, one selfie more with the prodigal son! How about a selfie here in front of the Sea of Galilee? Or better yet, hold on, I'll walk on the water one more time!*

"That's super helpful, Sister Theodora, thanks," Claire said. "Okay Sister Samantha. A statement about cheese, please?"

"No comment," Sister Samantha said, looking directly at Claire.

"No comment? You have nothing to say about cheese?" Claire didn't look as surprised as Sister Agatha felt.

"Sister Samantha, I am sure that Claire just wants...." She stopped when Sister Samantha picked up her phone and glancing at it, tapped the screen.

Sister Theodora looked from one to the other, nervously yanking off her headscarf.

"Sister Samantha, please put your phone down, if you will. Surely you have something to say about cheese making for Claire's article?"

Sister Samantha dropped her mobile into her lap. "No," she said. "I really don't."

"That's okay," Claire said, standing up. "Not a problem." They watched as she turned and walked across the room, stopping at Sister Callwen's group.

CHAPTER 4

"He doesn't want to get up on his feet, is all," Sister Agatha said. Bartimaeus, the Abbey's old Shetland pony, a favorite of all the nuns but especially Sister Agatha, lay on the floor of his stall in the pony barn. Sister Callwen and Ben Holden, the Abbey sheep herder and all-around-farmhand, stood next to Sister Agatha gazing down at him. The pony's sides heaved; his eyes were open but staring. Sister Agatha draped a prayer shawl over his bony frame and piled the floor with clean straw. She knelt next to him and stroked his ears on the silky part of his thick winter fur.

"When a horse, or in this case, a Shetland pony, lies down and won't get up, isn't that a cause for concern?" Sister Callwen asked, turning to Ben.

"Maybe he just wants a bit of a lie-down," Sister Agatha said, hating the fact that her voice broke.

The sisters had rescued the pony ten years earlier from a questionable petting zoo in the village when they realized that it was blind, and that the owner was about to sell it to the proverbial glue factory. The sisters had led the pony up Church Lane and to the Abbey by bribing him with the pieces of peppermint that Sister Matilda always carried in her habit pocket. He had settled contentedly into his new life at the Abbey and the nuns named him Bartimaeus, after the story of the blind beggar in the Gospel. Sister Callwen had said at the time that he certainly fit his name, since he was not only blind, but also a shameless beggar. Bartimaeus would stand at the edge of the fence facing the kitchen door of the Abbey neighing and stamping a hoof until someone appeared with an apple or a sugar cube. Of late though, he had stopped begging. He only wanted to stay in the barn, in his warm stall.

"Should we get Dr. Ross?" Sister Callwen asked. Tupper Ross had served the animals of the Abbey for years, rushing up Church Lane at all hours during lambing time or when Sister Harriet found a sparrow with a broken wing in her winter rose garden.

Ben looked from Bartimaeus to Sister Agatha and then cast a quick glance at Sister Callwen. "He's old, Sisters. You understand that, right?"

"I understand no such thing," Sister Agatha said. "And anyway, we're all old."

"We don't actually know his age," Ben said. "But Tupper thinks he's getting up there."

"What exactly is 'up there'?" Sister Callwen asked. Bending down, she adjusted the prayer shawl, tucking it in around the pony's thin flanks. Sister Agatha wondered about Sister Callwen's claim to dislike animals.

"A little pony like this one could live to be near 30 years, I would think. Old Bart here must be past that."

"I will agree that he is not in the prime of youth, but he isn't anywhere near.... near.... the end," Sister Agatha said. She coughed to regain her composure. "Get Tupper Ross out here and maybe he'll have some vitamins or special feed for him." Pulling up her habit skirts, she squatted next to the pony again and stroked his fetlock. "Right, old boy?" she said softly. He nickered gently and then to everyone's surprise heaved himself up to his feet, tossing his head and nearly knocking Sister Agatha backwards. "See there," she said, standing up quickly and taking a little hop to keep from falling into the water trough. She dusted off the front of her apron. "Like I said, a bit of a lie-down on a cold day. And who could blame him?" She picked up the curry comb and ran it over the curve of the pony's back. Sister Callwen retrieved the prayer shawl from the straw and folded it slowly. She and Ben shared a long look.

"You haven't forgotten that I'm leaving on holiday in the morning," Ben said, as he forked sweet-smelling timothy hay into Bartimaeus' manger. Ben was heading to Yorkshire for a sheep dog competition and a visit to his daughter in Thirsk.

"You'll be seeing that new grandson of yours won't you, Ben?" Sister Callwen asked. She placed the folded shawl onto a stack of feed bags.

Ben offered a rare grin. "I will. Three months old now. A wee bairn. I'll be gone ten days and so if the old boy goes down again, call Tupper yourself. Sister Elfrida has him on speed dial."

Anxious to avoid the topic of Bartimaeus' declining health, she told Sister Callwen about Sister Samantha's curt response to Claire in the cheese barn.

"What do you think made her respond so abruptly to Claire? To such an innocuous question?" Sister Callwen asked.

Sister Agatha pulled her woolly hat further over her ears. "No clue. Maybe it's nothing."

"I am a little concerned since Reverend Mother specifically told all of us to be as welcoming and gracious as we could to Claire. And yet, Sister Samantha expresses this sulky hostility." Sister Callwen wrapped her muffler around her neck. She was enveloped in azure blue-- jumper, mittens, hat, and scarf. Sister Winifred did not take color choice lightly and she was spot on with Sister Callwen. A cool, calm blue fit her to a tee. "We live in *community* and grievances need to be aired. Discussed openly without rancor."

"Should we take it to Reverend Mother?" Sister Agatha asked, thinking that she was already not telling Reverend Mother about the photos that Claire took against the wishes of Reggie. Although, everyone knew Reggie could be persnickety about his cathedrals. But she also had not mentioned the presence of an upsetting ex-boyfriend. Although that certainly qualified as personal and no one's business, which is exactly what Reverend Mother would say. Sister Agatha found very little to be outside the bounds of her business. Of course as both a detective and a writer, such an attitude made perfect sense. At least that was always her argument.

"It's probably a tempest in a teapot and we would do well to leave it alone. Maybe Sister Samantha was just out of sorts. The move to Gwenafwy Abbey has been a huge adjustment for the young sisters. From Los Angeles to Pryderi! I can't imagine."

"We should keep an eye on her."

"I can't believe I am saying this, but why don't you do some gentle snooping. See if there is a problem that we could head off before it gets out of hand. Maybe Sister Samantha is feeling homesick and just needs some friendly encouragement."

Sister Agatha grinned as she pulled open the heavy kitchen door. "Are you asking me to act like a detective?" Sister Callwen was generally opposed to her sleuthing on the grounds that it wasn't really within the jurisdiction of good nun behavior.

"I said 'gentle.'" Sister Callwen removed her woolly hat and smoothed her already perfectly tidy hair.

Sister Gwenydd looked up from the long worktable, flour smudged on her habit. The spacious room, fragrant with the aroma of cinnamon, offered a welcome respite from the cold.

"Just ask around with the other sisters and see what you can find out. Start with our Sister Gwenydd here." Sister Callwen slid out of her coat as she crossed the kitchen and opened the door to the warming room. She turned back with a smile. "She always seems to know what's going on in the Abbey."

"Ask me what?" Sister Gwenydd said.

"What do you think of Sister Samantha?" She watched as Sister Gwenydd deftly arranged doughy circles dotted with currants across a floured cookie sheet. Sister Gwenydd, as young as any of the new nuns from Los Angeles, had joined Gwenafwy Abbey last summer under unusual circumstances--on the lam from a false murder charge. Sister Agatha found her to be sharp, funny, and as observant as any detective. If Sister Samantha harbored secrets, Sister Gwenydd would already know about them. Or she could find out.

"What about her?" Sister Gwenydd asked.

She waited as Sister Gwenydd slid the sheet of currant-laden Welsh cakes into the oven and then dusting off her hands on a white towel, took a seat. Sister Agatha hated to stir up trouble at the Abbey and Reverend Mother adamantly discouraged gossip. She pried the lid off the gingerbread tin that sat in the middle of the table. One piece left. She tilted the tin towards Sister Gwenydd. On the other hand, was this really gossip?

Sister Gwenydd shook her head and poured two cups of tea.

Sister Agatha described the interaction between Claire and Sister Samantha in the cheese barn.

"Well, who knows?" Sister Gwenydd responded after thinking a moment. "I've heard that she is not the happiest person. And that her religious vocation has sometimes come into question."

Agatha's eyebrows shot up. "What do you mean?" A nun's call to life in a religious order is very private. Between the woman and God. To question the validity of another's vocation was serious business indeed.

"Well, she grew up, I guess, in a very privileged household. And then the family lost everything. Recently. I don't know why or what else happened. But instead of going off to the college of her dreams, she joined the order."

"Well, that doesn't seem so bad," Sister Agatha said. "I mean maybe she felt she was following God's direction."

Sister Gwenydd shrugged. "As you know, I'm the last person to question someone's vocation." They both sat for a moment remembering the previous summer when Sister Gwenydd had found herself placed in handcuffs at the Buttered Crust Teashop.

"True," Sister Agatha said finally. "But why not simply give Claire a quote about cheese?"

"No idea. Do you want me to find out?"

"Dig around a little. If you can do it discreetly."

"I'm pretty busy. With the feast of the Epiphany and all." Sister Gwenydd glanced at the timer on the range. "But I'll see."

Sister Agatha pulled her red jumper off over her head. "Is it hot in here?"

"The range overheats. You have to keep an eye on it."

"By the way, I noticed that Claire wasn't at dinner tonight. She usually doesn't miss a meal."

"She went into the village."

"Did she say why?"

"She said she wanted to check out 'something interesting'. I guess you do that a lot when you're writing a story. She seemed preoccupied. Reminded me of you when you have your investigator's hat on and you're hunting down a clue."

Sister Agatha felt a small flush of pride. "Did she say what the 'something interesting' was?

"No. I would have asked but she seemed in a hurry and I needed to get these Welsh cakes started. I have a lot more cooking to do with all the extra nuns. I've told Sister Elfrida that I need an assistant. The problem is, I don't want to share my kitchen."

"Understandable. One more thing. Does Claire have a boyfriend?"

"Don't know, why?" Sister Gwenydd placed their teacups in the sink and wiped down the oilcloth table.

Sister Agatha told her about the man in the window of the Buttered Crust Teashop and the silver car parked outside.

"What kind of car?"

"An Austin Healey Vantage."

Sister Gwenydd let out a low whistle as she folded a stack of dish towels. "Nice." The timer dinged and she slid the Welsh cakes out of the range and onto the counter.

"Indeed. But she seemed very unhappy to see him."

"Did they talk?"

"No. In fact, she couldn't get away fast enough."

"Well, just because a guy has an expensive car doesn't mean he isn't a total loser."

"Of course."

"If you don't mind, I'm going into the warming room, I have some menu-planning to catch up on and I like to do it while I watch The Great British Bake-Off."

"Right," Sister Agatha understood. She was known to binge-watch *Midsomer Murders* when she was about to start a new chapter in her book. Inspector Barnaby never failed to inspire.

CHAPTER 5

Sister Agatha craned her neck and surveyed the chapel. *No Claire.* All around her, the nuns' voices blended together in the opening hymn for vespers, *Abide With Me.* Moonlight dimly lit the backs of the stained glass windows as Reverend Mother stepped into the small pulpit at the front. The young reporter had faithfully attended chapel services since she had arrived –not that she was a believer—she had announced her firm atheism early in her stay at the convent; but rather, attending chapel helped her immerse herself in the life of the Abbey. But apparently not tonight. Maybe she felt adequately immersed without going to chapel three times a day, Sister Agatha thought to herself as she opened her hymn-book. Not everyone shared the sense of peace that she experienced whenever she stood in her usual pew, stained-glass windows shimmering, incense floating in the air.

Launching into the second verse of *Abide With Me*, she felt a quiet contentment. The polished wood altar table stood front and center. The small pulpit off to the side. All the nuns, new and old, stood raising their voices in the ancient hymn. All was right with the world. Except where was Claire? Why would she still be in the village this late? And why had she missed dinner? Sister Gwenydd had last seen her going to town in the early afternoon. She also wondered about the handsome man in the Buttered Crust Teashop.

She and the other nuns sat in the pews and listened as Reverend Mother spoke the opening prayer. She closed her eyes and sang along softly the final verse, *Abide With Me.*

Hold Thou Thy cross before my closing eyes
Shine through the gloom and point me to the skies
Heaven's morning breaks, and earth's vain shadows flee
In life, in death, O Lord, abide with me.

Sister Agatha slipped her hymnbook into the back of the pew rack when hot tears pushed against her eyelids. An old Anglican hymn often sung at times of death. Sister Agatha dug through her jumper pocket for a tissue and finding none was just about to use her sleeve when Sister Callwen slipped her a neatly folded and perfectly pressed handkerchief. Sister Agatha smiled as she dabbed her eyes. Sister Callwen *would* have a handkerchief at the ready. And an embroidered one at that.

As the sisters turned back to the psalter for the final responsive psalm, Sister Agatha realized that Sister Samantha was not present either. Now that was truly out of the ordinary. The sisters only missed the daily office if they were sick or unavoidably detained at some important work of the Abbey. Perhaps Sister Samantha was ill and that was the reason for her sharpness this afternoon.

Compline ended with a rousing benediction read by Sister Harriet-- a thrilling passage from Teilhard de Chardin. As the nuns gathered their things to leave the chapel, Reverend Mother called them back. She had stepped into the pulpit and was staring at her mobile.

"A text from Father Selwyn," she said. "He's at hospital with the Archbishop. Former Archbishop, Reggie, I mean. It seems that Reggie has had some sort of medical episode and they may keep him overnight. Father Selwyn requests that we hold him in prayer." Reverend Mother slipped her mobile into her habit pocket and closed her eyes as though to start praying immediately.

"What kind of medical episode?" Sister Callwen interrupted.

"He didn't say," Reverend Mother said, opening her eyes and then stepping down out of the pulpit. "I know that Reggie has been putting off getting a pacemaker. Perhaps that's it. I'll send a text in an hour or so and get some details."

"*Medical episode* could be anything from a shattered fibula to a coronary infarction," Sister Agatha said. She liked to get things straight when it came to medical terms and had practically memorized *Medical Forensics for Beginners*. Especially Chapter Seven "The Good, the Bad, and the Really Ugly."

"Or he could have had a bout of indigestion, panicked and called the ambulance," Sister Callwen added. "Don't let that imagination of yours overwork, Sister Agatha. As I recall, our Reggie has a penchant for the dramatic."

"Either way," Reverend Mother said, pulling on her green hat and wrapping the matching muffler around her neck. Sister Winifred had chosen *sea foam green* for Reverend Mother which was, of course, exactly right. "We shall know more in the morning, I suspect."

"You're not going out, are you, Reverend Mother?" Sister Callwen said as she watched her button her anorak. "So late? In this weather?"

"Just a brisk walk in the garden. You know. Clear my head."

Sister Callwen raised her eyebrows. She took a dim view of

spontaneous walks in the garden, especially after nine o'clock. "You'll catch your death," she said.

Sister Agatha shivered. She never liked that phrase, *catch your death*. Too macabre for day-to-day living. She liked to keep death between the pages of her novel. She and Sister Callwen watched while Reverend Mother pushed open the heavy chapel door and stepped into the moonlit night.

CHAPTER 6

Sister Agatha awakened slowly from a deep sleep. The wisps of a dream lingered. A pony, mane and tail flying, cantering across a green meadow, a brilliant blue sky above. A young girl with braids and a yellow dress clung to the reins and shouted with laughter.

It was the girl's laughter that had awakened her. The dream was so lovely that she lay for a delicious moment, feeling young and content, as if the sun on the meadow still warmed her face. But as she came fully awake, the loveliness of the dream slipped away; chilly air seeped under the heavy blankets and a ghostly gray moonlight fell across the stone floor. She remembered, sitting up, that Sister Matilda had told them at dinner that there would be a wolf moon tonight-- a moon so bright that it was said that it could set wolves howling.

She lay back, trying to hold on to the splendid image of the pony and the girl, flying across the meadow. She seldom dreamed with such clarity. Maybe Bartimaeus had come to her in a dream because he had... *Good heavens*, she thought. *I'm being ridiculous.*

Swinging her legs over the side of her bed, she pulled on heavy wool socks and a pair of snow pants over her flannel pajamas. She would simply check on him. Pop out to the barn and see how he was doing. Was the barn warm enough? Did he have plenty of hay? Was he still...? She couldn't even bring herself to think about it. *With Ben on holiday, she should be paying closer attention anyway.*

She layered her red jumper over her pajama top and then buttoned her anorak over the whole thing. The red muffler and her woolly hat finished off the ensemble. She closed her bedroom door softly behind her and crept along in stockinged feet carrying her sturdy snow boots, one in each hand. She continued down the long hallway, almost slipping on the steep stairs, and then entered the Abbey kitchen. She stopped to pull on her boots. The moonlight was so bright she didn't even need to turn on a light in the kitchen. Boots tightly laced, she grabbed an apple from the wooden fruit bowl on the table, opened the kitchen door, and stepped out into the winter night. She caught her breath in the cold air. As the door shut solidly behind her and she panicked for a moment, then patted the pocket of her anorak. Yes, she had remembered her keys.

A light dusting of snow had made the flagstones slippery and she took a few cautious steps. She paused for a moment, taking in the hushed stillness of the Abbey grounds. In the eerie light of the wolf-moon, the new snow had feathered each tree, bush and building leaving it unnervingly phantom-like. She jumped as a rasping, metallic sound broke the silence. The wrought iron gate at the end of the Abbey drive. She would have known the sound of the latch anywhere. She opened and shut that gate almost every day. She waited, holding her breath. In a moment, the gate clanked shut. Had someone entered the Abbey, closed the gate behind them, and was now walking down the long drive toward her? Or had they opened the gate to leave and were now heading down Church Lane?

She stood perfectly still, too terrified to walk forward to the barn and too terrified to turn around and face what might be coming up the drive. Just when she thought her feet had frozen solid to the ground, she took two steps backwards so she could at least stand hidden in the shadow of the hedgerow. Unfortunately, the heel of her boot hit a frozen rut in the ground, and she fell backward into the hedgerow, half-sitting in the prickly branches. She struggled to get upright, but the loud rustling of the leaves made her stay perfectly still again. A branch poked her in the back, and another jabbed her in the head, her woolly hat knocked askew. She waited, stiff with cold and horribly uncomfortable. Finally, she decided no one was coming down the drive from the gate. Maybe they had already paid the Abbey a late night visit and left? But who? And why?

She extracted herself from the hedgerow and hurried to the pony barn. Only when she reached the barn, did she dare turn and look behind her. No one. Perhaps the eerie shine of the moonlight on the snow and the late hour were sending her imagination to ridiculous heights. Maybe she imagined the sound of the gate. *Not likely.*

The warm air of the pony barn, mixed with the aroma of hay and fresh cut oats, enveloped her and her fright dissipated somewhat. The barn, built of field stone in the 1700's, stayed mildly warm even in the dead of winter. She pulled the cord that dangled from an oaken beam and the single light bulb dispelled the darkness, though creating some creepy shadows in the corners. She pulled a few more brambles from her hair and coat and went to Bartimaeus's stall.

Well, he was alive, but she didn't like how he looked. He stood with his head lowered, nose to the floor. She couldn't tell if he was resting while standing up as ponies were known to do, or if his arthritic bones wouldn't let him lie down. The memory of Tupper gently suggesting that she begin to think about euthanasia, flashed through her mind.

She stroked the fur around his ears where it was silky. She started to wipe the tears out of her eyes with her jumper sleeve when she remembered Sister Callwen's embroidered handkerchief still in her jumper pocket. She smiled as she dug it out. The old pony nickered gently and turned his head to look at her. She blew her nose and then stuffing the handkerchief back in her pocket, dug her cold hands into the thick brown fur of his winter coat. "Why, you're warm as toast, old boy." He nuzzled her with his velvety nose for a moment and then let his head hang low again. He perked up again when she offered the apple, nimbly taking it off the flat of her hand.

"There you go, laddie." She picked up the prayer shawl that had been tossed on top of the feed bags and draped it over his back. "You don't want to lie down?" She stroked his mane. "Even this late at night, you'd rather stand?" She forked a generous pile of fresh straw underneath him, fluffed it nicely, and then tugged on his halter until he slowly lowered himself into the soft bed.

"Your old bones creak as much as mine do. But isn't it nicer to lie down at night?" She knelt next to him and stroking his fetlock and told him all about her dream. "Someday soon, Bart, you will gallop across a meadow, just like old times." Her voice caught and she rummaged again for Sister Callwen's handkerchief. She recited a prayer for a restful sleep from the Common Book of Prayer and told him goodnight.

As she shoved the barn door solidly shut behind her,; clouds heavy with snow had covered the moon. She strained to see her hand in front of her face. She realized she was also listening intently for any noise. Had she really heard the gate? Perhaps the wind had rattled it. But the wind hadn't arisen until she was in the barn. She walked carefully back along the flagstones. Why hadn't she brought a torch? One would never think that she had once earned every single Girl Guide badge.

At the kitchen door, she yanked off her mitten and retrieved the key chain from her jumper pocket. The key wouldn't fit. She fumbled and tried the next key on the chain. No luck. She fingered the square key chain with her fingers. "Twmffat!" *Idiot.* She had grabbed her library keys. She resisted the urge to kick the kitchen door. *Girl Guide indeed.* Unless she wanted to share Bartimaeus' stall, she had to find a way into the building. There was always shouting until someone heard her, but the embarrassment of being caught outdoors during one of the coldest nights of the year in her flannel pajamas was almost as unappealing as spending the night in the pony barn.

She remembered that sometimes the back door to the Abby would not always shut properly. One had to slam it to get it to latch and lock. Could she be so lucky that it might be open? If it wasn't, she would have to throw rocks at Sister Callwen's window which wasn't an attractive prospect at all.

She pulled her anorak collar up and wrapped her scarf more tightly and began the walk around to the back of the Abbey's main building. She had to feel her way along the limestone wall and reaching the corner, grope carefully around it to the back. The clouds scudded across the sky and the moon shone bright again. She went along slowly until she found the handle of the small door. Just as she grabbed the handle with both hands to give it a tug, praying that it was unlocked, she froze. Someone was watching her. She turned very slowly and looked over her shoulder in the direction of the dovecote, andnd then flattened her back against the stone wall, holding her breath.

Two figures stood at the door of the dovecote, the guest cottage at Gwenafwy Abbey. One was taller than the other, both wearing heavy coats. The door to the dovecote cottage opened and for one second, they stood in the circle of light. The next minute they stepped inside and the door pulled shut behind them. They didn't seem to force the door. Whoever it was, had a key. Claire returning from a late night in the village with a guest? The boyfriend? The windows were shuttered, but a thin line of light at the bottom of the door leaked out. Claire must be entertaining for the night.

If it was the boyfriend, then where was the Aston Healy that the boy drove? They must have crossed the Abbey grounds without coming down the drive, which meant that they were on foot. Surely the two of them hadn't walked to the Abbey from Pryderi? But they were young, and it was less than a mile, so maybe they had.

Stiff with cold, she lurched over to the backdoor. She managed to grab the handle, and yank as hard as she could and to her great relief, it opened. Stepping in, she slammed the door shut, pulled the deadbolt, and then leaned against it to catch her breath. There were no windows in the stairwell, so she hurried up to the second floor and then quietly down the hall to peer out the window facing the front drive. Silent and snowy. No tracks that she could see.

She leaned her forehead against the cool windowpane. She couldn't stop thinking of Bartimaeus, his head drooping. He was a long way from the cantering young pony in the green meadow with the blue sky. A cloud moved in front of the moon and once again, the night turned black as pitch.

CHAPTER 7

The next morning, the sisters gathered at the long breakfast table laden with Sister Gwenydd's heartiest of breakfast choices. Steaming platters of sausages, a heaping bowl of baked beans and a serving of tomatoes canned from Sister Matilda's prodigious vegetable garden. Last summer had been a bumper crop in marrows, tomatoes and kale. The sisters had been improving their fiber consumption ever since.

As Sister Agatha spooned tomatoes onto her plate, she glanced around. *No Claire.* She felt a fleeting frisson of anxiety mixed with a bit of guilt. Should she have told Reverend Mother immediately about the man Claire had brought back with her? But Claire could have male guests. It wasn't as if she was one of the nuns. She would tell Reverend Mother everything as soon as breakfast was over. She tucked into her sausages and tomatoes.

Sister Samantha sat at her spot at the table, cheerfully chatting with Sister Theodora. She certainly seemed happier. Maybe the cheese barn moment was nothing more than a young woman settling into a new situation. Sister Agatha decided that she had once again put the cart before the horse and was glad she had not bothered Reverend Mother with it. Reverend Mother sat at the head of the table, sipping tea, and discussing plans for the Feast of the Epiphany with Sister Gwenydd, her plate holding only a piece of toast and a single sausage.

"Any news on the Archbishop?" Sister Agatha asked. "From Father Selwyn, that is?"

"Good heavens," Reverend Mother replied. "I forgot to check." She picked up her phone and tapping it, looked up, her brow furrowed. "He's home," she said. "Father Selwyn says that he was released at midnight last night."

"Poor Father Selwyn," Sister Callwen chimed in with a cluck of her tongue. "Up half the night taking care of the Archbishop."

"They've been friends for years," Reverend Mother said. "Ever since Reggie was the Bishop of Asaph."

"So Reggie was the original Suzanne Bainton?" Sister Gwenydd asked, as she slid a replenishment of sausages onto an empty platter. Sister Gwenydd's menus were so enticing that Sister Harriet had instituted a new workout schedule at the Pryderi gym and a walking regimen for anyone who would join in.

"Reggie was Bishop of Saint Asaph for ten years, and then ordained to the position of Archbishop of Wales. Until he recently retired," Reverend Mother said.

"So will Suzanne become Archbishop of Wales someday?" Sister Gwenydd asked taking her seat again next to Reverend Mother.

"Archbishop of Canterbury *and* Archbishop of Wales if she has her way about it," Sister Callwen said.

"I doubt Suzanne Bainton will stop there. I expect her to go to the Vatican and be made pope," Sister Winifred said, frowning into her tea. The nuns had a tenuous relationship with their bishop. She had both saved and imperiled the life of the Abbey a year ago. A stickler for budgets and protocol, the Bishop occasionally tangled with Reverend Mother.

"Please sisters," Reverend Mother said. "Let's turn our attention to the Feast of Epiphany which is almost upon us -- only a week away. I have placed Sister Gwenydd in charge and I am sure she has tasks for all of us."

"What exactly happens at a Feast of Epiphany?" Sister Juniper asked. Sister Juniper was a tall, lithe young woman. She had the whitest teeth and most glowing complexion that Sister Agatha had ever seen. She knew that Sister Juniper had grown up in Malibu and that she had spent her days surfing and rock climbing. That is until she took vows. Sister Agatha admired her across the table. Youth itself could be so annoying. All that clear skin and bright eyes and no double chin. "I know what *Epiphany* is," Sister Juniper said. "We celebrated Epiphany Sunday at the Sisters of Transfiguration. But we never had a feast."

"Well, the most important thing about the feast is the cake," Sister Gwenydd said. "And I have great plans." A loud knock at the door interrupted her. Not a timid knock Sister Agatha noticed, but a bold knock; the knock of someone who wanted something. And someone who wasn't waiting for an invitation. The door pushed open and Constable Barnes stepped in. "Reverend Mother," he said, tipping his head in her direction. "Sisters." His eyes swept the table and if Sister Agatha didn't know better, she would have thought he was taking attendance. "Could you come down to the beach with me? By the cliff walk."

"The beach," Reverend Mother said standing, her linen napkin sliding to the floor. "Whatever is it, Constable?"

"That young guest of yours, Claire MacDonagh. Has she gone missing?"

"No," Reverend Mother said at the exact same moment that Sister Agatha said "Yes."

Everyone turned from Constable Barnes to Sister Agatha.

Sister Agatha didn't feel that it was appropriate to blurt out Claire's late night activities. "The beach? At the cliff walk?" she asked. "What's going on, Constable?"

"Is she alright?" Sister Samantha spoke up. The only one to speak, Sister Agatha noticed.

"No, Sister," Constable Barnes said, in his quiet rumbling voice. He was the only person that Sister Agatha knew whose voice could rumble. It was wholly arresting. Almost like Father Selwyn's pulpit voice, but not quite. "I'm sorry to tell you sisters this, but Miss MacDonagh is dead."

Only the senior nuns accompanied Constable Barnes and Reverend Mother to the beach below the cliff walk, just a mile from Gwenafwy Abbey. In the squad car on the ride over, Sister Agatha quickly recounted seeing the two figures at the dovecote door last night.

"And you didn't think to call the constabulary, Sister Agatha? When you saw a strange man on the grounds at two in the morning?" Constable Barnes spun around and glared at her in the backseat.

"I thought I recognized him as the boyfriend...or ex-boyfriend...from the morning. At The Buttered Crust. It seemed like Claire's private business."

"Why did you think one of them was Claire MacDonagh?"

"Because they had a key, so I assumed it was Claire. You know, opening the door."

Constable Barnes let out a snort and grabbed the radio receiver from the dashboard. Sister Agatha and Reverend Mother listened as he told the dispatcher that he wanted the dovecote searched.

"Sorry," she said after he had slammed the receiver back into the holder. "I thought it was a late-night rendezvous."

Claire lay face down, her leg bent, her flyaway red hair now matted with frozen blood. Streamers of seaweed had rolled in with the tide and gathered in clumps that lapped at the toes of her water-filled boots. Dr. Beese, Pryderi's medical examiner, knelt next to her.

Sister Agatha wrapped her red muffler around her face, partly for warmth and partly to hide the emotion that was threatening to overtake her. She looked around for Sister Callwen, her port in every storm, but she stood with her arms around Sister Winifred who openly sobbed. Sister Agatha was glad the younger nuns had not come along.

"A selfie gone tragically wrong," Constable Barnes said. He handed a plastic bag containing a mobile phone to Reverend Mother. She looked through the bag and let out a gasp. Sister Agatha leaned in. The smiling face of Claire looked back at them. "The time stamp on the phone shows that she took this picture around 5:03 last night. Just as the sun was going down." The Irish Sea glinted in the background, giving a glow to Claire's red hair.

"But if she fell off the cliffs at 5 PM, then what about the..." Sister Agatha stopped as Constable Barnes shot her a thunderous look. Apparently, he didn't want anyone to know yet about the two people seen at dovecote. Obviously, it hadn't been Claire and her boyfriend. Or at least it wasn't Claire. The tall thin man did fit the body type of the young man in the Buttered Crust Teashop. If Claire had been dead by 5 PM, then who was at the Dovecote at two o'clock the following morning? And why?

"You mean she fell off the cliffs taking a picture?" Sister Callwen said from where she stood, her arm still around Sister Winifred.

"Happens more than you want to think. These young people, they just have to snap a photo. She must have lost her balance and tumbled backward," Constable Barnes said.

"Dr. Beese," Sister Agatha said in the direction of Pryderi's medical examiner who knelt next to the body of Claire. "Do you concur? Was it death from falling backward off the cliff?"

"Not death by falling, Sister Agatha." Dr. Beese stood up,

brushing sand off her black silk pants, and straightening her long cashmere coat. "Death upon impact. Internal hemorrhaging."

"Did she die quickly?" Reverend Mother asked.

"I would like to say 'yes' but..." Dr. Beese looked up at the cliffs and then back to Claire's outstretched body. "She is lying at the bottom of the highest point on the cliff walk." Dr. Beese paused again. "Which means she fell about twenty meters onto the sand. She may have hit the rocks as she came down or perhaps missed them and..." Dr. Beese paused and cleared her throat. "And did a complete free fall." Sister Agatha noticed that Dr. Beese, always unflappable, paused and coughed into her hand. "I will make a guess that the time of death was 5:10 last night."

"That's awfully precise," Sister Callwen said. "Five ten exactly?"

"According to the phone, she took the selfie at 5:03. I would say she was dead in approximately five minutes. That is, of course, if she died immediately." Dr. Beese knelt beside Claire's body once more. "And let's hope in God's mercy that she did."

CHAPTER 8

"Horrible business," Father Selwyn said, frowning. "How is Reverend Mother?" He fingered his prayer beads. Tall and balding, with a slight paunch that spoke of too many buttered scones, Father Selwyn chose to wear the traditional black cassock and dog collar. But although his garb was conventional, his theology was not.

"Shaken," Sister Agatha said. "We all are." She could just hear the sonorous tones of *O Light of Love, By Love Inclined* drifting down from the choir loft as Emerick Scoville, St. Anselm's church organist, prepared for Sunday. She needed the refuge of Father Selwyn's office at the church. The presence of her old friend, the steady supply of tea and cakes, the piles of old books all gave her the feeling that things were right with the world. Yet, they most certainly weren't.

"What did Parker have to say?" Father Selwyn placed a Welsh cake on Sister Agatha's plate and then took one for himself, biting into it and crumbling buttery flakes on his cassock. Sister Agatha loved Welsh cakes. A cookie, scone, and pancake rolled into one, dusted with sugar. The tea kettle whistled, and she watched as Father Selwyn poured steaming water into the teapot.

"I don't know. I wasn't able to stay to talk with him but I'm desperate to know what he is thinking. I had to leave for my noontime library meeting." Sister Agatha was on the Library Committee for the Pryderi Public Library, a post she took very seriously. "But he's promised to meet with me first thing tomorrow morning."

Father Selwyn raised his eyebrows. "You left the scene of a crime in the hands of law enforcement? What's happening to you, Sister? You're slipping."

"I had no choice, duty called. We had a guest speaker and I was to introduce him. Fascinating topic. 'Arsenic and Old Books.' Did you know that librarians can be in danger of poisoning from medieval manuscripts? The bindings were often decorated with green paint mixed with arsenic."

"Do you handle a lot of medieval manuscripts at the Gwenafwy Abbey Library?"

"Well, no. But it just goes to show that being a librarian-- even an Abbey librarian-- is not without its risks. People should think of that when they get cross about overdue fines and being asked to stop chatting so loudly."

She took a bite of the Welsh cake. "Bevan seems to be adding more butter to his Welsh cakes these days. Tell him I approve." Bevan Penrose, Father Selwyn's very competent and entirely devoted administrative assistant, not only kept St Anselm running, he also kept Father Selwyn supplied with Welsh cakes, raspberry crumble, and lemon squares. In the past, Bevan had tried to switch him over to green smoothies, fresh fruit, and tofu bites, but it hadn't taken.

They ate in silence for a moment staring at the fire burning in the small grate. "So is this a case for Scotland Yard?" Father Selwyn said, interrupting the quiet.

"Not sure. A woman is found dead at the bottom of the cliffs," she said, brushing crumbs off her habit front. Sister Agatha shivered even though the room was warm. She pictured Claire going backwards over the cliff and her stomach dropped. She forced herself to take several calming breaths. Father Selwyn's office, in fact Father Selwyn himself, always had the slightest aroma of cinnamon mixed with candle wax. She was never sure if the office aroma of cinnamon was from the cakes and cookies that Bevan put in front of Father Selwyn or if it was that Father Selwyn himself used cinnamon-scented soap. She wanted to inquire but it seemed a little intimate to ask one's vicar. Even if he had been your best friend since the Third Form. The cinnamon scent helped her regain a certain calmness. "If it were all a horrible accident, then why would someone break into her room?"

"She falls over a cliff at five o'clock in the evening and two people enter her cottage—with a key, or so it seems—at two in the morning?"

They sat without speaking for a long moment.

"Did Claire have enemies, do you suppose?" Father Selwyn stretched his long legs and smoothed his cassock.

"A good journalist always has enemies."

"But I thought she worked for *The Church Times*? They don't exactly cover stories on the cutting edge. Unless you count that scathing article about the royal visit to the Commemoration of Conwy's ancient yew tree."

"*The Church Times* was right to criticize. They should have sent the Queen. Although Prince Charles did bring a certain gravitas to such an occasion." She ignored Father Selwyn's eye roll.

"Royal visit aside, I doubt Claire has ever offended anyone through an article in *The Church Times*."

"Could you ask around, though? You have more clergy friends than I do. Find out if anyone has had an interview with Claire that went awry. You know how sensitive clergy can be."

Father Selwyn grunted but did not disagree.

Sister Agatha dug around in her jumper pocket. She located her favorite silver fountain pen and made a few notes on the inside cover of *Murder on the Orient Express*. She hadn't had a chance to start a Murder Book. She frowned. "I need to get organized. I feel an investigation coming on."

"Well, then may I suggest another cup of tea and a Welsh cake? You may need it."

Sister Agatha climbed the steep stairs to the attic library. She had wanted all day to steal away to her desk and launch her investigation. No one understood how much effort and planning a solid investigation required. Notebook selection, new fountain pen, establishment of evidence protocols, list of suspects, research. Of course there wasn't any evidence yet, but one wanted to be prepared and not caught on one's back foot.

But it wasn't just the investigation of Claire's murder that called for attention-- she feared her novel was dying on the vine. The rough draft lay in a jumble of digital pieces, and Bates Melanchthon seemed to suddenly lack direction. In the attempt to inspire herself, she had started to craft an agent's query letter. Sister Agatha had very strong opinions on where she wanted to find an agent—London or New York City. Anything else would be settling. And with a traditional publisher. No self-publishing for her. She could barely admit it to herself, but the truth was, she had no idea where to begin with self-publishing although Sister Harriet, who was very skilled in the self-publishing world, had offered to show her the ropes. Sister Harriet had two graphic novels under belt; both based on biblical stories for readers under the age of ten. The books had seen more than modest success-- especially with the Sunday School crowd-- and Sister Agatha appreciated her help. But she really wanted an agent. Partly so she could be reassured that there was someone out there-- a professional--who liked her work. So far, she had only shared her writing with Father Selwyn and Reverend Mother and they both loved it. But neither were exactly objective. However, she wanted an agent for another reason that she had never told anyone. She longed for the day she could pick up her mobile, look at it and say to anyone within earshot, "Sorry. I have to take this. *It's my agent.*"

She sighed and heaved herself up over the last step of the narrow staircase. She either needed to get back to the Silver Sneakers program at the Pryderi gym with Father Selwyn or she absolutely had to lay off Sister Gwenydd's Welsh cakes. Neither idea appealed.

She opened the door to the library, flipped on a light. *Her sanctum sanctorum. Her Holy of Holies.* She slid in behind her writing desk which was tucked into the north-facing dormer; the window gazed out across the Abbey grounds. The moon had risen hours ago, and its beams shone so bright that one could read a book while standing in Sister Matilda's herb garden.

She turned her attention from the window to the wall above her desk and the two note cards she had taped up nearly a year ago: "Seek ye first the Kingdom of God, and all these things shall be given unto you." *Matthew 3:6.* She closed her eyes and said a swift prayer. Then, opening her eyes, she read the other card. "The secret of getting ahead is getting started." *Agatha Christie.*

Opening the bottom drawer of her desk, she peered thoughtfully at her stash of colorful notebooks. Endlessly pragmatic and no-frills in almost all matters, she had one slightly embarrassing weakness-- she absolutely loved a new, fresh notebook. But not just any notebook. Only the expensive, cloth-covered, hand-bound ones that could be found at Smythson of Bond Street in London. The advertisement on the Smythson website read "minimalist, yet powerful," which was exactly how she thought of herself.

Each page of a Smythson notebook was watermarked; every binding, handmade; every spine carefully stitched; every page, gilt-edged. Just opening a new notebook-- the slight snap of the binding, the feel of the smooth top page, the gentle aroma of paper and ink-- sparked her creativity and at that moment, when she touched the clean, empty first page, the possibilities seemed limitless. The expensive notebooks were somewhat at odds with her vow of poverty, but fortunately Reverend Mother firmly believed that all-poverty-and-no-online- shopping made for a dull life. Even a cloistered life. Consequently, she had quietly approved the notebooks as long as Sister Agatha didn't overdo it. After all, Reverend Mother ordered *Nike Air Pro V* basketball shoes from a store on Oxford Street. And Sister Agatha knew for a fact, they weren't cheap.

The start of a real murder investigation called for a new note-book—a Murder Book. Her last notebook had been blue for Advent but now the season was Epiphany and the color of Epiphany was white and she did have a very nice egg-shell white moleskin with gilt-edged pages.

She used her notebook for any investigating or sleuthing that she might be doing as well as for all her writing ideas. So some-times she might jot down a bit of breakfast table conversation concerning something that seemed a tad on the suspicious side (although it usually wasn't) listed next to something like: "have victim bludgeoned with rolling pin." In a pinch, she had used the notebook for Sister Gwenydd's grocery list on a trip into the village andso items such as *three kohlrabi and a jar of bouillon* might be cheek to jowl with *antimony very efficient for quick death.*

Of course, Chief Inspector Rupert McFarland would never have approved. He always insisted that a detective's notebook be kept orderly. She could hear his voice on his online podcast *Write Now:* "Update and organize! Shipshape in Bristol fashion! You don't want to miss an important clue, just because you've spilled tea on your notes!" She never missed the podcast and often refer-enced her notes while sleuthing. The only shortcoming of Inspector Rupert McFarland was that he wasn't an Anglican nun. He never had to combine a trip to the village for kohlrabi and bouillon with a suspect interview and a search of the crime scene.

She listened as the bell in the village tower chimed twelve gentle peals. She would be sleep-deprived at Matins tomorrow morning, but this couldn't wait. Frowning, she peered at the crisp first page of the new notebook, her fountain pen poised-- but only for a moment. She wrote the word CLUES at the top, giving it a double underline. She sat back and thought for a moment and then wrote quickly:

Victim absent from Gwenafwy Abbey the entire afternoon and evening of her death. Where was she? In the village? Abbey? Boyfriend? Other?

Who might have seen her during the above time?

Room entered several hours following victim's death

missing key? green rucksack?

Did the victim have any enemies?

Again-- boyfriend?

Sister Samantha?

Journalism connection?

Just how well did anyone at the Abbey know the victim?

Did Reverend Mother thoroughly vet her?

Probably not. Trust was the hallmark of Reverend Mother's personality. Also her most unnerving weakness. She made a note to call *The Church Times* and conduct a more thorough background check.

She sat back and read over her list.

Sister Samantha seemed to be the closest thing to an enemy she could think of. But wasn't that a terrible stretch? She didn't particularly like Claire, that was clear. *But was she an enemy?* Claire had somehow offended Sister Samantha. People have killed for less.

The most disturbing entry under the heading *Clues* was that Claire's room had been entered following her death. Did the two people—one tall and one short—kill Claire and then return to the Abbey to search her room? Who was it? And what were they looking for? Or did the people in her room have nothing to do with her fall over the cliff? Was it really a horribly tragic selfie?

Her list suddenly seemed a bit lackluster. A young woman falls backwards while taking a selfie. Her private room is entered. Did that add up to murder? Sister Agatha capped her fountain pen and closed the notebook, looking out over the moonlit night. What would Armand Gamache say? Or Inspector Barnaby? Kinsey Millhone? She jumped as her phone pinged--a text from Deputy Parker Clough.

Can you meet me in the village early tomorrow?

She texted back. *Where? And why?*

The Buttered Crust. Before I go on my shift. I have something you might want.

CHAPTER 9

Sister Agatha peered into the steamy windows of the Buttered Crust Teashop. She stamped the snow off her boots and blew on her freezing hands having shoved her bright red mittens into the pocket of her anorak. On a balmy spring day, the fifteen minute walk from Gwenafwy Abbey to the village center was pleasant, the sweeping views of sheep and croft, babbling brook and patch-work fields, left one feeling inspired if not downright exhilarated. But sometimes, the walk was just plain cold.

She could see Parker sitting alone at a back table, hunched over his mobile. Ordinarily a serious young man, his face broke into a ridiculous grin. He must be texting Lucy, she thought. Lucy Pembroke had been a visiting artist at Gwenafwy Abbey last Christmas. Thrown together by unfortunate circumstances, Parker and Lucy's relationship blossomed into an unlikely romance. Sister Gwenydd, who always knew about such things, had said that they were "trying to make the long distance thing work." The look on his face made it pretty clear that something was working.

She pushed through the door to the cheerful jingle of the over-head bell and the friendly chatter of early morning diners. The usual clatter of cutlery and plates mingled with the friendly noise of a satisfied clientele. The fragrant aroma of baking bread, cardamom, and ginger filled her senses. The Buttered Crust Teashop could always be counted on for an onslaught of sensory comfort. She unwound her muffler, pulled off her woolly hat to the detriment of her short gray hair, and headed across the room to Parker.

"Officer Clough," she said smiling as she pulled a chair out across from him. "Bora da." *Good Morning.*

"Bora da, Sister," he said, standing up. "It's good to see you. Although perhaps not under the present circumstances."

"The present circumstances are what I am hoping you want to discuss," she said, taking a seat and looking around for Keenan, a recent graduate of Father Selwyn's confirmation class and now a waiter at the teashop. "However, first things first." She removed the new cream-colored, gilt-edged notebook from her jumper pocket and placed it on the table. Instead of labeling it *Murder* in bold letters on the binder as she usually did, she had taken Reverend Mother's advice and instead written it in small print on the inside cover. Reverend Mother always encouraged the subtle approach. Next, she uncapped her newest fountain pen, silver with a stainless steel nib.

"I've already ordered your favorite--a pot of tea and two Welsh cakes." Parker Clough said.

"Diolch," *thank you* she said approvingly. Parker Clough reminded her of how men in Wales used to be. Her father's generation. When people knew what was important in life—a work ethic, frugality, good manners. "Have you heard from Lucy?" she asked. Keenan, appeared at the kitchen door and she motioned him over. He began a slow trudge in their direction.

Parker nodded, the ridiculous smile reappearing. "She's doing well. Her portrait business has gained a bit of ground and she has a gallery show in a week."

"Good for her. I always thought she had talent. And the ability to stick with things. Very important these days. Do you Zoom?"

"Mostly *ooVoo*. Better for international calls."

"Ah...right. Definitely, a better choice." She must remember to ask Sister Gwenydd for an update. Sister Agatha hated to appear behind the times. She looked around for Keenan and as he often did, he appeared just as she despaired of ever getting her tea. "Thank you, Keenan," she said as he placed a small white teapot and two crispy Welsh cakes crumbled with butter and sugar on the table. Chocolate and flour smudged his white apron. "Does the apron mean you are training to work in the kitchen?" she asked.

"I guess. Not for long though."

"Oh?" She poured tea into her teacup and added sugar and milk. "And why not? Apprenticing oneself to bakers as skilled as those here at the Buttered Crust sounds like quite an opportunity."

"Yeah well, not my thing." He emitted an exhausted sigh and gazed at the empty chair as though he might fall into it.

"No? You could learn to bake. Wouldn't that be an advancement for you? You know, over waiting tables." *And he couldn't be any worse.*

"It's not the baking. They want me here three hours before the place opens." Keenan shrugged. "I mean, seriously? It's still dark out." He ambled off, waving to a gaggle of schoolgirls who came through the door in a burst of cold air and laughter.

Sister Agatha stirred her tea. "I weep for the future."

Parker nodded, biting into a very healthy-looking bran muffin. He carefully wiped his fingers on a paper napkin and then leaning back, gave her an anxious look. "Perhaps you know, Constable Barnes left for a two week holiday this morning."

Sister Agatha lifted her eyebrows. "Did he now? Where did he go?"

"He wouldn't say. Though we've taken bets on Honolulu or caravan camping at Bron-Y-Wendon."

"I'm pulling for Honolulu."

"He's afraid he'll get a work-related call. I guess Mrs. Barnes threatened to leave him at the curb if they don't have at least one uninterrupted holiday before he retires."

"Can't blame her. Does this mean you are in charge?"

"In a way."

She thought Parker was about to add something and then stopped himself. "In a way?" With the Constable out of town, she could certainly make progress on the murder. Her mind began to race with possibilities.

"In the day-to-day workings of the constabulary, then yes, I am in charge, as you put it. However..." His voice trailed off. He picked up his teacup and then studiously set it down in the saucer.

"However what?"

"However, the Constable told me...and I quote... 'do not let Sister Agatha drag you down a rabbit hole with the Claire MacDonagh case.'"

"Ha! Rabbit hole indeed." She broke her Welsh cake in half, and without taking her eyes off Parker, bit into the pastry. She chewed and swallowed. "You would think that after all the invaluable assistance I gave him last time there was a murder in Pryderi on his watch, he would have more faith in me."

"Yes. Well." Parker looked around as if to see if they were being watched. And then he pulled two evidence bags out of his pocket. One held a mobile phone; the other, a flash drive.

"Even so. I thought we might, off the record, do an exchange of information. Which means that first, you tell me everything you remember about the two people you saw at the Dovecote last night. And then, I'll share something with you."

Her heart trilled. Usually she had to burrow her way into an investigation, convincing Constable Barnes of her value. But now, it was as if Parker was handing her an engraved invitation. "Anything you want, but I did give a complete statement yesterday to Constable Barnes."

"I know, just tell it again to me."

She went through her description of the two people. They sat without speaking for a long moment.

"Do you think we could say that the tall one was male and the other, female?"

"Maybe. Though I jumped to that conclusion last night because I assumed it was Claire and her boyfriend, or ex-boyfriend. He's tall-- or what I could see of him that morning here at the Buttered Crust-- and Claire is...was... on the short side and well, not heavy, but a bit plumper at least than the boy. But now we know that Claire wasn't there at all. She was lying at the bottom of the cliff." Sister Agatha took a deep breath. "Which makes me equally unsure about the identity of the tall person."

"And you can't make a guess about gender?"

"Not with confidence."

"Alright then," Parker said and opened the bag with the mobile. Taking it out, he pressed a key, waited, and then tapped the screen a few times. He handed it to her, and she found herself gazing at the smiling photo of Claire, the selfie that she snapped just before falling to her death. She swallowed hard and grabbed a paper napkin to dab away the tears.

"Sorry." She hastily placed the phone on the tabletop. "Going backwards over the cliff. It's so... so horrifying." Very few people knew it, but Sister Agatha had only two big fears in life. A fear of literary rejection, and a fear of heights. On occasion, when she had to climb up into the barn loft to toss down hay for Bartimaeus, she could barely complete the task without her stomach somersaulting. But this morning even the act of *imagining* going over a cliff made her stomach drop.

"Her phone is mostly photos of people her age, an older couple who are likely her parents. Lots of selfies. Some recent shots of Gwenafwy Abbey and Pryderi. Three photos from Reggie's. But not nearly as many photos as most Millennials store on a phone. It could be that she downloads them. Also, there were only two messages on the phone. Both sent in the early afternoon. To someone named Peter. And he responded to her. Nothing particularly interesting in the texts."

"Peter is her cousin. He's in Snowdonia and he might be coming to visit."

"Okay. Makes sense, then. One of the messages to Peter is cryptic though." He flipped through his notebook and then slid it over to her: *"Fear them not therefore: for there is nothing covered, that shall not be revealed; and hid, that shall not be known." Matthew 10:26*

"That was a message to Peter?"

"Yes. With a smiley face."

"No other text messages?"

"All deleted. And all messages in her email account are deleted also. Except one that came in today. Her prescription at Sweny's Pharmacy is ready for pickup."

"She is very meticulous about deleting, isn't she? Do you think that's of interest?"

"Hard to say. People are getting cautious these days about security. If the case goes much further, I'll take the phone to Wrexham. They have special software to find deleted texts and emails. It's outside the Pryderi Constabulary budget, though. I would need permission from Constable Barnes."

"Oh dear. We don't want to contact Hawaii."

"Or the caravan park at Bron-Y-Wendon."

Sister Agatha took a sip of tea and stared at the selfie of Claire. She could almost look at it now without feeling queasy. Disturbing how quickly one habituates to violence.

"Can we be certain that it was not an accidental fall?" Parker Clough looked at her closely.

"If it were accidental, why would two people steal her key and break into her cottage before her body was discovered?"

She couldn't help but notice his use of the word 'we'.

"Why, indeed?" Parker picked up the other evidence bag, with the flash drive. He slid it across the table to her. "The weirdest part was-- nothing of value was taken as far as I can tell. Other than her laptop. Whoever those two were, they left cash and two credit cards in the desk drawer. And they were smart enough not to leave prints. They wore gloves and wiped everything down."

Sister Agatha picked up the evidence bag. "They took the laptop but left a flashdrive?"

"That's because it was rolled up in a sock in her sock drawer."

"Ha! Inspector Rupert McFarland said just last week, 'always check the socks!'"

"Well, as usual, your Inspector is spot-on. Where do you think I keep the family silver?" Parker gave a rare grin.

Although Parker was an extraordinary young man with impeccable manners, Sister Agatha had never known him to reveal a sense of humor. This must be the influence of Lucy who was nearly a stand-up comic.

"Anyway, the only thing on the flash drive is a file labeled "TL64".

"What's in the file?"

"Nothing. Empty."

"But labeled TL64?"

He shrugged and finished off the last bite of his bran muffin. "Could be meaningless."

She turned to a new page in the notebook and wrote TL64. *It was clearly a code. How much more Agatha Christie could one get?* She made a note in her murder book. *Re-read The Postern of Fate.*

"By the way, did you find her green rucksack?"

Parker Slough's eyebrows shot up. "I didn't even know there *was* a green rucksack." He dug through the pocket of his navy blue deputy's vest and pulled out his own notebook, black plastic with a wire spiral.

She watched as he took a few notes using a very ordinary ball-point pen. *Professionals. How can they even hope to solve crimes when they are so lacking in style and imagination?*

He frowned and looked up. "I did notice there was no purse, but since her wallet was in the drawer, I thought maybe she didn't carry a bag or anything."

"All women carry a bag. *Good heavens.* Claire's key was in her rucksack. Which is most likely how they got in the door without forcing it."

He sat back, his brow crinkled, looking at her. "But that would also mean ...." His voice trailed off.

"Mean what?" Sister Agatha sat up straight.

"Well, aren't there others at Gwenafwy Abbey with a key that fits the dovecote?"

"What are you saying?"

Parker cocked his head at her. "Come on Sister. You're too good at this to tell me you haven't had the same thought? It was pitch dark last night and you could really only tell that it was a tall person and a shorter person at Claire's cottage door. Both bundled up in winter clothes."

The cheerful conversation of the Buttered Crust seemed to fade around her as she looked hard at the young officer. "Of course I've thought of it. I just don't like it." She paused, remembering the two figures in the moonlight. Tall and short. Reverend Mother and Sister Callwen. *Never.* Sister Samantha and Sister Juniper. *Impossible. Or was it?* "Doesn't the fact that I heard the front gate open rule out one of the nuns? None of the sisters would be at the gate. They would have come from the main building."

"What if they were returning from the cliff walk? People often return to the scene of the crime. And you didn't hear a car, right?"

"No. Definitely no car."

He wrote in his notebook for a moment. "Are you positively sure about all of this, Sister? I mean, you were probably tired. It was late."

"I know what I saw."

He tapped his pen on the table. "Describe the man you saw at the Buttered Crust again, please."

She gave her description of the tall young man and recounted Claire's hostile reaction. This time she remembered the silver car. An Aston Healey Vantage.

"Really? That will help in tracking him down." He made more notes. Keenan wandered in their direction and she waved him over.

"Keenan, has there been a tall young man in here lately? A stranger to the village? Early 30's, blond hair?"

Keenan looked at her blankly. "Maybe."

"Maybe, yes? Or Maybe, no?"

"Just maybe."

"He drove a silver Aston Healey Vantage," Parker added.

Keenan's eyes lit up. "Oh the chap with the car. That's the car I want someday. I could definitely get a girlfriend with a car like that." He looked out the front window as if the car were about to magically appear on the curb.

"Did you get his name?"

"Whose name?" Keenan looked back at her.

"The man who drove the car."

"Sorry." Keenan shook his head.

"Did he talk about anything with you?"

"Complained a lot. Didn't like the service here."

"Imagine that?" Sister Agatha exchanged a glance with Parker. "What else did he say?"

"He liked the dining room at the Hotel Pryderi better. And I said to him, well, yeah, who doesn't?"

"Is that where he was staying? Hotel Pryderi?" Sister Agatha began to bundle her things into her carryall. She had just enough time to get to the hotel and then back to Gwenafwy Abbey to help Sister Matilda and Reggie with some sort of greenhouse project. Reggie wanted to explore gardening as a retirement activity and

Sister Matilda was only too happy to get him digging in the dirt. Gardening wasn't Sister Agatha's forte, but Sister Matilda had asked for her especially. And one didn't say 'no' to Sister Matilda.

"I guess." Keenan's eyes had wandered back to the front window. Two young women came through the front door, and without another word, he wandered towards their table.

"Good grief. Of all times for Constable Barnes to go on holiday." Parker tipped back his tea and while draining the cup, glanced at his mobile. "I have to get back to the station. Take the evidence with you and see if you can make any progress on it. Call me straight away if you do. And I hate to ask this, but do you have any time to stop by the hotel? Just see if the guy is still there and get his name if they will give it to you. Don't do anything else. I would send an officer, but if he sees a uniform, he might take off. And remember, we have no solid evidence that it was him at the dovecote last night. And we certainly don't have any evidence that he...had anything to do with what happened to Claire." He stood looking down at her, his hands stuffed in the pockets of his unbuttoned anorak.

"What's wrong?" She looked up at him. "You don't look like yourself."

"I just keep thinking of Lucy. You know, last Christmas." he said, leaning in and with a low voice. "She practically died because it took me so long to figure out what was going on."

"Nonsense. You were johnny-on-the-spot when she needed you." Sister Agatha didn't want to add, the obvious fact, that Claire was already dead. It wasn't like he could save her now anyway.

"I guess you're right." He stood to his full 6 feet three inches and gave her a polite nod, turned and wove his way out through the crowded tables.

She removed the mobile from the evidence bag and tapped the screen. The smiling face of Claire stared back at her. The Irish Sea in the background, a rocky drop off right behind her. Her eyes filled with tears and she gave herself a shake. *Time to get to work.*

. . .

If there was any information to be obtained, Sister Agatha was certain that Marjorie Atkinson, day clerk at the Hotel Pryderi front desk, would know it. And would tell her. They had worked the Tea and Cakes Table at St. Anselm's Christmas jumble sale together. A bonding experience if there ever was one.

"*Bora da*, Marjorie," Sister Agatha said walking up to the gleaming front desk. The lobby of the Hotel Pryderi, normally peaceful with deep carpets and quiet piano music in the background, was especially calm on a weekday at midmorning.

"I'll tell you right now, Sister Agatha. The answer is 'no,'" Marjorie Atkinson said in a firm voice, turning from the computer screen on the long front desk. "I'm not volunteering for another event at St. Anselm. I have barely recovered from the Christmas jumble."

"No, no. I'm not here recruiting volunteers. I promise," Sister Agatha said. "I just wanted to ask you about a guest you might have staying at the hotel."

"Oh." The relief in Marjorie's voice was obvious. "Ask away then." She turned back to her computer screen and tapped on the keyboard. "But if you don't mind, I'm going to keep working. We're about to get slammed. The St. Anne's girls' choir from Tenby is arriving for the music festival in Wrexham."

"Wrexham doesn't have its own hotels?" Sister Agatha asked.

"They do. But I guess this choir qualified late and couldn't get a reservation. So they're going to stay here and take the bus to the Cathedral." Marjorie switched from keyboard to pen and began to make check marks on an open ledger book. Sister Agatha leaned in. "Do you have a young guest staying here, a man who is from out of town? Tall, young, handsome."

At that Marjorie looked up. "Handsome?" she said and grinned. "And exactly how do you define handsome?" Marjorie closed the ledger book and placed her pen on the counter. She looked directly at Sister Agatha.

"I don't know. Handsome. Mr.-Darcy-handsome. Only with blond hair." Sister Agatha paused for a moment. "And drives a silver Austin Healey Vantage."

"Oh. The broken-hearted-boy. Hate to tell you, but he left early this morning."

"This morning?" Sister Agatha felt her heart drop. A day late and a dollar short as Sister Callwen always reminded her. "What did you call him?"

"'The broken-hearted-boy'."

"Why?"

"I'm not supposed to talk about the people who stay here." Marjorie paused. "But then this isn't private or harmful in any way. And it happened in public, right here in the lobby."

"What happened?"

"No, I don't mean something bad happened. I mean, it was sweet. Funny. Cute, even."

"Sweet, funny, cute? Tell me." Sister Agatha pulled out her notebook and silver fountain pen. "First, what time?"

"Not sure what time exactly." Marjorie paused and thought for a moment.

"Timing is very important here." Sister Agatha said, forcing her voice to remain calm. *Why was the public always so difficult in helping in a murder investigation?*

"Alright. Half-three, then. I'm pretty sure. Your Mr. Darcy came downstairs with a huge bouquet of flowers. From the Just-For-You Florists." Marjorie paused. "Don't you like it when visitors buy local?"

"Yes, love it. Who were the flowers for?"

"I asked him. And he was very talkative about it. He kind of blushed and he said he was meeting his girlfriend, and he was going to give them to her and then propose to her. He pulled a ring box out of his trousers' pocket and everything."

"And then what?"

"And then what, what?"

"Did he say or do anything else?"

"He said something like 'wish me good luck' and he left."

"And then?"

"And then I got the phone call from St. Anne's."

"How did he seem when he was talking with you?"

"Very happy. Maybe nervous."

"Nervous, how?"

"Nervous like 'I'm going to propose to somebody, and they might not say yes.'" Marjorie glanced at her computer screen and began to click on her keyboard. "If you don't mind sister. The choir's ETA is twenty minutes and counting. I've got to get back to work."

"Could you give me his name?"

The two women looked at each other for a long moment, Marjorie's fingers poised over the keyboard. "Not sure I feel comfortable doing that."

Sister Agatha forced herself to remain silent. Inspector Rupert McFarland often said, *give a witness enough time and they will eventually spill the beans.*

"I suppose it's okay. His name was Bickford Chadwick. And he registered for four nights. But then early this morning, he checked out. Two nights early. Although...."

"Although, what?"

"Well, I guess he overdid things at the pub, Saints and Sinners, and Ansel gave him a ride back to the hotel. You know Ansel. Never lets someone drive if he doesn't think they should. My shift was over by then."

"So, he was at the pub until late? How late?"

"Sorry. All I know is what the night manager told me."

"And he left early this morning?" Sister Agatha said.

"Before I came in, and I'm here by eight o'clock."

"Thanks. I owe you."

"Don't ever ask me to volunteer at the church again and we'll be even."

"Is it tea that you want, Sister?" Ansel asked her, standing behind the bar and holding up a white teapot. Ansel always seemed at ease, no matter how busy Saints and Sinners was on a Saturday night. Of course, it was barely noon now and the place was empty. His crisp white apron was spotless and tied smartly around his waist, his closely cropped beard and sandy hair neatly combed. His green eyes snapped at her. "I thought it was Guinness you fancied?"

"I would love a Guinness," Sister Agatha said. "But I've no time for one today. I need to get back to the convent to work with Sister Matilda in her garden."

"Garden?" Ansel said. "You can garden in the middle of January?"

"In the greenhouse. Sister Matilda and Reggie Thurston have dreamed up a huge gardening project. And apparently, I'm to help them. A cup of tea would be splendid." She waited as he poured the tea and then began. "Two nights ago a young man here at Saints and Sinners, got drunk and you had to give him a ride back to the Pryderi Hotel. Is that correct?"

"Indeed." Ansel shook his head. "Too much money to spend and too much time to waste. By the time I noticed how pissed he was, it was too late to cut him off." He was the only barman she knew who made a living off running a pub, but always exuded a slight distaste for drinking. She waited and watched as he began polish the top of the bar.

"Would you mind giving me a little more information about the young man?"

"I don't know much other than the fact that he drank malt whiskey, flashed a lot of money around, and made a complete idiot of himself."

"He was young, right?" Sister Agatha wanted to make sure they were talking about the same person.

"Youth is practically a requirement to drink like that."

"But not just young, good-looking, wealthy, maybe drove an Aston Healey?"

Ansel folded the dishtowel and dropped it on the bar. "That's him. When I saw the car, I knew I didn't want him getting into it."

"And you took him to the Hotel Pryderi."

Ansel nodded as he lifted a tray of clean glasses up onto the bar.

"When, exactly?"

"Exactly? Closing time. One o'clock."

"When did he come back to pick up the car?"

"No idea. The car was on the curb when I went home last night, and it was gone this morning."

"Can you think of anything about him that struck you? That you found interesting?"

"He couldn't stop going on about his girlfriend. *Most beautiful woman in the world. Smartest person he ever met. The love of his life.* The drunker he got, the more he carried on. I guess he proposed to her and she turned him down." Ansel shook his head again. "Maybe she'd seen him drink."

"He said he proposed to her?" Sister Agatha wrote rapidly.

Ansel nodded. "And if I had been that Kate person, I would have said 'no' too. Although he did drive quite the car."

"Kate?" Sister Agatha stopped writing and looked up. "He said his girlfriend was Kate?"

Ansel nodded.

Sister Agatha stared at the bar top for a moment. So the boyfriend wasn't in Pryderi to see Claire. He was here to propose to someone named Kate. Is that why Claire was so upset—she knew about the other woman? And who *was* Kate? A better question, did it matter? "And you took him back to the hotel at what time?"

"Like I said, just after closing time—one o'clock."

"You're sure about the time and the woman's name?"

Ansel nodded. Sister Agatha made a few quick notes. "What time did he come into the pub?"

"Early. Otherwise I wouldn't have noticed him right away. Five o'clock, I think. Could have been later. Half five. Stayed till closing," Ansel shook his head. "Could barely walk by the time I poured him into my car."

Sister Agatha laid her pen down. *Five or maybe half five?*

"Why are you so interested in this guy?"

"I'm not sure I am anymore."

CHAPTER 10

"So, he wasn't in Pryderi to see Claire. He was here to see someone named Kate. And not just see her, but to propose to her." Sister Agatha said, as she settled into the love seat in Father Selwyn's office. Winter sunlight streamed in the stained glass window and a fire burned in the grate. She dug her mobile out of her red jumper pocket and texted Sister Matilda. Maybe they could get started on the planting project and she could jump in later. "Which means he most likely wasn't anywhere near Claire the night that she died. And when Claire said he was her ex, she meant it. She must have known all about the other woman—this Kate person—and that was the source of her anger that morning in front of The Buttered Crust."

"Did you get a name for him?" Father Selwyn asked, taking a seat in one of the two the club chairs on either side of the fireplace.

"Bickford Chadwick. I did a quick Google search. The Chadwick's are an old family in London. In fact, Bickford's great uncle was a Viscount."

"Goodness," Father Selwyn said as he opened a package of digestive biscuits. "And you are confident that he was proposing to another woman at the same time that Claire died?" He leaned over to the electric kettle perched on the edge of his desk and pressed the button.

"Claire died at five o'clock that afternoon according to Dr. Beese and the time stamp on the selfie. Marjorie saw Bickford leave the hotel at half-three with a bouquet of flowers. Oh. And I double-checked with Just-For-You-Florist. The card was made out to a woman named Kate and he had them enclose a very endearing little poem about how much he loved her." She waited while Father Selwyn poured a cup of tea for each of them. "By five o'clock – or maybe a little later-- he was at the pub drinking and according to Ansel, stayed all evening and got rollicking drunk. I don't see much time in there to murder anyone out on the cliffs."

"So, while Claire lay dead on the sand, her ex-boyfriend was off proposing to another woman and then drinking off her refusal?"

"Looks like it." Sister Agatha took a digestive biscuit out of the package when Father Selwyn held it out to her. "I had a perfectly good suspect. And now.... nothing."

"Well, don't dismiss him yet. It sounds a little too neat and tidy to me."

"That's true. *Beware of the case tied up with a bow!*"

"Inspector Rupert McFarland?"

Sister Agatha nodded, her mouth full of biscuit.

"What else do you have?"

She swallowed and brushed crumbs off the front of her habit apron. "Parker did give me the evidence from the crime scene."

Father Selwyn's eyebrows shot up. "Should he have done that?"

"Of course he should have! Think how much I've assisted that constabulary over the past year." She ignored his eyeroll. "The problem is that the evidence is maddeningly brief. And I need your help." She opened her notebook and removed a folded piece of paper. "Take a look."

Father Selwyn sat up straight which forced him to draw in his long legs and peered through his spectacles. "TL64?"

"The label on an empty file on a flash drive and hidden among her socks."

"An empty file? That doesn't sound particularly suspicious. What does it mean?"

"No idea—but it reads like a secret code."

"It does?"

"Has no one read *The Postern of Fate*? Anyway, read what I copied below. That was sent in a text message to her cousin, Peter. It was the last text that Claire sent before she died."

He read aloud, "'Fear them not therefore: for there is nothing covered, that shall not be revealed; and hid, that shall not be known.'

"And it had a smiley face."

Father Selwyn leaned back again in the wingback chair. "A smiley face. Interesting. The context of the verse is Jesus addressing his disciples. Was Claire a scholar of the bible?"

"Claire was an acclaimed atheist. She only seemed interested in religion as it pertained to the story she was writing."

"So why would she send a bible verse to her cousin? Is he religious?"

Sister Agatha sat up and leaned forward. "You are asking the wrong question. The question we need to answer is, why that verse? Why send that particular verse the afternoon of the day she dies?"

"Well, when Jesus said this to his disciples, I believe he was encouraging them to speak boldly about his mission. To proclaim his message of love."

"And she writes that to her cousin and puts a smiley face?" They both sat in stumped silence for a moment. "Did you know Constable Barnes is out of town?" Sister Agatha finally said.

"I do remember Emerick complaining that he was missing his bass section. How long?"

"Two weeks."

"Better work fast."

"I plan to." Sister Agatha popped the last of the biscuit in her mouth and stood. She pulled on her anorak and squashed her woolly hat over her short gray hair. "Believe me, I plan to."

Sister Gwenydd was up to her elbows in macaroni.

"Lunch?" Sister Agatha asked, coming into the warm, fragrant kitchen. First, a cup of tea, then potting plants.

"The new sisters told me that they love mac and cheese. Not exactly a Welsh dish, but I thought I would try to make it for them."

"How do you think they're doing?" Sister Agatha asked, pulling a chair up to the table, and sliding the teapot over. She peered in. One sodden tea bag on the bottom. She went over to the stove to put the kettle on and then rinsed out the teapot in the sink.

"Well, for the most part, they seem happy," Sister Gwenydd said, stirring the macaroni noodles with a large wooden spoon. Considering that they've been here for only two weeks. And that they traded sunny California for snowy North Wales."

"You must like having some young women your own age at the convent." Sister Agatha watched as the young woman put the pasta aside and poured warm milk into a mixing bowl.

"I do like it," Sister Gwenydd replied, without looking up from her mixing bowl. Sister Agatha watched as she added butter and flour and then whisked vigorously. "But..." she trailed off, concentrating as she stirred the roux into the bowl of macaroni.

"But what?"

"It's an adjustment, that's all."

"Like how?" Sister Agatha poured hot water into the teapot over two bags of Welsh Brew.

"Reverend Mother would probably say I am being uncharitable. You won't repeat this? You'll keep it to yourself?"

"Of course."

Sister Gwenydd grunted and looked at her with raised eyebrows. Although Sister Agatha liked others to keep her secrets, she proved notoriously bad at secret-keeping herself.

"Except if Reverend Mother asks me a direct question, then you know I'll give it all up. Like a perp interrogated by Armand Gamache." Louise Penny's Quebec detective was a comrade in arms with her. An imaginary one, of course.

Sister Gwenydd spooned the macaroni and cheese-roux into a large casserole dish, smoothed it over, and slid it into the range. She fiddled with the thermostat for a moment. "I've kept an eye on Sister Samantha, like you asked. And you're right. She seems... I don't know...not into it."

Sister Agatha opened her notebook. "What do you mean?"

"For one thing, nothing is good enough." Sister Gwenydd wiped her hands on a linen towel and took a chair across from Sister Agatha. "She thinks we are... *antiquated.*"

"Antiquated!" Sister Agatha clattered her teacup into the saucer. "Ridiculous. We have all the latest in technology. Netflix, Wi-Fi, GPS in the minivan." She didn't like any criticism of Gwenafwy Abbey. Unless she was the one doing the criticizing.

"The Wi-Fi only works in the attic. Which is driving the new sisters a little crazy."

"Tell them about the barn loft. Great signal and you get to enjoy the lovely smell of fresh hay and horse manure. Well, pony manure." She poured a cup of tea for Sister Gwenydd and topped off her own cup.

"Not everyone thinks pony manure is a lovely smell."

"Their loss."

Sister Gwenydd walked quickly to the end of the kitchen and shut the door to the warming room. The first floor below the dormitory housed the kitchen, the long dining room that the sisters called the refectory, and the warming room where the old monks had kept a roaring fire throughout the winter. The sisters now used the warming room to relax during the evening-- reading, knitting, and watching Netflix. She walked back over to Sister Agatha and sat down across from her. She took a breath and peered around the room.

"Good heavens!" Sister Agatha exclaimed. "Do you think someone is hiding in the larder? Just say it."

"Alright then. Sister Samantha doesn't like Reverend Mother. And she even made an offhand comment about a vote of no-confidence."

"Doesn't like Reverend Mother?! A vote of no-confidence? A young nun still wet behind the scapular!" Sister Agatha glared across the table. "Millennials! *I weep for the future.*"

Sister Gwenydd suppressed a smile. "Well, it may not be as bad as that. The other nuns don't agree with her at all and it seems that Sister Samantha has a reputation of being kind of a Moaning Minnie."

"You did defend Reverend Mother, didn't you?"

"Well of course! What do you take me for? Without Reverend Mother where would I be today?" It was now Sister Gwenydd's turn to glare across the table.

"Okay. Sorry. It's just that I have other worries about Sister Samantha and now with this."

Sister Gwenydd got up and checked the thermostat to the old range. The door to the warming room remained closed. Closed door conversations in a common space, such as the kitchen, violated a well-respected practice at Gwenafwy Abbey. Reverend Mother insisted on total transparency among the sisters. But Sister Agatha didn't always agree, and she had reason to think that Reverend Mother wasn't always following her own rule. Of course she would never say so. In her mind, Reverend Mother was above reproach.

"So tell me. What have you found out?" Sister Gwenydd's eyes snapped with interest. "About Claire, that is? Because you practically promised to bring me in on your sleuthing."

Sister Agatha filled her in on everything she had discovered about Chadwick Bickford. She didn't tell her everything about the text message or the flash drive.

When she was done, they both sat in silence for a moment. "It's hard to believe isn't it?" Sister Gwenydd said quietly. "Sometimes, I'll be doing something, and I'll be thinking oh, I need to tell this to Claire. And then I remember she's gone." Sister Gwenydd grabbed a nearby dishtowel and wiped her eyes. "So Claire died while this ex-boyfriend was proposing to another woman." She looked up. "What a horrible person."

"Ansel called him an idiot." They both laughed, their grief relieved by laughter for a moment.

"If you want to sleuth, then continue to keep an eye on Sister Samantha. Tell me straight away if you detect anything unusual." Sister Agatha took a last sip of tea and stood, smoothing out the front of her blue habit. "One more thing, help me find out the whereabouts of every member of the Abbey at the time of Claire's death."

"Every member of the Abby? Surely you don't suspect... oh, I guess you do." Sister Gwenydd gave her a long look. "No one is going to appreciate being asked where they were on the night of a murder."

"They never do."

"When you say 'everyone' you don't mean...."

"Yes. Including Reverend Mother."

"Reverend Mother isn't my concern." Sister Gwenydd stood up and put their tea things in the kitchen sink. She turned back. "It's Sister Callwen I'm afraid of."

"It's time you accepted the fact that we're all just a little afraid of Sister Callwen. I also count her as one of my best friends." Sister Agatha pulled on her woolly hat. "Unfortunately, I have to go to the greenhouse."

"And I need to read up on cakes. You can't have an Epiphany feast without a king's cake."

CHAPTER 11

She glanced out the window over her desk and stared out. The sunny winter day had turned into a cold night. Ben Holden had sent her a text and assured her that Bartimaeus was warm and comfortable and she need not check on him in the middle of the night.

She poured tea from the thermos she had brought from the kitchen and then picked up her silver fountain pen, determined to update her notebook. *A detective is only as good as his notes!* Inspector Rupert McFarland had repeated many times in his podcast. *Write neatly, write often! Penmanship is a detective's best friend!* Sister Agatha skipped a few spaces and wrote as neatly as she could, *no rucksack, money untouched, flash drive left in socks, biblical text message (smiley face), most texts and emails deleted, boyfriend proposes to someone named Kate, file labeled in cryptic code possibly connected to article on miniature cathedral.*

Next, she took the evidence bag from her top desk drawer and removed the mobile. Fingerprints weren't a possibility since the salt water had washed over it. She made a note that there were identical scratches on each side of the phone and then snapped a few quick photos of the scratches with her own mobile. Next, she clicked the start button. Nothing. Either the battery had gone dead since Parker had given it to her, or the phone had given up the ghost. Maybe the salt water was too much for it. She knew some mobiles were amazingly waterproof since Father Selwyn had dropped his in the baptismal font once and didn't realize it until the next morning when the ladies from the Altar Guild found it.

She was pleasantly surprised to see that she could plug Claire's mobile in with her own power cord and even happier when the screen brightened and indicated that it was charging. In a moment, it buzzed and like Jesus from the tomb, it came to life. Picking it up, she felt a jolt. A photo of Claire, red hair blowing and wearing a bright green sweater, with a young man, stared back at her. Her screen shot was of the ex-boyfriend, Bickford Chadwick. Sister Agatha felt a wave of sadness. He proposed to someone else and yet Claire kept his photo on her mobile. Ansel might have been right in his characterization of the young man.

Sister Agatha made a few notes and then turned back to the photo. Claire's head was turned slightly towards Bickford so that you could just see her eyes. She clearly gazed at him with a look of youthful love. Tousled blond hair, brown eyes, a tattered fisherman's knit sweater, one arm around Claire, he looked directly into the camera. Sister Agatha couldn't decide what she thought of his look. Not quite so in love as Claire? She looked closer. They stood under a sign on a green field with tall waving grass. "Snowdonia Bird Centre." Was Claire a birder? She had never mentioned it, but then what did that prove? Perhaps the boyfriend was? Or maybe they were out for a lark in the country and snapped the photo. And Snowdonia was a short train ride from Pryderi. And wasn't the cousin in Snowdonia?

She knew that Reverend Mother had unsuccessfully tried to contact Claire's parents, hiking in the Himalayas. What about Bickford? How had he taken the news of Claire's death? Had anyone told him? Not if he had left town before the sun even rose, which meant he left before they found Claire's body.

On the other hand, was he the murderer and somehow just managed to make it appear like he had a solid alibi? Boyfriends were always suspects in murder mysteries. And not just in fiction- - in real life. What was that awful statistic that she had just read? More than half of the murders of women are at the hands of an intimate partner? She added a note: *find out who Kate is. Does Bickford really have an alibi?*

She clicked on the icon for *Gallery* and felt another jolt. The selfie popped up. She shuddered and said a brief prayer and then forced herself to really examine it. In one sense, it looked entirely normal. If one didn't think about what happened only a moment later. A happy, bright-eyed smiling young woman. Her life ahead of her. Could she enlarge the photo and print it? Which meant technology, and that called for a younger nun.

Are you awake? She texted. Surely Sister Gwenydd was up. In her youthfulness, she was both a night owl and an early bird. Sister Agatha's phone chirped.

Not really.

What does that mean?

I was asleep till I heard your text.

In the attic. Pressing tech question.

K.

What did *K* mean? Sister Agatha wondered. She hated to ask and risk of sounding antiquated. Maybe sister Samantha had a point. Just as she was Googling "urban slang", Sister Gwenydd came through the door. "It means okay," she said, without asking. She crossed the long room to Sister Agatha's writing desk.

"I knew that," she replied, as she clicked out of Google.

"What's up?" Sister Gwenydd pulled a chair next to Sister Agatha's desk. She shoved her thick brown hair back into a pony-tail which was Sister Gwenydd's customary signal that she was ready to work. Sister Agatha quickly filled her in on the evidence that Parker Clough had given her.

Sister Gwenydd let out a low whistle. "No kidding? I knew I liked Parker. Is he still hooked up with Lucy?"

"Apparently they zoom and do other things."

Sister Gwenydd raised her eyebrows. "Other things?"

"Like oovoo. Or something."

"Oh." She yawned again. "Well, Lucy could do worse than Parker Clough."

"What a thing to say. She could do much worse than a Welshman!" Sister Agatha looked askance. "She would be smart to choose a man from Wales."

"So what do you want me to do," Sister Gwenydd said, picking up the mobile. "Oh my god," she murmured. "The selfie. And right at the edge of the cliff." Sister Gwenydd set it down, her face pale.

"I want to know if it can be enlarged. For a closer look?"

"Did you download it?"

"No. Can you just get into her mobile like that? Don't you need her password?"

"You're in her mobile now, Sister. Which is a good argument for a password protected phone. It's amazing that someone like Claire wouldn't protect their phone. But people are like that. Either too trusting or just lazy."

Sister Agatha wanted to remark that Claire MacDonagh was neither trusting nor lazy, but instead she stayed quiet and let Sister Gwenydd work.

"I don't suppose your mobile is connected to your printer?"

Sister Agatha looked at her blankly. "I didn't know it could be."

Sister Gwenydd sighed. "I'll do it for you later."

She watched as the young woman tapped and swiped the screen a few times. "There. I emailed it to you. Open it on your computer. If you give me a minute, I could download everything from her phone?" Sister Gwenydd looked at Sister Agatha.

"That seems a little intrusive. At least at this point. We could save drastic measures for later. I want to respect her privacy as much as possible. Although Parker told me almost all of it is deleted."

A few clicks and swipes by Sister Gwenydd and a moment later, they stared at the selfie now splashed across Sister Agatha's computer screen. "Enlarge it," she instructed. "And now again, the top right corner." She waited as Sister Gwenydd tapped the screen. "Again."

They both stared at the enlarged, grainy photo, not speaking. The bell in the village clock tower chimed softly.

"I'll need to call Parker," she finally said.

Sister Gwenydd nodded not taking her eyes off the screen. "What about Reverend Mother?"

"I hate to wake her up, but...."

"But don't you think..." Sister Gwenydd's voice trailed off.

"Sister Winifred? Yes. But let's start with Reverend Mother. She'll know what to do. Print several copies, would you?"

Sister Gwenydd nodded and in a moment the printer on the other side of the room began clicking and churning.

"Meet you in the kitchen," Sister Agatha said.

Reverend Mother took a sip of her tea without taking her eyes off the print-out. "Talk me through this," she said. "And could you turn the heat up a bit, please, Sister Gwenydd. It's colder than usual in here." Sister Agatha had found Reverend Mother in her office hunched over a finance report that looked almost as ominous as what they found in the selfie.

"I hope you aren't getting a cold," Sister Agatha said.

"Nonsense. I'm without my good jumper is all. Sister Winifred is repairing it. I tore the cuff the other night."

"Ah. Yes. Sister Winifred," Sister Agatha said shooting a glance at Sister Gwenydd and pulling a chair close to Reverend Mother. She used her silver fountain pen as a pointer. "This is, as you can tell, an enlarged print of the selfie as it appears on her phone. Do you see this?" She pointed to a gray spot at the edge of the photo.

"I think so. Sort of," Reverend Mother said leaning in and adjusting her spectacles.

"Now look at it. This is the same selfie photo but enlarged once again. This blur is Claire's left shoulder. This is the top of the zipper on her coat. And here is the object." Sister Agatha pointed to the edge of the photo. "See the rectangle. Can you read it?"

"It looks like two letters."

"Right," Sister Agatha said, replacing that print out with the next one and even more blurry enlarged photo. "We enlarged it again and focused just on the square at the edge."

"Oh my goodness," Reverend Mother said, leaning in. "It says *SW*."

Sister Agatha lifted the bottom edge of her jumper. Sewn onto the edge was a small rectangular tag with the initials *SW*. "Sister Winifred. It's her signature label. She puts one on everything that she knits from prayer shawls to potholders."

"I know that," Reverend Mother said, her brow furrowed, her voice tight. "Is it possible that Claire is wearing the scarf and it blew into the picture?"

"No. Look at the selfie as it appears on her mobile screen." Sister Agatha pointed to the cheerful photo of Claire smiling into the camera. "She isn't wearing a scarf. And she told me once that she never wears them. I think someone else was wearing a Sister Winifred scarf and it blew into the picture."

"So you are saying that not only was someone at the cliff, they were wearing a scarf knitted by Sister Winifred?" Reverend Mother spoke slowly as she stared at the page. "But that doesn't mean that it was someone from the Abbey. I mean, there are lots of Sister Winifred labeled scarves out there. She sells them at the St. Anselm Christmas jumble every year. Everyone in the village seems to have something knitted by her." Reverend Mother looked at the photo again. "Father Selwyn has a Sister Winifred scarf."

"I am not saying that I think it's a person from Gwenafwy Abbey. Not definitely, anyway."

"Good heavens, Sister Agatha! What do you mean 'not definitely, anyway'? Do you actually think that a sister from Gwenafwy Abbey would shove someone over a cliff?" A frosty chill had blown into the room.

"Actually," Sister Gwenydd chimed in. "There is no evidence that the person in the scarf pushed her. Although they must have seen her fall, at the very least. They were certainly standing next to her."

"And did nothing." Sister Agatha added. "And likely took the opportunity to go to her room in the dovecote and ransack it."

"Which would mean that the person in the scarf, knew she was from the Abbey and knew she was staying in the guest cottage."

"Or they figured it out when they went through her rucksack." Sister Agatha looked again at the blurry photo. "They also were familiar with the Abbey buildings." She paused; Reverend Mother looked as if she were about to interrupt. When she didn't, Sister Agatha continued. "And they used Claire's key to gain entry. Or rather, they most likely used the key they found in her rucksack." She cringed under Reverend Mother's glare but continued. "Whoever got into the dovecote used a Gwenafwy Abbey key. How ever they might have attained it."

"No one from Gwenafwy Abbey would have done this." Reverend Mother, eyes blazing, turned to her. "I know my sisters. I've known these women for years. What you are suggesting is preposterous."

"But there are ten new sisters. You don't know them."

The room fell silent. Sister Agatha stared down at the oilcloth tablecloth, while Sister Gwenydd gently swirled the tea at the bottom of her teacup. Reverend Mother stood and walked to the window. She stared out at the winter night. When she turned around, her face was drawn. "I will concede that you could have a point. A weak point. But, a point, none-the-less." She walked past them and opened the door that led into the warming room. "You will take all of this evidence to Officer Clough immediately following breakfast tomorrow morning. We will say nothing of it to anyone." She turned around and gave them each a withering look. "And that includes Sister Winifred."

CHAPTER 12

"Are you sure?" Parker said, staring at the print-out. The Pryderi constabulary was as quiet as Gwenafwy chapel--though warmer. It also smelled like cleaning chemicals, fragrant tea, and the slight whiff of old cigarette smoke although Constable Barnes had banned smoking a decade ago.

"Look more closely," Sister Agatha said. "You'll see it."

Parker Clough flipped on the desk lamp and leaned in. "Holy Mother," he said quietly. "*SW*. I see it now. He reached into his desk and pulled out a plastic magnifying glass, not at all unlike the ones in the kindergarten room at St. Anselm.

"SW," he said again, holding the glass over the page. "And you're sure the SW is Sister Winifred?"

Sister Agatha unwound her red scarf and laid it across the desk. Parker Clough slid its label under his desk lamp. He let out a low whistle. "How many of these scarves do you think are out there?"

"Possibly hundreds. Sister Winifred has made one for each of us at the Abbey, including Ben. And it's not just scarves, everyone gets a matching sweater, hat, and mittens. All labeled." Sister Agatha put her arms out like a scarecrow standing in the garden.

"You see--red sweater, red scarf, hat, and red mittens. Sister Winifred put me in red because she thought I would be less likely to get lost in the crowd. Everyone has their own color especially chosen by Sister Winifred. Reverend Mother is green. Sister Mildred is purple. Sister Callwen, an azure blue."

"But your hat's brown?" He nodded towards her head.

"I lost my red one and had to settle for what was left in the scrap bag."

"What color is this scarf, would you say?" He held the photo up to the light again.

"Burgundy."

"Would she remember who she might have knitted a burgundy for?"

"Possibly."

"So who else has a Sister Winifred knitted ensemble? "

"Father Selwyn, yellow. Emerick Scoville, black."

"Black?"

"He's a musician."

Parker grunted and held the page up to the light, staring at it again.

"Not only that, she sells scarves, hats, mittens, and potholders at all the fundraisers: St. Anselm, Women's Institute, the Abbey. They go as fast as Sister Gwenydd's Welsh cakes."

"So half the village could own a scarf from Sister Winifred?"

"Don't leave out the village of Grenfell. Macie Cadwalader, the new priest at St. Mary, is pink. She wanted white stripes, but Sister Winifred has a solids-only rule. Unless a child wants a Hogwarts scarf and then she throws out the rule book."

"This at least narrows it down to North Wales. Which means it wasn't Bickford Chadwick." Sister Agatha quickly filled him in on what she had learned about the young man. "I doubt a young man who can buy an Aston Healey would shop at a jumble sale."

"Did you get a last name for Kate?"

Sister Agatha shook her head.

"I can't recall anyone in the village named Kate who is the right age to be proposed to by someone like this Chadwick fellow."

"I had wondered that. I don't know a Kate either."

"What if 'Kate' is a ruse?"

She liked the way Parker thought. "You mean he just made out like he was proposing to his girlfriend, in order to murder Claire? Regrets his actions and so he goes and gets himself hammered at the local pub?"

"It wouldn't be unheard of."

Sister Agatha wrote rapidly in her notebook. "Can you run a check on Bickford Chadwick? He's already left town."

"Better than that. I'll alert Scotland Yard." Parker tossed his pen onto his immaculate desk and stood abruptly giving the impression that he was about to take some sort of decisive and immediate action. Sister Agatha started to rise to her feet in the spirit of the moment, when he sat back down and stared out the window, his brow furrowed. She followed his gaze. Reggie pedaled down Main Street on his bicycle, wearing a large felt hat, brim flapping. He looked as if he were about to go airborne. Probably on his way to the Buttered Crust or his daily trip to the Pryderi Public Library. Fortunately, his fall the other night wasn't slowing him down. He had certainly been enthusiastically planting seedlings in the greenhouse yesterday.

She turned back and looked at Parker. His youthful face had gone from determined to dubious in matter of moments. "What?"

"I was just wondering if I should call Constable Barnes. You know, get his advice." A horn blared. They glanced out again just as Reggie crossed the street, his handlebars and front tire wobbling. A car screeched to a halt, just missing him, the driver leaning again on the horn. Reggie waved gaily as he bumped over the curb and continued down the sidewalk.

"Didn't Constable Barnes' wife say she would leave him if he took a single work-related call? Do you really want to be responsible for the break-up of a 39-year-long marriage?" She paused and gave him a hard look. "And anyway you are perfectly capable of solving this murder on your own. With help from me, of course."

"Right," he said, absently staring down at the photos. "So we now have solid evidence that Claire wasn't alone on that cliff when she fell. Someone stood next to her and that person wore a Sister Winifred scarf." Sister Agatha watched as he neatly lined up a stack of manila file folders, squaring them with the corners of the desk. "And whoever was up there with her most likely pushed her." He then placed in a row six perfectly sharpened pencils making them parallel to the bottom of the files. "My opinion, anyway. Or if they didn't help her fall, they walked away from the scene." He took off his glasses and carefully polished them with a folded bit of cloth from his top desk drawer.

Of course Sister Callwen likes young Parker. Sister Callwen thought tidiness was the sign of an ordered, if not ethical life. Sister Agatha rather thought it was the sign of not enough reckless abandon and chocolate.

"I'll need to meet with Sister Winifred immediately," Parker said.

"You can't. Reverend Mother wants to be the one to tell her."

"Why?"

"Because...well, she didn't come right out and say it exactly, but I would imagine that she doesn't want anyone to think that she thinks...you know." Sister Agatha watched as Parker stood up again, his six foot frame seemed to fill the small room. He crossed the floor in two steps and closed the door and then returned to his desk, squeezing in behind it.

"You're saying that she doesn't want anyone to think that one of the nuns was involved?" He paused, holding her in a steady gaze. His eyes were a deep blue. Is it any wonder that Lucy fell so hard for the young officer? "What do you think, Sister Agatha? Does the presence of this scarf change your mind about anything?"

"No! Absolutely not." Sister Agatha fingered her detective's notebook and glanced out the window again. Traffic flowed smoothly. Reggie must be off his bike and settled with a cup of tea at the Buttered Crust or perusing the new-arrivals section of the library.

"You're sure about that?"

"Of course, I'm sure." Sister Agatha took a breath and fingered the label on her red scarf. "Except...."

"Except what?"

"Except a good detective explores every option, foregoing a conclusion until all the evidence has been weighed carefully."

"And who said that?"

"Me, actually."

Parker picked up the blue stress ball from his desktop and tossed it from hand to hand and then set it down. They both watched as it rolled off the desk and bounced on the floor. She never understood why everyone was so intent on relieving stress. Sometimes the presence of a little stress is what got the job done.

"You're thinking of something and not telling me," he said.

Sister Agatha looked across the desk at Parker. "All that I am thinking is that I'm certain it was not one of the old nuns-- *older* nuns, that is. But, and I hate to say it, we have ten new nuns that we know nothing about. A reality that should give anyone pause."

Parker retrieved the ball off the floor and dropped it in the drawer. "I hate the thought of suggesting such a thing to Reverend Mother." He shut the drawer with a slight bang.

"Well, yes."

Parker Clough looked around the room as though he had lost something.

"What is it?"

"I'm not trained as a detective. You know that."

"But you are a very good policeman. Brave. Fearless, even. We saw that last year." Parker flushed pink from his collar to the roots of his black hair.

"I did what any policeman would have done."

"And you are a Welshman. Born right here in Pryderi. A Welshman never gives up."

"You're not going to start humming *Men of Harlech,* are you?" Parker gave her a rare grin across the desk.

"Don't be cheeky." There were some things Sister Agatha didn't joke about and *Men of Harlech* was one of them.

Parker looked at her for a long moment, tapping his pencil on the top of the desk. "If I call in the detectives from Wrexham, they're going to slam Gwenafwy Abbey into lock down, turn the place upside down. Interrogate everyone, confiscate Sister Winifred's knitting bag, and who knows what else. I don't think that's what you need up on the hill right now."

"Goodness, no." Sister Agatha held her breath. The detectives from Wrexham would ruin everything. Cut her right out of the investigation. And more to the point, had any one of them ever read Agatha Christie?

"So I was thinking, that for the moment anyway, you and I could try to get to the bottom of it ourselves. Quietly. We have a little more than a week before Constable Barnes gets back and if we haven't figured something out by then, he can call in the big guns."

Sister Agatha's eyes snapped as she dug into her jumper pocket locating her fountain pen and white moleskin notebook with the gilt-edged pages which she opened with a bit of ceremony. "In that case, we need to stop talking and start thinking."

Parker reached over to the small side table and pushed a button on an electric teapot. "I'll put the kettle on."

CHAPTER 13

"Curds must be heated very slowly," Sister Callwen's voice rang out above the subdued chatter of the nuns, who were gathered in the processing room of the cheese barn for the second of the cheese tutorials. "Please, sisters. If you could just give me your full attention. Perhaps all mobiles could be turned off and placed in apron pockets."

Sister Agatha reluctantly dropped her mobile into her pocket. She wished desperately that she could dash to her desk in the library. But no such luck. She was stuck here, watching curds warm.

"Diolch," *thank you*, Sister Callwen said as the room fell momentarily silent. "Would one of the new sisters please tell me what we added to the solution earlier in the process?"

Sister Theodora raised her hand and simultaneously called out, "Milk."

"Well, yes," Sister Callwen replied. "The entire process begins with a milk base. But what did we add to the milk?"

"Rennet," Sister Samantha said in a flat voice. Sister Agatha noticed her slouching posture and bored face. But on the other hand, just how exciting is rennet? The boisterous rowdiness that usually accompanied the new sisters whenever they were in a room together was missing today, the sorrow of the community, palpable. Reverend Mother had insisted that focusing on the tasks of the Abbey would go far in helping everyone as they each dealt with Claire's death. Therefore, work as usual continued.

"Correct," Sister Callwen said. "Now, everyone listen carefully. You must stir *consistently*. Never cease to stir for the entire time that you are heating the curds." She paused and looked around the room until everyone was listening. "And this next part is essential...you must stir *gently*. Think of the curds as delicate flowers." Sister Agatha resisted the desire to roll her eyes or perhaps just give in and bang her head against the wall. Sister Callwen took cheese-making a little seriously.

She took a quick inventory of the room. Most of the older nuns stood grouped around the back wall. Reverend Mother gave Sister Agatha a warm smile and then she went back to tapping on her iPad. *I guess iPads are allowed, she thought.* Sister Winifred sat on a stool and knitted, while Sister Harriet leaned against the wall and sketched with a charcoal pencil. She noticed that all the young nuns-- including Sister Samantha-- diligently took notes. A few had spiral notebooks and pens while others had electronic tablets. Sister Agatha pulled her notebook out of her jumper pocket and admired its cream-colored moleskin cover and gilt-edged pages. Could she ever switch to an electronic tablet? She slid the notebook back into her jumper pocket. *Never.* She was grateful to Sister Winifred for designing the jumper with pockets large enough to stash her detective's notebook, silver fountain pen, Girl Guides knife, prayer book and latest Agatha Christie re-read.

"Once the curds have completely firmed," Sister Callwen went on. "Then it's time to drain the whey." She pulled up a ladle-full of curds and spooned them into one hand. Then she squished the curdish mass together into a ball. The young nuns leaned in eagerly, eyes bright with interest.

Well, they couldn't be faulted for a lack of enthusiasm.

"When you can form the curds into a ball-- and when they are a bit squeaky-- then they are ready for the next step."

She realized that Sister Callwen was in her element. She hadn't appreciated how skilled Sister Callwen was at teaching. And she had to admit, the positive attitude of the new nuns was having a good effect on the older nuns. A fresh energy had entered the community.

"Ladle the curds out of the whey, without haste, into a mold like this one." Sister Callwen held up a blue plastic cylinder.

Had Armand Gamache ever been kept from an investigation because he was required to separate curds from whey? Very doubtful.

"And now," Sister Callwen said with a flourish. "If you will all follow me to the other end of the processing room, I will show you how to properly place the newly formed curds into the press." Sister Agatha slipped through the side door and with her head down, walked as fast as she could along the walk to the Abbey's main building. One can only handle so much cheese in a day.

"I like this spot," Sister Gwenydd said brightly from where she sat in the attic library as Sister Agatha came in the door. Sister Gwenydd, excused from cheese-making due to her many hours in the kitchen, sat sideways in an overstuffed upholstered chair, her legs and stockinged feet draped over the side. A pile of culinary magazines lay scattered on the floor around her and sunlight poured through the attic windows onto the chocolate brown carpet. Sister Agatha's librarian's heart trilled. Sister Gwenydd wasn't known for being a big reader and yet she had found her way to the new reading nook. *The very reason a library should find a way to welcome everyone.*

"*Bore da,* Sister! You're enjoying my new reading nook? Splendid," Sister Agatha said as she heaved her carryall onto the long worktable in the center of the room.

"Listen to this." Sister Gwenydd turned a page or two and then read aloud, "'My dinner consisted of a liver pâté remarkably similar to library paste –if that library paste had been mixed with the glutinous mass of seaweed one finds left on the sand after the tide had gone out.'" Sister Gwenydd dropped the *Modern Cuisine* onto her lap. "I hate to admit it, but I love reading snarky reviews of other people's cooking. It makes me feel better about my own." She paused; her brow crinkled. "Do you think that makes me a bad person?"

"Only if reading bad reviews of fiction authors makes me a bad person. I always think, if they're that bad and they got published, there's hope for me." Sister Agatha dropped into the chair behind her worktable. Her writing desk and computer, at the opposite end of the long room from the reading nook, beckoned her. But a librarian's first duties were to her patrons and she had ordering to do. "So you like those magazines? Glad I didn't throw them out." Sister Agatha looked to Sister Gwenydd for a response, but she was staring at the page.

"You won't believe this."

"What?"

"You know who wrote that horrible review?" Without waiting for a response, Sister Gwenydd stared at her, her eyes wide. "Claire."

"Our Claire?"

"Yes..." Sister Gwenydd flipped through the pages. "I guess she was a food critic at one time. I mean I know she's a journalist and that she said she took on lots of little jobs when she started out, but this is crazy. Claire was a *food* critic." She began to rifle through the other old magazines. "Oh wow...she had a regular column." Sister Gwenydd skimmed another review. "And she was *not* nice. Oh *snap*."

"I thought she was a muckraking kind of journalist who was looking for that one big breaking story. Why would she write food articles?"

"I would imagine she wrote anything she could, if it would bring in some money."

"True. Paying the rent drove Dickens to write *The Christmas Carol*. And Louisa May Alcott wrote *Little Women* to pay the grocery bill." Sister Agatha paused for a moment. "How does a chef feel after a review like that?"

"How do you think they feel? Devastated. Angry. A single bad review can destroy a career."

"Would they hate a review enough to kill the reviewer?"

"You don't think?" When Sister Agatha didn't respond, her face turned thoughtful. "With some chefs, maybe. Their egos are huge, and the stakes are high. But high enough to murder?" She paused. "I hate to say it, but maybe."

"Can you do me a sleuthing favor, Sister Gwenydd?"

"Of course." Sister Gwenydd looked at Sister Agatha, her eyes gleaming.

"Find out if Claire ruffled any feathers in the cooking world. See if she does have an enemy. Especially someone local. We need to see if there's anyone out there who might kill when they read that their pate was compared to library paste."

CHAPTER 14

The packages of McVitie's Jaffa Cakes stood artfully arranged in a tall pyramid at the center of one of Sister Agatha's favorite stores, The Fatted Calf, which sold mostly farm-to-market organic meats and locally grown fresh produce. But one could also find a tempting array of baked goods and sweeties.

She was on an errand for Sister Gwenydd who required two large cans of green enchilada sauce for pork chili Verde because she heard that the new nuns loved it and she thought it might make them feel at home. Apparently when you live in California, pork chili Verde is something you enjoy. Sister Gwenydd would be disappointed that the Fatted Calf had only one small can of green enchilada sauce. It was the best that The Fatted Calf had to offer according to Mildred who was working the register this morning. Sister Agatha had procured the small can when she came upon the tower of McVitie's Jaffa Cakes. She dropped it into her carryall and leaned forward, reaching for the top box. Sponge cake, orange-flavored jam, chocolate. Does life get better?

"She's a young woman, red hair? Claire MacDonagh," a man's voice said from the cash register on the other side of the cake tower.

Sister Agatha stood back on her heels and strained forward to hear over the low chatter of the store. She was sure that she did not recognize the man's voice. Listening hard, she could still only catch snippets of the conversation. "A reporter for *The Church Times*." The man continued, "Do you know where she might be staying?"

Mildred's soft voice was drowned out by the two old men who stood a few meters away, arguing loudly about football. She shot them a withering look which they completely ignored. Apparently, the *Cefn Druids* versus the *Cardiff Mets* required loud voices. Even in the grocery.

"She's what?" the man said. "No. It can't be." His voice distressed.

"I'm afraid so, sir. I'm so sorry to tell you," Mildred said, her own voice now distressed.

She reached into her carryall and pulled out her murder notebook and a pen. *A stranger in town inquiring about Claire.* And only two days after her death. Sister Agatha wanted to get a good look at the man without revealing herself. She thought Mildred murmured something else to the man and then whatever was said next was thoroughly drowned out by a truck going down main street. The two old men had moved on to a spirited discussion of the *Llandudno Amateurs* and Sister Agatha couldn't hear a thing.

"Perhaps you could talk with Constable Barnes," Mildred said.

"Constable Barnes?"

"No wait. I'm sorry he's out of town. I think his deputy is covering for him."

"And what is the deputy's name?" The man's voice shook, and Sister Agatha wanted nothing more than to get a glimpse of him. He was clearly Irish. He had a brogue as lovely as anyone from Dublin.

"Deputy Parker Clough. You'll find him at the police station. On Main Street."

"Thank you. That's very helpful. I'll just be going."

"Are you sure? Perhaps the manager could bring you a glass of water. Or a cup of tea?"

"You're very kind, but no. I won't trouble you any longer. I'm fine. Just a bit shaken up is all."

Sister Agatha could stand it no more. She removed her notebook and fountain pen from her jumper pocket and then leaned as far as she could, without disturbing the Jaffa Cakes, to peer around at the man at the register. Unfortunately, she forgot how bulky she was in her red jumper and she bumped into the middle tier. The pyramid began to tumble from the top, one or two cakes at first, and then the cakes began to tumble in a cascade onto the floor. She struggled to take a step forward to begin to catch the boxes. But in her effort to avoid stepping on the already fallen cakes and to grab those that were mid-air, she lost her balance. Arms flailing, she fell forward, her murder notebook and fountain pen flew out of her hand and skidded across the tile floor. At least the pile of cakes was mercifully soft. She quickly got to her feet but then, her right foot slid on a cake that had burst from its packaging and under a coating of chocolate and orange jam, her feet went out from under her and she sat down rather hard smashing even more boxes of cakes, a few of them acting as chocolate and orange jam explosives. Shoppers left their baskets and ran to the destruction site. She heard the crackle of the loudspeaker. "Clean-up in aisle four. Sister Agatha has fallen in the Jaffa cakes."

"Is this yours?" She heard a voice say.

She looked up into the piercing green eyes of a middle-aged man. He squatted on his heels beside her. He had her notebook in one hand and her fountain pen in the other. His salt and pepper hair was cut short. He wore hiker's pants; a frayed green jumper and hiking boots. His face had the ruddy complexion of someone who spent much of their time out of doors. "Are you okay? You've taken quite a fall." She reached for her notebook but instead he held onto it, his index finger inside the front cover. He slipped her silver fountain pen into his jumper pocket and offered his hand.

"I'm fine. Thank you," she said grasping his hand and careful not to step on the few remaining intact Jaffa cakes, rose to her feet. Two boys in white aprons scurried around picking up smashed boxes and stacking them to the side. Mildred had closed her register and rushed over.

"Sister Agatha! Was the floor slippery?" She shot a glare at the two stock boys. "You didn't mop without putting up a sign, did you?"

"We haven't mopped all day," one boy answered. He balanced a stack of cakes in his arms. "Do you want us to save the ones that aren't smashed?"

"Of course I want you to save the ones that aren't smashed! Sister, if you are quite alright, I must get back to the register."

"I'm so sorry.... I don't know what happened." Sister Agatha looked at the cake carnage all around her. "Let me pay for the smashed cakes. It's all my fault."

"Never!" Mildred said. "It wasn't your fault at all. I am sure the stack of boxes was unsteady, that's all." She gave the boys a withering look and hurried off.

"I'll take that please," she said to the man in hiking boots, gesturing to the notebook.

"Are you sure you're perfectly fine?" He put one hand on her should and held the murder book in his other.

"Indeed. No worse for the wear." She looked at the murder book.

He handed to her with the front flap open, the small letters *Murder* evident. "You've given your journal an interesting name?" He smiled with his eyebrows raised. "And this is yours." He handed her the fountain pen. "It rolled across the floor when you fell into the cakes."

"Thank you again." She took the fountain pen and dropped into the front pocket of her habit. "Now if you'll excuse me." She drew herself up to her full height, trying to regain what dignity she had left.

"Sister Agatha, if you're all done shopping...." Mildred called out.

"I've one can of green enchilada sauce. For Sister Gwenydd." She headed towards check-out, trying not to limp.

"No, no," Mildred said. "It's on the house. You just go." Sister Agatha was not certain, but she thought she might have heard Mildred say *please go* under her breath.

"Well, thank you then," Sister Agatha said. She smoothed her hair and shook out her apron. The man was still standing there. He seemed to be watching her. It suddenly hit her. The cousin. Claire's cousin who was going to visit. *Of course.* "You're Peter," she said.

"I am indeed. Peter MacDonagh. How did you know?" His voice registered surprise.

"Claire told me all about you. You're on a walking tour in Snowdonia and you might come to Pryderi to visit."

"Yes. And here I am, but...." His voice trailed off. "The woman at the counter told me that Claire...that she...." His deep eyes grew bright with tears. "Tell me it's not true."

Sister Agatha placed a hand on his arm. "I am so sorry," she said softly. "We have been trying to reach her parents, but apparently they are hiking in the Himalayas and are off the grid."

He nodded, the color having drained from his face. "I'm not sure, but I think she must have listed me as next of kin. While they are on this latest expedition."

"In that case," Sister Agatha said. "Come with me and I'll tell you all about it."

Sister Agatha took stock of Peter MacDonagh as he sat across from her at The Buttered Crust. She thought they both needed a cup of tea after the events at The Fatted Calf. He seemed a nice sort of man. Early 40's, athletic, his shabby hiking clothes gave him the look of a student on holiday, but his sharp haircut, gold wedding ring, and expensive hiking boots spoke otherwise.

"So you are Claire's cousin, are you?" she asked, pouring tea into his teacup. "She spoke very highly of you. I guess I had it in my head that you were younger."

"Well, I like to think I am younger as well. Claire is my dad's younger brother's daughter. He is nearly ten years younger than my dad and Claire was born late to her parents. So we are about fifteen years apart in age."

"I wish we could reach her parents." Sister Agatha took a sip of tea. "We are so sorry about what happened. They need to be told."

"I'll do my best to reach them. I told them to keep at least one mobile turned on, but they said it would ruin the 'liberation of being off the grid.'" He grimaced and then looked at his tea. Sister Agatha waited. One thing she had learned from Father Selwyn was to wait. To give people who were grieving a chance to feel whatever it was that they were feeling.

Peter looked up, his eyes welling. "What exactly happened?"

"At this point, all we know is that she went off the edge of the cliff onto the beach. About a twenty meter drop." Sister Agatha went on to explain Constable Barnes' theory that she was snapping a selfie. She left out the two individuals who ransacked her cottage and stole her laptop. She already liked Peter and usually followed her instincts, but it was too soon to trust him with any further information about Claire. She certainly didn't tell him about the Sister Winifred scarf.

"When, exactly?"

"Tuesday. At about five o'clock. That was the time stamp on the selfie."

"It must have been beastly windy on the cliffs. What in the world was she doing out there? No one goes for a stroll in that weather."

"Haven't you just come from a walking tour of Snowdonia?"

He gave her a slight smile. "I hike all the time. Well, when I am not teaching. Medieval studies at University College Dublin. We're on winter break. But Claire wasn't one for cliff walking outdoors. She was more for sitting over her computer or chasing down a good lead."

"Was she chasing down a good lead?" Sister Agatha peered at him over her tea.

"What do you mean?" He gave her another piercing look. He must have made a few students squirm in his time.

"I mean, do you think that Claire might have had an enemy due to her journalism efforts? Someone about whom she might have written something explosive or offensive? Did she have an enemy?"

"An enemy? I thought my cousin fell backwards taking a selfie. Which, by the way, does sound like something she would do." He shook his head and his eyes took on a faraway look, a look of pain. "Her poor mother. You don't know what this will do to her."

"I'm sorry," she murmured.

"Claire didn't have an enemy in the world. Except..."

"Except?"

He blew out his breath. "A bonny lass she was. Smart as a whip...." He paused for so long, Sister Agatha almost broke in. She was glad that she didn't. "Claire was her own enemy. Our Claire struggled with depression. I'll talk with the medical examiner, but I am afraid that she...."

"Took her own life?" Sister Agatha said softly. "She didn't seem at all depressed at Gwenafwy Abbey. Not in the least."

He shook his head and drained the last of his tea. Sister Agatha filled his cup again and watched as he added sugar and milk. He looked up; his green eyes faded. "She hid it. I am afraid that perhaps she found herself in one of her dark moods and just.... you know.... stepped back over the cliff."

Sister Agatha decided to share at least some of her findings with him. He deserved to know. "It might have been that her boyfriend proposed that night to another woman. A woman named Kate."

Peter very slowly set the teacup back in the saucer. For a moment, Sister Agatha was reminded of Parker and how he very neatly aligned the items on his desk. "Say that again?"

She filled him in on the whole drunken proposal by Bickford and the response that Claire had had when she saw him in the window. "So maybe she heard that he had proposed to another woman. Well, I don't know. It would be very hard." Sister Agatha frowned. "I realize that you know Claire far better than I do, but that just doesn't seem like the Claire MacDonagh that I spent time with."

Peter was staring at her. "When did this proposal take place?"

"Two nights ago. The same night that Claire died."

"Where is the boyfriend now?"

"Ex-boyfriend."

"Right."

"We don't know. But Parker Clough is chasing him down."

"Parker Clough?"

"Deputy for Constable Barnes. Wonderful young man. I think he's calling Scotland Yard."

"Ah-ha." Peter blew out his breath. "Sister Agatha, something tells me that you know more that you are revealing."

She raised her eyebrows. "And why would you think that?"

"Well, for starters, you're carrying a murder book."

Sister Agatha remained silent. What was there to say? She couldn't deny it.

"And you ask questions like a detective."

She felt her face grow warm with pride.

"And you remind me of someone, I hope you don't mind me saying?"

"Who?"

"The great Agatha Christie, of course."

Sister Agatha looked at Peter with bright eyes. She picked up her woolly hat and pulled it on over her short, gray hair. "Would you like to go back to the Abbey with me, Peter? So we can really talk?" They both stood.

"There's more?"

"Indeed. Much more. I would tell you everything now, but I must leave for our Epiphany planning meeting. And I promised Sister Gwenydd that I wouldn't be late."

CHAPTER 15

"When I first joined the Abbey," Sister Gwenydd said to the new sisters who had gathered in the Warming Room around the crackling fireplace. "I didn't know Epiphany from Advent." *Now that's an understatement*, Sister Agatha thought as she settled into her favorite chair at the back of the pleasant room.

"So if an epiphany feast isn't in your tradition," Sister Gwenydd continued, clicking on a power point. "Don't worry about it. You'll be up to speed before you know it." Sister Gwenydd had hardly attended church before she joined the Abbey, but the sisters at Gwenafwy had found her a quick study. More important, the young woman's culinary expertise had saved the convent from an early death by take-away fish and chips. Now they feast on lamb cawl, Welsh rarebit, and homemade glamorgan sausages.

By the time she and Peter had climbed Church hill and returned for the meeting, she had told him everything-- the concerns about the library paste review, the photo with the scarf in it, the two ominous figures seen at the dovecote door. The theft of the laptop. She liked Peter so much that she did something she had never done before; she gave him her notebook to read. He was Claire's family after all. He tucked it in his coat pocket and promised to guard it with his life. She left him sitting outside of Reverend Mother's office. She knew that it would be a great weight off Reverend Mother's mind that a family member had shown up.

"The western church," Sister Gwenydd continued. "Adopted 'the twelve days of Christmas' culminating on the eve of Epiphany, or 'Twelfth Night' in about the fourth century." She clicked to the next slide on her power point. "By the fifth century, however, it was established that that was the night on which the Magi arrived."

Good heavens, Sister Agatha thought. Does she think none of us know the story of the magi? But then Sister Gwenydd was also a newbie when it came to the liturgical year. Hadn't she told Reverend Mother that Christmas had always meant poppers and beer and that this last Christmas Eve was the first time she had ever attended a vigil? Sister Callwen had protested when Reverend Mother placed Sister Gwenydd in charge of the Epiphany Feast planning committee. The Gwenafwy Abbey King's cake feast was an annual crowd-pleaser. The guest list was so long that revelers spilled out into the kitchen and dining room. Last year the weather had been mild and some of the younger guests ended up having a celebratory beer in the pony barn. Putting a newbie like Sister Gwenydd in charge was just like Reverend Mother, Sister Agatha thought. The energy of youth is what we need, she had said reassuring Sister Callwen and the others. Our Lord was young, don't forget!

"Keep in mind there is nothing in the bible that identifies the Magi as male." Sister Gwenydd was really warming to her topic.

Of course there were women on the journey. Someone had to cook and clean up! Sister Agatha almost said aloud.

"And even the fact that there were three magi isn't in the bible. Which surprised me," Sister Gwenydd said. "And... believe it or not, they weren't even Kings. That comes from a much later, non-scriptural tradition."

"Now wait a moment, Sister Gwenydd," Sister Elfrida said, looking up from her ledger. She sat at a table in the far corner of the room, her laptop open. "Let's not throw the baby out with the bath water here."

"It's true though, Sister Elfrida. And you like facts as much as anyone."

Sister Agatha noticed a smile on Sister Elfrida's face as she turned back to her screen.

"We will still have a king's cake and everything. I'm only pointing out that some of the story is clearly pagan."

Sister Agatha looked back at Sister Elfrida who was now gazing over her spectacles at Sister Gwenydd. Only Sister Gwenydd would throw around the word *pagan*. Although the sisters did share a few pagan beliefs, such as the Welsh belief in fairies, it wasn't something to just bandy around.

"Well, let's move from myth to menu," Sister Gwenydd said.

A decided snort from the back table.

Sister Gwenydd handed out menus and cooking assignments to each of the new nuns. She might have been a bit freethinking, but she certainly was organized. Just then, Reverend Mother slipped in the side door and motioned to Sister Agatha to follow her. They stepped out into the hall and walked in silence to the far end.

"I have just met with Peter MacDonagh. A nice man. So awful for Mildred to have to tell him about Claire."

"I know," Sister Agatha said.

"I'm glad you were able to be present for him when he heard the news. Imagine hearing such a thing at The Fatted Calf."

"Indeed." It didn't sound as if Peter had mentioned that she had been buried under a pile of McVitie's Jaffa Cakes at the time.

"Here is your notebook. He gave it to me with deepest thanks." Reverend Mother cocked an eyebrow at her. "I've never known you to loan out your notebook, Sister."

"He seems like an honest person. Authentic." She hated feeling defensive. Had it been a good idea to let him read it? *Sister Callwen always did say that she was a bit impulsive.*

"I agree. Very sincere. He doesn't want the body moved from the morgue until he talks with her parents. I sent him to Dr. Beese to work out arrangements."

"Good," Sister Agatha said. They walked several paces down the hall in silence. Finally Sister Agatha could stand it no more. "Have you told Sister Winifred yet?"

Reverend Mother seemed to jolt out of a reverie that put her far away. "About the scarf? Yes. She took it better than expected."

Sister Agatha waited for more details, but Reverend Mother didn't offer any.

Reverend Mother took a breath and shoved her hands into the pockets of her blue habit, shuddering as though she were cold. "Why don't you update me on your meeting with Officer Clough?"

"He thinks someone was there on the cliff when Claire fell. And it is impossible to determine who based on the scarf. "

"Does he think she was pushed?"

Sister Agatha shrugged. "Who knows?"

"What do you think about Peter's thought that she died by suicide?" Reverend Mother said in a low voice.

Before she could answer, the door to the Warming Room opened and banged shut. Sister Samantha stepped into the hall, and stood for a moment, her back against the slammed door. Her eyes red and pinched as though she had been crying. She turned and hurried in the opposite direction and Sister Agatha expected Reverend Mother to call out to her. When she didn't, she was surprised. She then thought Reverend Mother would go after Sister Samantha, but she only continued her conversation about Claire. Sister Agatha remembered the comment from Sister Gwenydd about the vote of no confidence. Why was Reverend Mother so unconcerned? One of her young nuns leaves a meeting nearly in tears and she does nothing?

"Well, I need a walk," Reverend Mother said, after a few moments.

"Kind of chilly for a walk."

"Just a turn about the garden. You know, clear my head. Keep me informed, Sister Agatha. I'm counting on you. And could you check on Sister Samantha? I think she was headed towards the laundry room."

The warm, humid air and the aroma of clean fresh laundry was a welcome greeting to Sister Agatha. Blue habits hung in rows on long clothing racks, and next to them sat several baskets of socks and towels that needed sorting and folding. Sister Samantha stood at the long folding table with her back to the door. She yanked a towel out of one of the baskets, scattering three other towels onto the floor, gave it a vigorous shake and then folded it determinedly. She grabbed the next towel and subjected it to the same treatment.

Just as she went into the basket for the third towel, Sister Agatha cleared her throat. "Oh, Sister Agatha," Sister Samantha said as she turned around. "I was just...." She tossed the towel back into the basket, and then crossing the floor, flopped down in the one of the two canvas deck chairs next to the dryer.

Sister Agatha picked up the clean towel and finished folding it. Sister Samantha sat slouching, staring dejectedly at the floor looking both angry and ready to cry. The young sister was more petite than she had realized, the hem of her habit grazing her shoe tops. Her olive skin, pale as though her California tan had already faded. Dark circles ringed her brown eyes. Sister Agatha felt a twinge of guilt for not being more gracious with her. It couldn't be easy, leaving Los Angeles to come to North Wales, no matter how much the new nuns loved to talk about "the great adventure God set has set them on".

"How are you finding things? Here at the Abbey?" Sister

Agatha had to admit it was a lame question and the beleaguered Sister Samantha looked at her as if she had two heads.

"How am I finding things? Well, considering I just ran out of a meeting crying and now I'm hiding in the laundry room, then not so great. I am not finding things here so great."

All she wanted to do was put her arm around Sister Samantha and if she did, then how was she ever going to ask her where she was the night Claire died? What would Miss Marple do? Or Armand Gamache? Or Stephanie Plum? Well, Stephanie Plum would order a large pizza and then go out to the parking lot and discover that her car had been blown up.

"Are you hungry?" she asked. *Stephanie Plum it was, then.*

"I could eat," Sister Samantha said, blowing her nose on a clean dish towel.

Bingo. You could always depend on the young when it came to free food.

"I like the Welsh cakes, but they aren't for everyone," Sister Agatha said. "And Welsh Brew tea, but again, maybe since you're American, you'd like coffee?"

"Coffee and those cakes would be great," Sister Samantha said, gazing around. "This place is nice. Reminds me of home."

"They have tea shops like this in Los Angeles?" Sister Agatha's image of Los Angeles was mostly highways and brilliant sunshine. And tall people with perfect teeth.

"I'm not from Los Angeles. That's just where the convent is. I grew up in Brookline, Massachusetts. Near Boston. There are lots of little shops there. Not quite as quaint as this one, but similar. There's one you would like, Martin's Coffee Shop on Harvard Street."

Sister Agatha had not thought of the Buttered Crust as quaint. But maybe it was. If you were American. She looked around for Keenan. He saw her wave and seemed to indicate that he would be over to their table, or he was just scratching his head with his notepad?

"My parents used to go to Martin's every Saturday morning until..." Sister Samantha's voice trailed off.

"Until what?" Sister Agatha asked.

"Not important."

Sister Agatha noticed that the same hard look came over Sister Samantha's face as it did the day they were in the cheese barn and Claire had asked her for a quote. She was about to push her a bit further when Keenan ambled over to their table. He stood without speaking, his pen poised over his notepad, gazing at Sister Samantha. She guessed that his stint in the kitchen had ended. Probably badly. "I would like my usual," Sister Agatha said. "Double the Welsh cakes, and a coffee for my friend."

Keenan dragged his eyes over to Sister Agatha. "So you want a Welsh brew tea, double order Welsh cakes, and a...."

"Coffee." Keenan often had a difficult time when attractive young women were at the table. Apparently, this was the case even when they wore a habit and scapular. "And a cranberry scone." She waved off Sister Samantha's protest. "They're delicious. And you're too thin for this climate. You need a little more body fat to make it through the winter."

"It's the wind that is so cold here. And now I've lost my scarf from Sister Winifred."

"Do you want anything in the coffee? Like...I don't know," Keenan paused. "Milk?"

"You've lost your scarf? Where?" Sister Agatha forced herself to not pull out her notebook.

"Cream?" Keenan said.

"I don't know."

"You don't know if you want milk? Or you don't know if you want cream?" He shifted from one foot to the other.

"I mean, I don't know where I lost it. If I knew where I lost it, I'd go get it." She looked at Keenan. "Cream, please."

"What color was it, by the way?" Sister Agatha felt her wrists flutter.

Sister Samantha looked around. "Actually, this place is nothing like Martin's Coffee Shop. It's as if.... no one's in a hurry."

"Because no one *is* in a hurry. If I knew the color, I might be able to find it for you."

"That'd be great." She looked back at Keenan, "Forget the cream. Make it a skinny latte with double micro foam and a shot of espresso."

"The color?" Sister Agatha prompted.

"Burgundy. She said the color fit me."

CHAPTER 16

"I suppose that's one key I won't get back," Sister Elfrida said, peering at her ledger book. "I signed it out to Claire on January 2 for the guest cottage." She plucked a tissue out of the box on her desk. "So very sad. Such a young woman and filled with so much promise."

Sister Agatha stood for a moment. Finally she asked, "Does the key have any distinguishing characteristics?"

"If it is for a guest, I scratch the location of the door on the back of the key. Or if it is for one of the sisters, I put their initials on the back of the key."

Sister Agatha pulled her own door key out of her jumper pocket. Sure enough on the back *AL* in tiny letters. *Agatha Llewellyn*. She had never noticed before. "And the key to the dovecote?"

"*DC*, of course."

"Does anyone else have a key to the guest cottage?"

"No." She knew that Sister Elfrida kept meticulous records. "Of course, there are two master keys that can give access to the guest cottage."

Sister Agatha raised her eyebrows. "Who has them?"

"Ben Holden. As our caretaker he has a master key in case of emergency. A burst pipe or broken window."

"And Reverend Mother has the other one?"

"Yes, but good heavens." Sister Elfrida looked at her over her spectacles. "Sister Agatha, honestly."

"Of course not. Just gathering information." She would never tell anyone at the Abbey, but no one was exempt from suspicion. Not even Reverend Mother.

CHAPTER 17

Sister Agatha loved the feasts and celebrations of the Anglican faith. Her favorite was "Alban Elie" *Spring Equinox* which the nuns celebrated with a pig roast and a keg of beer. The air still had a wintry bite to it and so the roasting pig was also a warming fire as the nuns huddled, mittened hands cupped around glasses of warm beer, singing favorite hymns, and waiting on the succulent pork. Or "Gŵyl Absent" *Feast of the Patron* held annually in commemoration of the patron saint of a parish. That feast day began with a traditional black pudding breakfast. Since the nuns lived in Asaph parish, their saint was, of course, the good Saint Asaph, the first Bishop of St. Asaph.

But perhaps the feast of the Epiphany was her absolute favorite. Partly because it came after all the hustle and bustle of the Christmas season had ended. Epiphany, a time of bitter winds, short days, and the long slog of winter, needed a celebration. Especially one that featured cake.

With Sister Gwenydd and the younger nuns heading up this year's Epiphany celebration, Sister Agatha had noticed quite an uptick in decorating, baking, and other lively activities. She looked down the long decorated table; the nun's celebrations in the past had paled in comparison. The room was strung with small white lights and each plate had a candle next to it. In the center of the table sat the round king's cake which Sister Gwenydd had spent the previous day preparing. The ring of pastry, smelling deliciously of cinnamon and covered with creamy white frosting, was lavishly decorated with purple, gold and green sprinkles. Strings of gold beads adorned the edges of the tall cake plate (two of the California sisters who had attended Mardi Gras as undergraduates on spring break) and somewhere in the cake was hidden a tiny porcelain figure of the baby Jesus. Whoever discovered it in their piece would be designated as King or Queen and would preside over the day's festivities. Although Sister Agatha knew that the festivities really consisted of a cake and wine around the fire in the warming room.

The table, set with dessert plates, flowers, candles and tea things, was lined on either side by both nuns and guests. All the sisters were present—Sister Agatha noticed that Sister Elfrida and Sister Juniper were sitting side-by-side, chatting amiably. Sister Elfrida usually talked spreadsheets, budgets, and roof repairs while Sister Juniper was generally preoccupied with climbing, surfing, and hiking, but today, they seem to have found common ground. Several guests from the village had been included--in keeping with the Epiphany dictate to invite one's neighbors. Next to Reverend Mother sat Father Selwyn. Just the sight of the two of them together made her smile. Across from Sister Matilda and in deep conversation with her, was Reggie. She thought she heard him say the words *primrose* which was Sister Matilda's most recent acquisition for the trellis in last summer's new prayer garden. Sister Samantha looked better than she had for a while. The young sister wasn't exactly chatting and laughing like the others, but she seemed relaxed and composed as she sat quietly at the far end of the table. Parker Clough had also been invited and had pulled up a chair on the other side of Reggie. She was glad Reverend Mother had put him on the guest list. Everyone from

Gwenafwy Abbey was there with only Ben Holden missing, still in Yorkshire visiting his new grandchild.

She looked up as Reverend Mother tapped on her wine glass and asked for everyone's attention. Sister Gwenydd had come in still wearing her long habit apron and taken a chair next to Sister Samantha. Not another person could have been crammed into the refectory.

"I want to welcome everyone to our annual celebration of Epiphany. Thank you to Sister Gwenydd and to her committee for putting together such an extraordinary day. I know that I have never chalked a lintel on so many doors nor seen such a lovely cake." Reverend Mother paused while the group broke into enthusiastic applause. "Now let us gather our hearts in the spirit of worship as I turn the service over to Father Selwyn and the Archbishop." She smiled in Father Selwyn's direction and he stood, clearing his throat.

"From Advent wreaths to Christmas Eve service to tongues of fire on Pentecost, candlelight is an essential metaphor for those of us who travel a journey of faith. He gestured to the center of the table where four tall candles flickered, representing the magi and Jesus. Or as Sister Gwenydd put it, three men and a baby. "These lighted candles remind us that the feast of Epiphany marks the *theophany* of Christ. By the recognition of Christ in his baptism by the Father and the Holy Spirit. In other words, the trinity." Father Selwyn picked up the small candle by his plate and lit it from one of the central candles in the middle of the table. Then each person took the small candle that had been placed next to their plate and the flame from Father Selwyn's candle was passed down from one end of the table, back up the other until the long table of nearly thirty people was lit by candlelight.

Sister Agatha caught her breath at the sudden beauty reflected in the faces surrounding her at the table. She had not noticed before, but the lights in the room had been dimmed until the only light was from the candles and the sliver of light from under the kitchen door. What was it about candlelight that made the world warm and welcoming? She almost regretted her dependence on electricity. Except for Wi-Fi of course.

Father Selwyn nodded to Reggie who slowly pushed back his chair and stood. Sister Agatha noticed that his hands shook very slightly as he used his candle to read from his notes. "In the feast of Epiphany, we learn from the Magi how to pay attention to the light."

Sister Agatha's candle had begun to drip. They had never used so many candles in the refectory before. Sister Elfrida as building manager disapproved of excessive candle use.

"The Magi observed the heavens with great wisdom, but their efforts to find the newborn king also demanded a careful and perceptive reading of the Scriptures. So tonight we hold our candles up," Reggie held his candle up and waited as everyone followed suit, "as we ask for God's light to shine on us so that we may recognize God's presence in our midst." Reggie sat down and looked back at Father Selwyn who handed his dripping candle over to Reverend Mother. He gazed at the assembled group bathed in candlelight and raising his hands heavenward, said in the voice that Sister Agatha loved, "Peace be with this house and all who dwell in it, and peace to all who enter here."

He took his candle back from Reverend Mother and then looking around the long table said, "And now, in honor of Marie Antoinette and Sister Gwenydd 'let us eat cake!'" The group broke up in laughter and each person blew out their candle just as Reverend Mother switched on the lights. The spell for Sister Agatha was broken. But just as well, she thought, her candle was beginning to really drip, and she didn't think she could hold onto it much longer.

"Now remember," Sister Gwenydd said. "There is a porcelain figurine in one piece of cake. Whoever gets it is the king or queen of the party."

"Not that it means much," Sister Callwen said, leaning across to Sister Agatha.

"It ought to mean at least that you don't have to help with washing up," she whispered back.

"Take care everyone," Sister Harriet chimed in as her piece of cake was handed to her. "I broke a crown one Epiphany biting right into the baby Jesus."

"Actually, everyone might gently stab their piece with a fork before you just bite in. If you hit porcelain, you've got it," Sister Gwenydd said as she continued to distribute the generous triangles of white cake down the long table.

"I do think that when it comes to Epiphany traditions, we might have stopped with the candles and the chalking of the lintel," Sister Callwen said. "Dental work seems a risk."

Sister Agatha carefully probed her cake with her fork. No baby Jesus. Good. She liked to eat cake, not extract trinkets from it.

Sister Gwenydd was looking anxiously around the room. "No baby Jesus yet?" she asked, just as Sister Juniper called out, "I've got it!" They all turned and watched as she pushed aside a bit of frosting and tapped her fork against something hard. "The baby Jesus! I win," she said. "Oh sorry," she added quickly. "I'm always too competitive. My biggest weakness." Sister Juniper poked again with her fork; Sister Agatha noticed her forehead crinkled.

"It's not baby Jesus, that's for sure," Sister Juniper said. "Is this a joke?" She grinned quizzically at Sister Gwenydd. Reaching into her piece of cake with her fingers she picked up an object that at first Sister Agatha couldn't recognize. Then Sister Juniper wiped the cake and frosting off it and held it up between her thumb and forefinger. "It's a key," she said. "Is this some part of the celebration that they only do in Wales?"

All eyes turned to Sister Gwenydd who looked dumbstruck. "I didn't hide a key in the cake. I hid the baby Jesus. I pushed it right into the dough right before I put the cake in the oven." She looked at Reverend Mother who looked back, equally perplexed.

"Let me see that key," Sister Elfrida said and Sister Juniper handed it to her. She wiped it off with her napkin and flipped it over, holding it up to the light. She looked straight at Sister Agatha.

"What?" Sister Agatha said.

"DC," Sister Elfrida said. "Dovecote. The missing key to the dovecote."

"Interesting. The missing key shows up in the King's cake." Sister Agatha held her glass up for a refill. Father Selwyn obliged. The senior nuns, Father Selwyn, and Parker Clough were all gathered in Reverend Mother's office. Reggie had been feeling tired after all the excitement and Sister Juniper had driven him home in the minivan.

"Are you saying someone put a key into the cake that just happens to be the missing key that was mostly likely used to enter Claire's apartment when it was searched?" Parker Clough said, accepting the glass of wine that Reverend Mother handed him. "Thank you. I guess I can drink this. I'm not exactly on duty."

The Epiphany Feast had ended in chaos as the sisters and all the guests searched their pieces of cake for the baby Jesus. Father Selwyn found it in his piece. Although being declared king of the feast felt entirely irrelevant now. The missing key to the dovecote, signed out to Claire a week before she died, had been put into Sister Gwenydd's cake. But how and by whom? And most importantly, why? Sister Agatha had her notebook out and wrote furiously.

"They had to push the key into the dough." Sister Agatha added.

"How do you know that?" Father Selwyn asked.

"Because, had they put it in after the cake was baked, it would have been obvious to Sister Gwenydd when she decorated it. On the other hand," she kept talking as she wrote, "a key is thin, and metal is slippery." She finished the page and looked up; her fountain pen poised to continue writing. "Think about it. The key actually *could* have been poked into an already baked cake, then the frosting smoothed over. And with all those sprinkles, it could have gone unnoticed.

Sister Winifred's knitting needles clicked rapidly, a fluorescent pink scarf billowing from down to the floor. Her needles stopped for a moment. "How in the world could some perfect stranger do all this?" Sister Winifred asked, casting off. "Sneak into the kitchen, poke a key into a cake and not be noticed?"

The room stayed silent. No one looked at each other. The bell in the village clock tower chimed eight times. Sister Agatha slowly counted in her head. Finally, Parker Clough cleared his throat. "Did anyone see a stranger? Someone you didn't recognize...at the Abbey today?" Sister Agatha thought the young officer looked decidedly uncomfortable. She knew why. And she was glad he was here to say the difficult words and not make her be the one to bear bad news.

"What are you saying, Officer Clough?" Reverend Mother's voice had gone cold.

"I am saying, and I am truly sorry to have to say it, but we must look into this matter as an inside job. That one of the members of this community did it."

"Did *what* exactly, Officer?" Reverend Mother had gone from frosty to arctic. "Murder? Or just cake-tampering?"

Sister Agatha felt the thinnest of smiles twitch at her lips. *Cake-tampering. Only Reverend Mother.*

"At the moment," he said, "let's go with cake-tampering. We'll save murder for another day."

CHAPTER 18

For the hundredth time, Sister Agatha wished she could pick up a phone and call Inspector Rupert McFarland. What would he say to a key in the cake? She could make no sense of it. She pulled the curry comb over Bartimaeus's back and he flicked his tail in enjoyment. She breathed deeply. The fragrant hay mixed with the earthy smell of pony manure always had a calming effect on her. She traded out the curry comb for the metal comb and began to work on the tangles in his mane.

Whoever had the key most likely pushed it into the cake before Sister Gwenydd put it in the oven. Unfortunately, there had been a steady stream of people in and out of the kitchen that morning. Several of the young nuns, Sister Samantha among them, had gathered around the farm table for a last minute Epiphany planning session; as well as Sister Matilda and Reggie who had dropped by to borrow a muffin tin for seed starting; the repairman to fix the leaking kitchen sink. Even Reverend Mother had popped in to ask how the cake was coming along.

Two figures. Tall and thin. Short and plump. That could be any combination of Gwenafwy Abbey inhabitants. *Ridiculous.* She pushed the thought from her mind. She stood back and took a long look at Bartimaeus. Although not *unhealthy*, she had to admit that he wasn't his perky self. He didn't nicker cheerfully when she came in the door of his stall, nor did he stomp his front feet and switch his tail when she reached into her apron pocket for the bit of sugar from the kitchen. But his eyes were bright, and his ears flicked forward when she stroked the silky fur around them. And his velvety pony lips did snatch the sugar with all his usual greediness. She fluffed the straw on the floor of the stall and pulled the light cord, wishing the old pony "nos da" *goodnight.*

She stepped outside and a swirl of windswept snow scudded across the mostly bare ground. She picked her way down the flagstone path from the pony barn to the main building as the chimes in the clock tower began. Eleven o'clock. Late for her, since all the nuns rose before dawn for matins followed by a hearty Welsh breakfast. Straight ahead, she could see Sister Gwenydd through the kitchen window, sitting at the farm table. She appeared to be staring over a cup of tea. Probably thinking about the key in the cake. Sister Agatha thought she would join her. Just then something caught her eye. A weak yellow light seeped under the door of the dovecote. Someone was inside the guest cottage.

She sprinted to the kitchen window and knocked gently. Sister Gwenydd jumped and nearly spilled her tea. She gestured wildly at the younger sister, who made a face and disappeared from view. In a moment, she was slipping out the kitchen door, shutting it softly behind her.

"What is it?" she said in a loud whisper.

"Look." Sister Agatha gestured to the dovecote. The line of light was just visible.

"Who is it?"

"How would I know? Possibly Claire's killer."

"Or Sister Callwen doing some late night cleaning and organizing. Or Ben Holden checking the thermostat."

"Ben's out of town and Sister Callwen went to bed early with a cold."

"Maybe someone left the light on."

"No one has been in there. I'm sure of it."

"Should we call Parker?"

"By the time he gets here, they could be gone."

"They?"

"I'm thinking it's the two who stole her computer."

"It's freezing out here. What do you want to do?"

"I want to see who they are and what they are up to."

"Why do I let you pull me into these things?" Sister Gwenydd said. If a whisper could sound cross, her whisper did. Sister Agatha knew it was only because she was nervous, not because she wasn't up for the adventure.

"Don't worry. We have the element of surprise on our side. Follow me."

The two women began to walk as quietly as possible towards the cottage. Sister Agatha couldn't believe how loudly frost could crunch on the ground. The sliver of light below the door remained strong. When they reached the door, they stopped and then crouched behind a hollyhock bush off to the side.

"We could wait here and hit them over the head with something, as soon as they step out of the door?" Sister Gwenydd said.

Sister Agatha didn't want to explain that it might be Sister Samantha or Sister Juniper or Reverend Mother which would make hitting anyone over the head quite out of the question. Also, they had brought nothing to hit anyone with. "I'll go around the back. To the back window. You stay here."

Sister Gwenydd shot her a glance that seemed both exasperated and nervous. "Oh sure, leave me here."

"Come with me if you want, then."

"No, I'm fine. But what if they come out? What do you want me to do?"

Just then the line under the door clicked off. Both women pressed back as far as they could. The door opened and a figure stepped out. *Peter MacDonagh.* She put a hand on Sister Gwenydd's arm. This was one for Parker, not for her and Sister Gwenydd.

CHAPTER 19

"Just because Sister Samantha lost a burgundy scarf, doesn't mean the one in the photo was hers," Sister Gwenydd said, wrapping her own scarf tighter. She and Sister Agatha stood on the cliff walk near the spot where Claire had fallen. Although not as close to the edge.

"I want to find that scarf. It's evidence."

"But what are the chances that it's here? I mean who kills someone and then leaves something as obvious as a burgundy wool scarf?"

"Let's just do a search. You never know." Sister Agatha set off, studiously avoiding the precipice as she scanned the brown grass.

Sister Gwenydd walked closer to the cliff's edge. "Did you tell Parker Clough about last night? About seeing Peter in the dovecote?"

"We're meeting up later today. I wanted to look for the scarf before anything else. We should have conducted a search as soon as we saw it in the photo."

"Another thing—if the scarf were here, don't you think Parker would have found it?"

"Well, yes. But it can't hurt to look." They only had a week before Constable Barnes would return home. Sister Agatha wanted to have the murder all wrapped up by then.

"Stay away from the edge, please." A wind off the water wrapped their blue habits around their legs. She wondered if the person who had pushed Claire had climbed down to the beach to examine her dead body. To see if she really was dead.

"Even if we do find the scarf, how is that going to change anything?" Sister Gwenydd said, still staring at the ground. "Sister Winifred has knitted a slew of burgundy scarves. Remember the Pentecost knitting project? It was an endless array of all shades of red-- scarves, mittens, hats, vestments, prayer shawls. I have to say I don't entirely understand the obsession with liturgical colors."

"Liturgical accuracy is essential," Sister Agatha shouted, the wind whipping the words out of her mouth. It barreled ferociously off the sea and across the open field making it hard to talk. "The color of the season sets the worship mood. It's almost as if the colors have their own voice and they speak to us. Ask Father Selwyn sometime. He has very strong feelings about it. And anyway, you're only in a bad mood because you are still tired after last night." The two women had stayed up another hour in the Abbey kitchen drinking tea and talking over the case.

"I'm not in a bad mood. I just don't see the point. What will it prove if we find it?"

"I have to look. It seems important." Sister Agatha kicked a piece of frozen sod, as though it might be concealing the scarf or better yet, the killer.

"Did you question Sister Samantha about her alibi? Did you at least get that out of her?"

"She said she went to bed early that night. And that she wasn't feeling well."

"Do you believe her?"

"An alibi is only as good as it checks out to be."

"Who said that? Sherlock Holmes? Colombo? Jessica Fletcher?"

"I said it. I do think for myself on occasion, you know." Sister Agatha waited for the customary sarcastic response. When she didn't hear anything, she turned around. Sister Gwenydd was standing still, staring down at a tall clump of grass.

"What is it?"

Sister Gwenydd looked up. "A scarf. I think, anyway. It's frozen in the dried weeds." She kicked at the ground with her boots and then tugged yanked up a scarf, frozen solid. And although faded and icy, clearly burgundy. She handed it to Sister Agatha who flipped it over and they both took a breath. *SW* on a small rectangular label.

"What do you mean we can't have it fingerprinted?" Sister Agatha sat across from Parker in his office.

"We're not Scotland Yard. This office has no capability to fingerprint a piece of wool fabric that has been in the snow and ice for who knows how long. And as much as I want a real suspect in this case, there is no proof that the scarf belongs to either Sister Samantha, or the person in the photo. You've already said that Sister Winifred knits for half the parish."

"Yes, but it seems quite a coincidence doesn't it? She dislikes Claire and is openly hostile. She was nowhere to be found the night of Claire's death. Then she admits to having lost her burgundy scarf. We know that the killer wore a burgundy scarf with Sister Winifred's initials."

"No," Parker interrupted. "We know that the person who was at the cliff that night with Claire wore a burgundy scarf with Sister Winifred's initials."

"Fair enough. But you cannot so easily dismiss a burgundy scarf found not ten yards from the scene of the crime. Isn't that at least a little disturbing?"

"Truthfully, I feel more disturbed that we missed this scarf when we searched the area that morning."

"Oh." Sister Agatha realized she hadn't even thought of that. Why did they miss it? "You and the other officers weren't really searching as though it was a murder or a crime scene, though, right? You were thinking it was an accident."

"True, but it's a pretty big miss." Parker Clough looked at her from behind his desk. "I'll put it in an evidence bag. That's about all I can do with it. But take a seat if you have a moment. You said you had something about the cousin, Peter MacDonagh? Seems like a nice guy. Friendly. Heartbroken about Claire and who wouldn't be."

She described what she and Sister Gwenydd had observed the night before.

"Good heavens, Sister." He ran his hands through his hair and then quickly smoothed it down. "I'll bring him in. At any rate he's trespassing and possibly breaking in. Did you see how he got into the room? Did he have anything in his hands when he left?"

Sister Agatha had to think for a moment. "No. I don't believe he carried anything out with him."

"Okay. I'll deal with it."

"I ran a check on the boyfriend. No priors. On break from University. He might be worth pulling in. I want to talk to him, anyway, get some more details on his alibi."

"What is it, Parker? You look all jumpy?"

"Okay. I do know something about Sister Samantha that I need to tell you. And please don't jump to conclusions." Parked tapped his ball point pen on the desk pad and stared out the window, his brow crinkled. He finally turned back to her. "Anyway, when I talked with Lucy last night, I told her a little bit about our case."

Sister Agatha felt her heart thrill to hear him say 'our case'. Finally, law enforcement taking her seriously as a detective.

"Anyway," he went on. "Lucy is an artist, remember."

"I know."

"And so she has some connections in the art world. She knows something about Sister Samantha's family."

"Are they artists?" Sister Agatha's eyebrows shot up. "Interesting."

"No, not exactly. As soon as I said Sister Samantha's last name, *Camfield*, Lucy couldn't believe it. By the way, I would appreciate it if you didn't mention to Constable Barnes that I was discussing the case with someone--I mean, other than you."

"My lips are sealed." As if she would discuss anything about the case with Constable Barnes.

"Lucy immediately recognized the name--or she thought she did-- and she Googled it as we talked. It's the same family that she was thinking of and they had a daughter-- an only daughter-- named Kaiya-- who is the same age as Sister Samantha."

"But that doesn't make her Sister Samantha. Just because she had their last name and is the right age."

"And the family is from Brookline, Massachusetts. The daughter joined a convent in Los Angeles."

"Oh." Sister Agatha pulled out her notebook and uncapped her silver fountain pen. "Did the article say which convent?"

"The Sisters of Transfiguration. Does that sound right?"

"Bingo. It *is* Sister Samantha. What does Lucy know about the family?"

"The father, Cameron Camfield, was in the news for months a few years ago, for this big scandal at the Godwin Art Museum in Boston." Parker glanced at a page of notes on his desk.

"He was a whistle-blower, it seems, and he reported a history of discrimination at the Godwin. He accused a few higher-ups and Lucy said that the media hounded him relentlessly."

"For being the whistle-blower?"

"Yes. Whistle-blowers usually don't fare well."

"You would think they would. What they are doing is the right thing."

"Yes, well. Seems there was this one journalist, a woman from the *Boston Globe*, who made Camfield's life miserable. She hounded him relentlessly and basically ruined his career. He left the art world, went bankrupt. He and his wife divorced."

"Poor Sister Samantha. Sounds like her family fell apart."

"The family blamed the media, especially this one reporter. They've initiated a lawsuit against her and the Globe." They sat looking at each other. Sister Agatha remembered Father Selwyn once saying that everyone was fighting their own quiet battle. Well, Sister Samantha was mourning the loss of her family. At least, her family as she knew it. She suddenly remembered the comment about Martin's Coffee Shop. The memory of her parents going there every Saturday, but not anymore.

"Do you think that would that be motive enough for Sister Samantha to want to murder Claire? Because she triggered memories of this other journalist?"

"Revenge, fueled by grief? Sounds like a motive to me."

CHAPTER 20

"The prioress of the convent in Los Angeles filled me in before they arrived," Reverend Mother said. "She was worried about Sister Samantha coming here so quickly after all that had happened in her life. So, yes, I do know. But my question is, Sister Agatha, how do you know?"

"Lucy told Parker."

"Lucy?" Reverend Mother smiled. "Good heavens. Small world. So Parker and Lucy are still together? Well. That makes me happy. But how would she know anything about Claire?"

"Big scandal in all the papers. All over social media. And Lucy lives in Boston, remember?"

"Of course." Reverend Mother picked up the basketball that she kept on her desk for stress relief and tossed it from hand to hand. "Are you saying that you think that Sister Samantha could be so angry at the media that she would kill a journalist? And that journalist is Claire?"

"Familial loyalty is very powerful. Think of *The Godfather*."

"Honestly, Sister."

"Okay then, Tony Soprano." Reverend Mother had been a huge fan of *The Sopranos*.

Reverend Mother caught the ball with both hands and held it in front of her as if she was going to make a free throw. "What does Parker think?"

"He thinks it's possible. His exact word was 'worrisome'."

"He might be understating it a bit."

"There's more though." And Sister Agatha told Reverend Mother about the burgundy scarf.

"So Sister Samantha had a burgundy scarf that went missing. There's a burgundy scarf in the photo, and you found a burgundy scarf off the trail at the cliff walk?"

"Yes."

"Gracious," she said, setting the basketball on her desk. "I assume you have asked Sister Samantha where she was the evening of the murder?"

Sister Agatha noticed that Reverend Mother was now calling it a murder. She pulled her notebook out of her jumper pocket and opened it. "The suspect claims to have been in bed with a cold." Sister Agatha looked up and noticed a slight twitch in Reverend Mother's left eyebrow.

"Well, perhaps she was."

"Perhaps?" Sister Agatha looked closely at Reverend Mother. She cleared her throat and slipped her notebook into her jumper pocket. "Do you mind if I ask you something, Reverend Mother?"

"Ask away." Reverend Mother smiled as she turned to the stack of files on her desk.

"Where were you the evening of Claire's death?"

"Well, let me think," she said, glancing up at the ceiling. "I believe I had just finished leading Compline and then I went up to my office to get caught up on some paperwork. Yes, I was in my office." She selected the top page from a bulging file folder. "And now, Sister, if you will excuse me. It's a busy morning."

Sister Agatha nodded and turned towards the door. She wasn't sure if she had offended Reverend Mother or not. Should she say something to smooth things over? Before she could decide what to do, Reverend Mother called her back. She turned. "Yes?"

"By the way," Reverend Mother's warm smile faded. "Parker called this morning to ask if Peter MacDonagh had access to any of the buildings in Abbey grounds. Apparently, you had seen him enter the dovecote last night?" Reverend Mother didn't wait for an answer. "I had given Mr. MacDonagh a key to the dovecote so that he could retrieve any belongings of his cousin's that might still be there. Also, he wanted to see the last place that she had stayed in her short life. Somehow it seemed important to him." Reverend Mother paused, holding Sister Agatha in her gaze for a long, silent moment. "The next time you have a concern about activity at Gwenafwy Abbey, I suggest that you come to me first. Not the local law enforcement."

"Of course," she stammered. "I guess, I just...."

"That will be all, thank you. My *zoom* meeting with the bishop is about to start, and you know how she hates to be kept waiting."

CHAPTER 21

"A few nights ago, after vespers, she told us that she was going for a walk in the garden to 'clear her head.' The night Claire died. I remember it perfectly. And so does Sister Callwen. And then, yesterday, when I asked her directly where she was the night Claire died, she said she was 'in her office.'"

"Well, I don't know," Father Selwyn said, taking a seat in the wing chair next to the fireplace in his study. "It doesn't sound like much of a lie to me. You aren't saying that you suspect Reverend Mother?"

"I don't *want* to suspect her. And how is that not a lie?"

"Maybe she's not lying so much as maintaining some personal confidentiality."

"But this is a murder investigation. Don't you think she would understand that confidentiality has no place at a time like this?"

"Have you ever known Reverend Mother to break confidentiality?"

Sister Agatha reached for a digestive biscuit. She didn't know how long it would be before she felt like a McVitie's Jaffa Cake again. "Never. And I have known her for thirty years."

"An example to us all," Father Selwyn said, his mouth full of biscuit.

"Yes, but her strict standard of personal ethics makes a murder investigation difficult." She had finished telling Father Selwyn all about meeting Peter at The Fatted Calf (omitting the Jaffa cake fiasco), discovering the scarf, and finally, her remorse at not talking openly to Reverend Mother, when they were interrupted by a knock at the door.

Father Selwyn called out a cheerful "come in" and still the door stayed shut. "Come in," he repeated, standing up and crossing in two steps, opened it.

An older man, older than either Sister Agatha or Father Selwyn, stood tugging at his collar. Father Selwyn stepped aside and swept his hand towards the empty club chair. "Please join us. This is Sister Agatha from Gwenafwy Abbey up the hill. I am Father Selwyn, St. Anselm's vicar."

They waited for the gentleman to enter, but he continued to stand in the door. Sister Agatha wondered how long he had been standing there. Had he heard what they were talking about? Not that it mattered. She had never seen him around Pryderi and by Father Selwyn's response to him, the vicar hadn't either. He was a bit disheveled and though his faded clothes were clean, they were frayed and wrinkled, as if they had been slept in. His flimsy coat was not nearly warm enough for winter in Wales. The man had wrapped a faded trench coat around his thin frame, closing it with a belt that didn't match. Sister Agatha could see a flannel shirt and jumper layered underneath. He lacked a proper hat or scarf, though a pair of expensive-looking leather gloves stuck out of one pocket. He stood eye-level with Father Selwyn.

"I was wondering, Vicar, if the church had any provisions? You know, for someone a bit down on their luck?"

"Of course," Father Selwyn said, still standing. "You don't want to come in and tell us your situation? What kind of help do you need?" Father Selwyn smiled warmly. Sister Agatha always liked how he treated everyone as an honored guest.

The man ducked his head under the door frame and stepped into the room. "Maybe a tenner or two to get by?"

"I'm afraid I don't have cash available. But I can give you a food card and a ride to the shelter in Grenfell."

"Not going to any shelter. A tenner would do it," the man said, as he kicked the back of his heel with the toe of his other boot. His face took on a hard look as his eyes swept the office.

Father Selwyn opened the top drawer of his desk and withdrew an envelope. He flipped through the envelope for a moment then handed the man two cards that looked to Sister Agatha like credit cards. "Here are two coupons worth 10 pound sterling that you can use at Buttered Crust Tea Shop for a meal or you can purchase two bags of groceries from The Fatted Calf, just up the street. Now, do you have a place to stay?"

"I've a mate here in Pryderi. Thought I'd stay with him. But he's gone all high-horse with me and now he's not obliging." The man frowned.

"Well, if you find yourself without a roof over your head, come back here to the church and I'll give you a ride to Grenfell."

"Can't spare even a tenner then?" The man shoved the cards into the pocket of his trench coat. "I'm stuck out at that motel on the A55 with no gas for my car."

"Afraid not," Father Selwyn said. "But I could call the petrol station at the north end of the village. They'll fill up your car's tank and bill it to the church. What kind of car do you drive?"

"Ford Fiesta. From the '90's. Ancient, it is. Give me a tenner and I'll fill the tank myself."

Father Selwyn smiled and shook his head.

"How about a warmer coat?" Sister Agatha asked. "I'm certain we could do better for you. And a scarf and hat as well. And how are you outfitted for socks?" The Abbey had just finished the Annual Winter Sock-Hop. It was a sock collection to end all sock collections. They had at least two hampers full in the laundry room.

"No. I'm fine." The man tipped his head and turned to leave.

"I didn't get your name," Father Selwyn said.

The man turned back, one hand on the door. "Owen Wiley."

"And who is your friend here in Pryderi?"

"Bloke by the name of Reggie Thurston."

"The Archbishop?" Father Selwyn said, surprise in his voice.

"Yeah. One of you church blokes. And he won't even help out an old friend."

CHAPTER 22

Sister Agatha walked back to the Abbey lost in thought. Why hadn't she just asked Reverend Mother about seeing Peter in the dovecote? Or alerted her that there was an intruder on the grounds? She hadn't even considered talking with Reverend Mother. None of the other nuns would have responded by telling the deputy constable first.

She slipped in the side door of the main building and went straight to the chapel. She needed to be alone. The sunlight filtered through the windows, but she hardly noticed the peaceful beauty. When she had observed Peter in the dovecote, she just assumed he was up to no good. She was ready to add him to her suspect list. She had never even considered the reality that he was a grieving relative who had just lost a loved one.

What had happened to her?

And where was her trust in Reverend Mother? Was she getting so caught up in the investigation that she was forgetting her true calling-- a sister of Gwenafwy Abbey? She leaned forward and rested her forearms on the back of the pew in front of her. How could she so easily take Reverend Mother out of the picture like this? She sat up. Maybe it wasn't that she didn't *trust* her. It was that she didn't trust her as a *detective*. Reverend Mother was absolutely crackerjack at running the Abbey, but she wasn't that discerning when it came to good versus evil. In fact, she thought everybody, deep down, was inherently good. But Sister Agatha believed in evil-- as well as good, of course. She sighed. Maybe she could write Reverend mother a note of apology. She would ask Sister Callwen. She was always good at knowing what to do in these circumstances.

She leaned back in the pew and closed her eyes. For all her running around, she had made almost no progress on figuring out who had killed Claire. And the clock was ticking. When Constable Barnes returned, his first call would be to Scotland Yard and that would mean no more Sister Agatha on the case.

There were so many disparate clues: the missing rucksack, the key in the cake, the photobombing scarf, the strange set of letters and numbers, the bible verse, Sister Samantha's open hostility. Her head hurt just thinking of it. And what if Peter was right and Claire had taken her own life? Died by suicide. *No.* She thought of Claire's laugh, her snapping blue eyes, her passion about writing, her cheeky prose.

Maybe she should commit herself more fully to the life of Gwenafwy Abbey. Or at the very least, set aside this mystery and focus on the mystery that she was writing. She closed her eyes and said a short prayer for guidance. A familiar feeling of peace came over her as it often did when she committed herself to prayer. But the moment of calm was shattered as the chapel door flew open. She twisted around to see Sister Callwen framed in entranceway light.

"It's Bartimaeus," Sister Callwen said. "You'd better hurry."

CHAPTER 23

They raced to the pony barn. As Sister Agatha pushed open the heavy door, she was relieved to find that at least the barn was warm. In fact, it was toasty warm. Sister Elfrida had placed a heat lamp in the far corner. "We can't have the old boy suffering from the cold," she had said.

Stepping into his stall, her heart broke though. Bartimaeus was down, his sides heaving as if he couldn't breathe. Sister Winifred had created a special wool blanket for him from several old wool blankets no longer used at the convent. She had cut them into strips and then woven a heavy pony rug.

"Oh Bart," Sister Agatha said, pulling up her habit skirts and kneeling next to him. "Oh please, Bart," she said quietly as she smoothed his fetlock. She stroked the fur around his ears where it was silky. "You can't die now," she said. "You just can't."

"I've called Tupper on my mobile, but he is completely unavailable. He has an emergency delivery at Blackstone dairy. One of their best Guernsey's is calving early."

"I'm afraid it's too late even for Tupper," Sister Agatha said, her voice breaking. "Listen to his breathing. This is awful."

"I spoke very clearly to his office and said that we needed Dr.

Ross here. They said he would come straight from Blackstone, but it could be a few hours."

"A few hours will be too long," Sister Agnes said, tears falling on the pony's thick mane.

The barn door pushed open and to Sister Agatha's surprise, Peter stepped in. "I heard you had a horse down." He pulled off his woolly hat and started to unbutton his anorak. "Good god, it's warm in here," he said looking around.

"We have a heater running," Sister Callwen said sharply. "If you don't mind, Mr. MacDonagh, we are experiencing a medical crisis at the moment and we need privacy."

He walked around Sister Callwen and knelt on the other side of Bartimaeus, panting and heaving underneath his blanket. "Ah. A grand old Shetland. A Silver Dapple. I've not laid eyes on one of those for a while now.

"He is struggling to breathe, and we can't get the veterinarian." Sister Agatha wiped her eyes quickly and willed herself to be calm. "I am afraid he may not make it until he gets here. He's very old and.... and...."

"He's an old thing, alright," Peter cut in. "But I don't think he's about to die."

"How do you know? Do you know something about horses?" Sister Agatha sat back in her heels and looked at him.

"Yes indeed. You see, in Ireland my family.... We...." He paused. For some reason Sister Agatha thought he looked briefly uncomfortable but then regained himself. "I know about horses, you might say."

"Can you help him?" Sister Callwen asked.

Peter reached down and yanked the wool blanket off and tossed it in a corner. Then, he got to his feet and opened the door that led out to the meadow wide. A gust of winter air blew in. "Now turn off that heater," he said to Sister Callwen.

"Do you think this is a good idea? Tupper said to keep him

warm." Sister Agatha stood up; glad she had worn her heaviest jumper.

"Warm, yes. But not a sauna. Shetlands were bred in the northernmost tip of Scotland. They are meant to live in the open and survive the harshest of climates. Look at the deep furry coat on this chap. Between that heater and wrapping him up in a wool comforter, he's hyperventilating."

He gave Sister Agatha his hand and she stood up, reminded for the briefest moment of her rescue from the Jaffa cakes. She put it out of her mind.

"Let's get him on his feet and see if he'll take a drink."

Sister Agatha tugged on the pony's halter to no avail. Finally Peter shoved from behind and in a moment, Bartimaeus stood.

Peter held the water bucket while the pony took a long drink. When he stood up from the bucket, he tossed his head and nickered. "He does seem a bit more chipper, doesn't he?" Sister Agatha said, relief in her voice.

"I shall tell Sister Winifred that wool blankets are no longer needed for Bartimaeus," Sister Callwen said.

"Feel like a turn-about the meadow, Sister Agatha? He wants a bit of a walk, I would say." Peter caught hold of Bartimaeus halter and moved him towards the open door.

Sister Agatha pulled her woolly hat down over her gray hair. "Exactly what I feel like as well," she said.

"I will leave you to attend to him then," Sister Callwen said. "I really do think we need to change that pony's name to Lazarus."

Sister Agatha and Peter started off across the meadow with Bartimaeus walking along between them. It was a slow walk, partially because the pony was still getting his breath back, although he was looking much better, but also because the ground was frozen in treacherous ruts. She noticed that instead of old Wellingtons like her, Peter was wearing another pair of expensive hiking boots. He still had that schoolboy look of studied sloppiness that didn't seem to match his neat, almost military haircut. She took a long look at him sideways and for the first time, noted his handsome profile: broad forehead, aristocratic nose, determined chin. He didn't look much like Claire, but then cousins often don't look alike.

"I can't thank you enough for helping Bartimaeus. I never would've thought we were overheating him. It was just that when our veterinarian told us to keep him warm, we all went a little overboard."

"These ponies thrive on the Shetland Isles where it's either snowing or raining or both. They really weren't bred to live in a convent with nuns."

"Bart has done very well living in a convent with nuns, I'll have you know." Just as she said this, Sister Agatha stepped on the wrong side of the frozen ridge of sod and lost her balance, forcing Peter to reach across Bartimaeus and grab her shoulder. Neither spoke a word as she regained her balance, as well as a bit of her dignity. *Why am I always falling when I am with this man?*

"Aye, you've made him a contented pony all right. Other than nearly killing him with love, I think he's had a wonderful old age," Peter said.

"Well he does seem better now. And I am very grateful." They walked on for a few more moments in silence.

She couldn't stand it any longer. She had to inquire what he thought about the clues in her murder book. "So tell me, you took a look at my murder book and I know that you're a big reader of mysteries. I mean, you must be, if you know Agatha Christie so well. What is your opinion of some of the clues that I have discovered?" Sister Agatha tried to sound casual. Modest, even. "You know, in my attempt to investigate Claire's death."

Peter was silent so long that Sister Agatha almost thought he hadn't heard her question. Finally, he spoke. "Don't take this the wrong way, Sister. But I think that it's like old Bart here. My cousin Claire was very well cared for here at the Abbey." He paused. "And I appreciate it that you've worked so hard to figure out how she died."

"What are you saying?"

"I'm saying that I think you're trying very hard to prove something that didn't happen."

"What didn't happen?" Sister Agatha stopped and turned around, one hand on Bartimaeus' halter, the other on her hip.

"Don't get me wrong, I appreciate that you want to prove that she didn't take her life, but I don't think you can. I'm sorry, but if you knew Claire the way knew her....it wouldn't be so hard for you to believe."

Sister Agatha shook her head. "Claire was a very happy, upbeat person. With plans for her future life. I really can't imagine...."

"My cousin was good at *acting* happy. But she struggled desperately underneath it all, a great deal. And then the fact that her boyfriend came here to propose to another woman...well, it was just too much."

"You mean his proposal to Kate?"

"Yes. Kate. I think that was harder on Claire than we can imagine. And that's why she went out to the cliffs that day and ended her life."

"What about the fact that we have a photo of her smiling into the camera and the scarf of another person in the photo?" Sister Agatha stopped again and turned to him. "Obviously, somebody was there with her on the cliff when that photo was taken." Sister Agatha turned and began to walk again.

"Could it have been her own scarf that was blowing the wind?"

"Our own constable's deputy does not think it was hers." Sister Agatha pulled the halter to the left, and they turned to go back to the barn. Bartimaeus was decidedly perky again and breathing normally. "Anyway, what about all the other things. For example, the letters and number sequence: TL 64?"

"I meant to tell you. TL is Claire's grandfather's initials. On her mother's side. Thomas Lane. And his birthday is June fourth. So it was just a note about her grandfather's birthday. His initials TL and his birthday six four."

"Why would Claire make a file for her grandfather's birthday? And store it on a flash drive? And hide it in her socks?

Peter laughed. "Well, our Claire was a bit quirky. You would know that if you knew her as well as I do. I suppose that she just didn't want to forget his birthday."

"Okay. But if she were going to take her life, why did she plan for her grandfather's birthday, six months out?"

"Perhaps she made the file before she knew her boyfriend was here to propose to another woman? I think it was that proposal that threw her back into depression."

Sister Agatha walked on with Bartimaeus following, trying to digest this information. It made sense. Or did it?

"What about the Bible verse she sent you as a text message? About things being hidden and coming to light?"

"Well, I wondered about that, too." Peter shrugged. "Did Claire tell you she was really into scavenger hunts? Always setting up clues and conducting these elaborate games with her friends and younger members of the family? No doubt it was just an idea for a future lark."

At this Sister Agatha stopped. "I'm sorry, but that doesn't even make sense." She looked hard at Peter.

He laughed. "Well, it makes more sense than a secret code that explains her death as murder."

They had reached the pony barn and Sister Agatha waited while Peter pulled the door open. She led Bartimaeus in the stall and gave him a bit of hay. When she turned to leave, Peter stood blocking the door.

"In truth, my cousin's death has very little to do with you, Sister Agatha. You might do well to focus your energy on things here at the convent and stop trying to prove that there has been a murder. Your murder book is all very charming, and your reliance on mystery writers is unique, if nothing else. But you must admit, you hardly knew Claire. I watched her grow up and I know first-hand the demons she wrestled with. Give her the respect she deserves. Let her rest in peace." And with that he pushed shut the door and left Sister Agatha and Bartimaeus alone inside.

CHAPTER 24

"That is the last time I let anyone read my murder book," Sister Agatha fumed. She had joined Sister Matilda and Reggie in the greenhouse where they were transplanting tomato seedlings. "I cannot believe such arrogance." She thumped a clay pot onto the worktable and jabbing a trowel into a mound of dirt, filled it to the top. "Of all the nerve. Telling me to focus on the needs of the convent and stop trying to see murder where there isn't any. He called my murder book 'charming'!"

"Please, Sister Agatha, careful with the seedlings. They're extremely fragile at this stage." Sister Matilda gathered spilled potting soil up off the table and gently tamped it down around the spindly tomato plant. "I am so sorry he didn't recognize your skills at detection. Maybe he isn't aware that you have cracked two murder cases already."

"You've what?" Reggie broke in. Reggie was draped nearly head to toe in a heavy gardening apron. He already looked pear-like, now he resembled a Christmas pear wrapped up for a fruit basket. "Murder cases?" He pushed his spectacles up leaving a smudge of potting soil on the bridge of his nose. He tilted his head back so he could squint at her through the lower part of his lenses. "Goodness. I didn't know you solved murders."

"Well," she began modestly. "I do have a reputation as a pretty good amateur detective. Even if *some people* do not appreciate me."

"And where did you learn such erudite skills?" he asked, gazing at her with admiration. "Have you taken an online class?"

"No. Nothing like that. I fell into it naturally. As I have honed my craft as a mystery writer, I've simultaneously developed some fairly shrewd detecting proficiencies. It was a natural progression, really." She picked up another clay pot and filled it with potting soil. "I'm working closely with Deputy Clough to find her killer."

"You don't say? I heard she took a selfie and fell backwards. Dreadful. And she was such a lovely young woman. But you think she was murdered?"

"Let's just say that Officer Clough and I are exploring all possibilities."

"She liked your miniature cathedral didn't she, Archbishop," Sister Matilda said.

"She did. It was so nice to sit and talk about it with a young person. They show so little interest normally."

"I believe she mentioned it to me at the last cheese tutorial. She wanted to know if I had ever seen it. I told her that everyone in the village had. Remember the Women's Institute presentation that you did?" Sister Matilda asked.

"Of course. Splendid discussion with the ladies, afterward." Reggie picked up another clay pot and began filling it.

"Did your friend Owen find a place to stay?"

Reggie's trowel clattered to the floor and he ducked under the worktable to retrieve it. Coming up, his heavy apron was askew and his eyes wide. "Owen?"

"He came by Father Selwyn's when I was there."

"Yes. Well. I sent him to Father Selwyn, of course. Owen is not in a good place in life. I was hoping Selwyn could be a sympathetic ear."

"I don't think he was seeking sympathy." Sister Agatha again stabbed her trowel into the mountainous pile of potting soil on the worktable and clapped the dirt off of her hands. Although she loved the steamy, tropical environment of the greenhouse on winter days, she had planted all the tomato seedlings that she had patience for. She tried to pitch in with the many gardening tasks at the convent, but she just couldn't fire up much enthusiasm today. Peter's comments had taken her aback.

"Oh?" Reggie tamped down the soil around a particularly frail seedling.

"He wanted money."

"Ah well, that's our Owen."

"Said he needed money for gas."

"Did he now?" Reggie clucked his tongue and placed the small pot containing the seedling into the tray. "Not to be trusted is Owen." He sighed. "Sad."

"He said you were old friends. Mates from way back."

"We were indeed friends at one time, when we were young. But, I fear, not anymore. And not for a very long time." He brushed the dirt off his hands and turned to face her. "Without breaking confidentiality, Sister, I can tell you that many years ago, Owen made choices that I couldn't abide." He gazed out the streaked window for a moment, and when he turned back, a look of pain had crossed the old man's face.

Sister Agatha felt annoyed at herself for bringing it up. But a stranger in town looking for money at the same time that a young woman ends up dead. She had to inquire.

"It's sad when one must end a friendship, isn't it?" Reggie untied his apron as the bells began for afternoon tea. "But sometimes, it's the only way forward."

CHAPTER 25

"I knew that the Archbishop had a good reason for not letting the old gentleman stay with him," Sister Agatha said as she pulled out a chair at the long farm table. The Abbey kitchen was redolent with the yeasty aroma of baking bread and something with cranberries, perhaps. Sister Gwenydd often sliced a loaf of freshly baked bread still warm from the oven and melted with butter for the nuns' lunch on a winter day. Although at the moment, she was rolling out a pie dough. "He's not to be trusted. And with Reggie's health being in question, a person as needy as this Owen Wiley might quickly become a burden."

"I wonder," Sister Gwenydd said, her brow crinkled. She stopped her rolling pin in mid roll and stared out the window, a flock of sparrows fluttered and chirped around the bird feeder.

Sister Agatha stirred her tea and waited. She had begun to consider Sister Gwenydd a detective-in-the-making and wanted to give her plenty of opportunity to arrive at her own conclusions.

"It is my opinion that people only tell part of the truth when they're telling something," she said, turning back from the window, and vigorously rolling again.

Sister Agatha opened her detective's notebook and made a lengthy note.

"You're not thinking of him as a suspect, are you?" Sister Gwenydd said.

"Everyone is a suspect at this stage of an investigation."

"Seems a bit far-fetched."

"Are you kidding? 'A stranger comes to town' is a classic bad-guy scenario." Sister Agatha took a sip of tea. "You really have to start reading the classics: Agatha Christie, Louise Penny, Anthony Horowitz. Not just watching Netflix."

Sister Gwenydd smirked. "As if you don't watch your share of Netflix."

"Only for professional development."

Sister Gwenydd smirked again. "Right."

"Moving on." Sister Agatha turned a page in her notebook. "How are you progressing on determining the whereabouts of each member of the Abbey the night of Claire's death?"

"It's not been easy. But I have made some progress." Sister Gwenydd put down her rolling pin and checked her phone. "I thought I was being subtle and then Sister Callwen bit my head off. She accused me of abandoning cooking for crime."

It was hard to get anything past Callwen.

"And then she accused me of becoming like you and blamed it on spending too much time with you."

Sister Agatha snorted. Well, that was a compliment!

"But I would say that everyone was present and accounted for the night of the murder."

Sister Gwenydd maneuvered the pie crust into the round pan. "Although, people do lie about alibis. Don't forget, *A Is for Alibi*."

"You read Sue Grafton?"

"No. I'm just messing with you. But people do lie." Sister Gwenydd crimped the edges of the pie crust, pricked the bottom with a fork and then slid the empty crust into the waiting oven.

It wasn't a pleasant thought, but it seemed increasingly more likely that someone at the Abbey was lying about their alibi. "You don't want to put the filling in that before you bake it?"

"I bake the crust first. I hate a soggy bottom."

Sister Agatha raised her eyebrows.

"One of the many weird things you learn in cooking school." Sister Gwenydd had graduated from the prestigious Leith School of Cooking in London. Her Food and Wine diploma hung on the kitchen wall right between the health department certificate and the hand carved crucifix Sister Winifred had brought back from the Holy Land. Sister Gwenydd paused and cocked her head. "Or maybe I learned it from watching the Great British Bake Off."

"I like that show. Though Paul Hollywood can be a bit of a sodder. He made that young lad, Andrew, cry. Who knew what a 'botanical-themed bake' was supposed to look like anyway?"

"Don't feel sorry for the bakers. If you're going to play with the big boys, you need to man-up."

"Speaking of bakers and such, any progress on the chefs that Claire might have offended with her stinging restaurant reviews?"

Sister Gwenydd dusted her hands off on a dish towel and took a seat across from Sister Agatha. "I thought you'd never ask." She leaned forward as she poured a cup of tea.

She noticed that Sister Gwenydd's eyes gleamed.

"The review by Claire that I read to you was from The Blue Moon Grille, in Cardiff. Very posh. And you know who used to be the chef at the Blue Moon?"

"Not a clue."

"Hubert Clethyn." Sister Gwenydd sat back and grinned at Sister Agatha.

"The chef at the Pryderi Hotel?"

"Yes. He's always talking about how he trained in Paris and everything. And how he used to be at the Blue Moon which is known for its French Cambodian menu. I wondered why all of a sudden Hubert was here in Pryderi. I mean the Pryderi Hotel is nice and all, but it's not exactly upmarket. Not like the Blue Moon."

"And thank goodness for that." Sister Agatha distrusted restaurants that served anything other than decent Welsh fare. "So you think that the bad review had something to do with his leaving Cardiff and ending up in the North Country in a small village?"

"I would put this week's grocery money on it. A bad review can be the beginning of the end for a chef. Or at least, it can derail a career."

Sister Agatha looked out the window just as the sparrows scattered and a red kite swooped in. "Do you fancy a bit of upmarket cuisine, Sister? Well, upmarket for Gwenafwy Abbey, anyway."

"Always."

"Good. Because I think it's time we had afternoon tea at the Pryderi Hotel."

CHAPTER 26

"I'm surprised Reverend Mother was so amenable to us coming to the Hotel," Sister Gwenydd said, picking up a menu. "She usually digs her heels in on anything this pricey."

Sister Agatha, accustomed to the bustle and noise of the Buttered Crust Tea Shoppe, realized she liked the elegant calm of the Pryderi Hotel. Not that she wasn't absolutely loyal to The Buttered Crust, but white tablecloths, starched napkins, crystal water glasses, and waiters in black who glided from table to table, made for a refreshing change.

"Sometimes when investigating murder, you have to do things a bit outside the box."

"You mean she doesn't know we're here?"

"She knows we're in the village. And that's honest. We *are* in the village."

"Sister...."

Sister Agatha shook out the snowy white linen napkin and spread it across her lap. "Any good investigation requires a certain amount of solid research."

"Well," Sister Gwenydd said, as she picked up a menu. "As long as we're here, we should enjoy ourselves."

"So, this is fine dining," Sister Agatha said, gazing across the dining room. "I could get used to this."

"This is *relatively* fine dining. Although I must say, these menu items are impressive. Escargot, beef carpaccio, foie gras."

"Foie gras?"

"Liver."

"For afternoon tea?"

"I asked to see a dinner menu. I'm curious about what Chef Clethyn has to offer."

A young waiter appeared out of nowhere to refill their water glasses even though they had hardly touched them. *Keenan could take a leaf out of this waiter's book.*

"My name is Jeffrey and I will be your server today. May I suggest the coronation chicken sandwiches to begin," he said in a smooth voice. "Followed by the fruit scones and clotted cream?"

Sister Agatha sighed. Any day with clotted cream was sure to be a good day.

"Perfect," said Sister Gwenydd. She handed her menu to the waiter. "And the Battenburg cakes and the Yorkshire curd tart."

"Of course, madam. The Battenburg is one of Chef Clethyn's specialties."

"Is Chef here today?"

"I am afraid not, madam. But do not be concerned. Our sous chef is most skilled, and your afternoon tea will be of the highest quality."

"But you indicated that Chef Clethyn baked the Battenburg cake?" Sister Agatha asked.

Jeffrey flushed and stood a bit taller. "When I said it was Chef Clethyn's specialty, I meant to say that it was one of Hotel Pryderi's specialties. Our sous chef made today's Battenburg cakes. Which I assure you, are delectable."

"Will Chef Clethyn be in later today?" Sister Agatha asked. She had met Hubert a few times in the village. He was sometimes seen shopping at The Fatted Calf, piling his cart with organic meats and fresh produce. She remembered him as a bit portly with a mop of curly brown hair.

Again it was hard not to notice the discomfort of the waiter. *Hubert Clethyn hadn't been sacked again, had he?*

The waiter leaned forward and said quietly, "I can tell you, I suppose, since you are sisters from the Abbey. But Chef Clethyn is...he is... missing."

"Missing?" Sister Gwenydd said in a whisper. "Since when?"

"Since Tuesday. Epiphany. He was supposed to make the King's cake and quite unlike him, he did not. We did not discover the dilemma until the last moment, and we had to quickly prepare a cake."

"When was he last seen?" Sister Agatha slid her notebook out of her habit pocket.

"Tuesday. At afternoon tea. But he left early. Just as we were starting the savories and tea sandwiches."

"Have you reported this to the constable?"

"No...."

She looked at Sister Gwenydd and then back to the waiter. "Why not?"

The waiter drew himself up to his full height and looked around the restaurant. He then leaned in. "Again, since you ladies are sisters from the Abbey." He lowered his voice almost to a whisper. "We are holding off."

"Why?" Sister Agatha found that she too was whispering.

The waiter took a deep breath and said a bit louder. "Because everything is so much more pleasant with him gone. The staff have begged for just another day without Chef." And with that, he clutched the menus and glided away.

Sister Agatha and Sister Gwenydd looked at each other. "The staff wants another day without him. Interesting. Are head chefs really that awful? Sister Agatha asked.

"Absolutely," Sister Gwenydd replied.

Sister Agatha opened her notebook and consulted the first

page. "Claire died at five o'clock Tuesday. If afternoon tea started at 3:00 that same day, could Hubert Clethyn have followed her to the cliff, and somehow helped her fall?"

"He could have," Sister Gwenydd said slowly.

"He could have killed her and then panicked and left town."

"Or searched her room that night and then left town. Maybe he thought she had written another review and that's why he took the laptop."

"We need to find Chef Clethyn."

"Agreed," Sister Agatha said, taking a sip of tea from the delicate china teacup. "But not before I have my clotted cream."

CHAPTER 27

It wasn't difficult to track down Sister Juniper. According to the other sisters, she divided her time between cheese-making and building the climbing wall. And since the latest cheese batch now sat in the aging room, she wasn't surprised to find Sister Juniper in the old dairy barn, wearing a tool belt, polka-dot Wellingtons, and her long blue habit pinned up over yoga pants. She looked exactly how Sister Agatha thought someone from California should look: tall, svelte, blond, *Amazonish*. Yet she seemed entirely unaware of her commanding physique.

"How is the, um, wall, coming?" she asked as she approached the far end of the barn where Sister Juniper stood, hands on her hips, tool belt dangling and staring upwards. Power tools, stray nails, and pieces of thick wood were scattered on the floor. A table saw sat in the middle of the room. Sister Agatha didn't even know the Abbey owned a table saw. A large piece of plywood covered the back wall from floor to loft. It was pocked with what looked like cut out rocks and little ledges. Sister Agatha wondered just how one climbed this wall. And more importantly, *why?*

"Progressing!" Sister Juniper flashed her million dollar smile at

Sister Agatha. *Americans.* You just had to admire their commitment to orthodontia.

"Are those little pieces to grab hold as you climb up?" she asked more out of politeness than actual interest. Sister Agatha doubted strongly that she would ever scale the climbing wall. Although several of the other sisters had certainly shown an interest.

"They are." They both stood necks craned, gazing upwards. "A fabulous way to exercise. Core *and* cardio. In fact, it is nearly completed. You'll love it."

"I'm sure I will." She made a mental note never to be available when climbing lessons were offered.

"Do you have time to talk for a moment?" She gestured to a few hay bales sitting off to the side.

"Of course," Sister Juniper said, unclasping her tool belt and tossing it on the floor. She plopped down. "What's up?"

Sister Agatha noticed it took her a little longer to lower to the hay bale. "I'll come straight to the point. Where were you on Tuesday at five o'clock?"

"When Claire died, you mean?"

She nodded, opening her notebook.

"Just like I told Sister Gwenydd, I was here in the barn. I missed most of dinner because I lost track of time. Which I know isn't good-- but I really wanted to get the wall finished. I sometimes forget about eating."

Sister Agatha found that annoying since not once in her life had she ever forgotten about eating. "You forgot about time because you were so close to finishing. But that was three days ago, and you are still not finished, right?'

Sister Juniper shrugged. "I hit some snags."

"Was there anyone with you Tuesday evening?"

"Why all the interest? I thought she fell backwards over a cliff taking a selfie." Sister Juniper looked directly at Sister Agatha, her expression open and thoughtful.

A little too thoughtful, perhaps. Most people shuddered when they said the words 'fell backwards over a cliff.' "I'm just gathering information."

"I came into dinner about five-thirty or so. It would be quite a feat to make it up to the cliff walk, shove someone over, and then get back all in 30 minutes."

Sister Agatha looked up from her note-taking. "I guess even someone as athletic as you would have a hard time moving that quickly." She paused for a moment. "Are you a runner, Sister Juniper?"

"I am."

"Long distance?"

"I prefer shorter races."

"It's a mile to the cliff walks from the Abbey. How fast can you run a mile?"

"In the snow? Wearing a habit, jumper, and my new Wellies," Sister Juniper stuck her foot out to reveal a red polka-dot Wellington. "Not too fast."

"But you could run it, if you had to?"

"Are you thinking that I shoved Claire over the cliff, hiked up my habit, and sprinted back to the Abbey in time for bread pudding?"

Sister Agatha smiled. "Ridiculous, I know. Sorry to interrupt your work." She stood. "If you'll excuse me, I need to get back to the library. I am terribly behind on my cataloguing." She felt Sister Juniper's eyes on her as she walked away.

"A missing key found in a cake, a very athletic nun with a weak alibi, a cousin of the victim telling me to back off, a strange code hidden among the victim's socks, two ominous figures at the dovecote the night of the murder, a Sister Winifred scarf at the crime scene and in the selfie, a stranger in town asking around for money, a suspicious and missing head chef. Oh, and a sick pony." Sister Agatha accepted the tea that Father Selwyn handed her. "My life is taking a downturn."

"Sick pony?"

"Bartimaeus. He's just not himself. I've started taking him for short walks on his halter just to keep him limbered up like Tupper said, but then he heads right back to the stable. It used to be that he was always wanting out. Now he seems content to stay in. And we nearly killed him with Sister Elfrida's heat lamp and a wool blanket."

Father Selwyn stirred his tea slowly, looking into the cup. "How old is Bartimaeus now?"

"Not that old."

"You're sure? As I recall, you got him when he was already well past midlife."

"If you are implying that Bartimaeus is dying of old age well then you're wrong. All he needs is a bit of a pick-me-up. I've started him on the extra magnesium in his grain and a better exercise regimen and I think it's working." She shot Father Selwyn a fierce look. "In fact, he wouldn't have even had that lying-down-and-not-getting-up episode if we hadn't almost smothered him." She was both angry at Peter for what he said about her detecting skills and grateful for possibly saving Bartimaeus' life.

"Right," he said quickly. "It's just that you..."

A knock at the door interrupted him as Bevan Penrose stepped in. "Reverend Thurston called and wondered if you could come by for a visit?"

"Of course," Father Selwyn said. "Tell him I will be by in about an hour." Bevan stepped out, closing the door behind him.

"Reggie really bounced back quickly after his fall."

"Yes and no." Father Selwyn frowned.

"I saw him in the greenhouse yesterday with Sister Matilda. He seemed fine."

"Well, good. Glad to hear it."

"How did he fall? "

"That's the concerning part. He doesn't remember."

Sister Agatha peered over her teacup, eyebrows raised.

"Well, he was just very vague on the details. At the hospital, that is. And other than being rather shaken up, he didn't seem particularly hurt."

"If he wasn't hurt, what took him to the hospital in the first place?"

"Frightened, I think. Which is unlike Reggie."

"Maybe he's frailer than we like to think."

"Maybe."

"Dementia?"

"Possibly, but it isn't something you casually bring up. Yet, cognitively, he doesn't seem like the old Reggie. Everything makes him anxious. Nervous."

"It's hard to accept when someone you love gets older. But it happens." Sister Agatha drained the last of the tea from her cup.

"It does. Perhaps that's a way that you could think about..."

"I have to leave now." She stood up and pulled on her woolly hat. "I want to stop by the Hotel Pryderi before my next library meeting. We are beginning a lecture cycle and it's just in the planning stages. Our moderator is pushing for a series on the history of the wool production in Wales which will never pull in the crowds. I need to be there to steer it off."

Father Selwyn stood with her. "Sister Agatha. Wait. I am adding Bartimaeus to my personal prayer list. He's going to be fine. I have a good feeling."

Sister Agatha blinked back the tears that sprang to her eyes. "Do you think so? Really?" She turned back to him; her throat suddenly tight. "Because everyone else is giving up. Sister Callwen told me that I should think of it as a hospice situation. That all we should be doing at this point is palliative care—making him comfortable until he, you know, until he.... But it isn't hospice. It really isn't."

"Of course it isn't! I will lift his name in prayer, and we shall fully expect a miracle."

Unable to speak, she smiled her thanks at her old friend and slipped out the door. Buttoning her anorak, she had to admit, with a friend like Father Selwyn, it was hard to go wrong.

CHAPTER 28

Sister Agatha gave a sidelong glance to the open door where Jeffrey stood with his arms crossed and his foot tapping. The sign on the door read *Chef Hubert T. Clethyn.* "Sister, hurry. Please." He gave a furtive glance down the hall. "If anyone finds out that I've let you search Chef's office, I'll get the sack."

"It's either this, or I call Parker Clough and report the chef as missing." Sister Agatha felt a little guilty that she had manipulated Hotel Pryderi's head waiter, Jeffrey, so effortlessly. But the coincidence of Claire's death at the exact same time that Hubert Clethyn conveniently disappeared, was too much to ignore.

"Well, at least speed it up." Jeffrey closed the door.

The cramped office had one window which overlooked the alley. Its gray panes indicated that possibly it hadn't been washed in its lifetime. A metal bookcase held volumes of dogeared cookbooks some of which spilled off the shelves onto the floor. Others were piled onto a rickety card table. Stacks of culinary magazines, invoices, spreadsheets, and unopened mail sat in a jumble on the desk. Sister Elfrida would make short work of his bookkeeping, that was for certain. An old club chair, its upholstery worn thin and its springs sagging, sat in the corner. Well, maybe Hubert

Clethyn wasn't exactly svelte. Most chefs weren't. Except Sister Gwenydd who did Pilate's videos every morning after Matins.

Sister Agatha stood in the middle of the chaos and took stock. Where to begin? At a glance, there was nothing incriminating in plain sight. Well there wouldn't be, would there? On one wall, across from the bookshelf hung a bulletin board covered with fliers, sticky notes, a board of health notice, several yellowed advertisements for farmer's markets, organic meat, and farm-to-table produce. A photo, curling up at the edges, was stuck in the corner of the bulletin board frame. It was of a younger Hubert Clethyn accepting an award. He wore a tuxedo and had an unruly mop of curly brown hair. Most of the pages on the board were crinkled with age, as though it were a time capsule. Nothing mentioned Claire MacDonagh. Only one page stuck up in the bulletin board was new. The order of worship bulletin from St. Mary's in Grenfell. She leaned in. Dated two weeks ago. *Interesting.* A church goer. Nice.

The desk chair groaned as she took a seat. She rolled back to a squeal of rusty casters and tugged on the middle drawer. Locked. If the drawer was locked, it must contain something worth finding. She lifted the blotter. Sometimes people left a key in the most obvious places. No luck. She tugged on the desk drawer again. Brute force wasn't going to work. But she couldn't help it and she rattled the drawer again.

The door opened, and Jeffrey stepped in glowering at her. "I can hear you out in the hall."

"Do you have a key for this drawer?"

"You said you wanted to look around, not go through his desk."

"I said 'search his office'."

Jeffrey pulled the door shut and locked it. "What do you think you'll find? A map to where he went?"

"Not exactly."

"Why are you here, Sister?"

"I'm concerned about Chef Clethyn's disappearance."

Jeffrey raised an eyebrow. He pulled out a folding chair and, setting it up underneath the dirty window, sat across from Sister Agatha. He tamped out a cigarette from a pack in his pocket.

"You can smoke in here?"

Jeffrey reached up and cracked the window. "We do it all the time." He withdrew a lighter and then breathed in while lighting the cigarette. He closed his eyes, clearly enjoying the first inhale. "I have to smoke. It's the only way I can keep my weight down. I stopped once and put on 30 pounds."

Sister Agatha cocked her head and took a long look at Jeffrey as if seeing him for the first time. Tall and thin. Her fingers itched to write in her notebook. Maybe not that tall. "You replaced smoking with food?"

"Not just food. *Milkybars*." He tapped the cigarette on the edge of the windowsill so that the ashes fell outside. "Now tell me, what are you looking for?"

Sister Agatha smoothed her apron over her habit. If she wanted access to the desk, she would probably have to tell Jeffrey the truth. At least a version of the truth. "Have you heard about the death of a young woman who had been staying at Gwenafwy Abbey?"

"Claire MacDonagh? Of course. They say she was taking a selfie and fell backwards." He inhaled smoothly and turned his head toward the window and exhaled. "Jesus. Who wants a selfie that badly?

"But does the name Claire MacDonagh mean anything to you? Had you ever heard it before?" Sister Agatha wondered if Hubert Clethyn had ever mentioned her. Of course, if you are carefully planning the murder of a person, you probably didn't go around ranting and raving about them. But you might-- if you had anger problems. And it seemed Chef Clethyn did. And anyway, she didn't know if he carefully planned her death. Maybe he followed her out to the cliff walk to confront her, and then one thing led to another.

She watched as Jeffrey lifted the pot with a deceased geranium and removed a key from underneath. He opened the middle desk drawer and reaching in, took out a manila folder. He opened it and handed her a stack of dog-eared articles. Some were yellowed and creased, a few others appeared to be newer. At a glance, she concluded that they were every article Claire MacDonagh might have written for *Modern Cuisine*. The top article had a thick red line through Claire's name.

Jeffrey grinned. "You should have told me that was what you wanted. He keeps them handy."

CHAPTER 29

"Any luck at the Hotel?" Sister Gwenydd asked, as she closed the oven door. An hour before lunch and the kitchen was filled with the aroma of lamb cawl. Before Sister Gwenydd had joined the convent, the nuns had been making do with take-away fish and chips or Wok-in-a-Box from the Golden Dragon on the A55. She had certainly improved their mealtimes and as Sister Callwen pointed out, their cholesterol levels.

Sister Agatha told her all about the articles as she reached into her carryall. "I made copies. There's only one that was written specifically about Chef Clethyn. Although all of them are on the scathing side, the one about him is particularly nasty." She handed them over to Sister Gwenydd.

"The one about him has Claire's name crossed off?" Sister Gwenydd looked up.

"In red ink."

"That seems pretty angry."

"It is also significant that he saved the articles, right in his middle desk drawer. That certainly indicates anger, if not obsession."

"And he's saved these a long time. Some of these are nearly 10 years old." Sister Gwenydd looked at her, her head cocked to one side. "Didn't you get the feeling Claire was younger? I mean she seemed young to me. Like early 20's. But these articles are a decade old. So even if she started writing for *Modern Cuisine* right out of journalism school, she had to have been in her 30's when she came here?"

"Well, she did seem young to me. But remember, the thirties are different for different people. Some people are very mature, others not so much."

"Parker Clough is in his early thirties, right?"

"I think so."

"I like the guy, but you have to admit, he was forty years-old the day he was born."

Sister Agatha laughed. "I expect Lucy will lighten him up a bit." She stirred her tea as Sister Gwenydd took a closer look at the article that Claire had written about Hubert Clethyn. "She had such a bold style of writing," Sister Gwenydd said. "It's on the edge of funny; yet, razor sharp at the same time. I wonder why she gave up *Modern Cuisine* for *The Church Times*. I mean, there's not a lot of cheeky in *The Church Times*."

"No. I hadn't thought of that. I wonder what her articles are like for *The Church Times*? Subdued in comparison, I would imagine."

"How could you go from biting commentary like these to a newspaper read by church ladies? It would be like if you were *sou chef* at Buckingham Palace and then suddenly found yourself on the morning shift at the Buttered Crust."

"Don't disparage the Buttered Crust." Sister Agatha was deeply loyal to her favorite teashop. "Or church ladies. Some of my favorite people are church ladies."

Sister Gwenydd grunted. "You know what I mean."

"I do." Sister Agatha stared thoughtfully at the stack of articles.

"Didn't she say that she was looking for that big breaking story?"

"Yes."

"So what was she doing here in Pryderi? A village in North Wales where the biggest excitement is the Christmas Jumble at St. Anselm?"

"She was on assignment. The article on Gwenafwy Abbey."

"I guess she had to earn a living, like the rest of us. Have you told Parker Clough yet? About Hubert Clethyn?"

"Haven't had a chance. But soon. I have a new plan."

"Oh?"

"We interview Nickolas, the sous chef, of course."

"Nickolas, do you have a moment?" Sister Agatha asked. She stood on the steps of St. Anselm's. She had hoped to talk with the sous chef away from the Hotel and Father Selwyn had told her that he attended the early morning yoga class.

"Excuse me?" he said, pulling a skull hat over his short graying hair. He turned and waved to the other yoga students as a group ambled across main street in the direction of the Buttered Crust. "Be right there," he called. He seemed to take her in in one sweeping glance. "I'm sorry, do I know you from..." he said politely.

"We've never met," Sister Agatha said. Feeling some need for credibility, she added, "Father Selwyn told me I might find you here this morning."

"Right. Of course. Wonderful chap, Father Selwyn. And a good yogi, at that."

"I don't know much about his yoga skills, but I wondered if you and I could talk."

"Will it take long? I've a busy morning and this is my only chance for a cup of tea."

"Only a couple of questions."

Nickolas shrugged and followed her back inside the church. They took a seat in a back pew. She introduced herself and then asked him what he knew of Hubert Clethyn and Claire MacDonagh.

"What do I know of them? What's to know?"

"Did Chef Clethyn have a grudge against Claire MacDonagh?"

"Why do you ask?" He pulled his phone out and checked the screen, tapped a few times, and then slid it back in his pocket.

"You know that she is dead, right?"

"Of course, I'm not living in a bubble. Everyone knows she took a selfie and fell backwards off the cliff." He grimaced. "But what does this have to do with me or Chef?"

"Did Chef Clethyn ever talk with you about Claire MacDonagh?"

"Sister Agatha, since you don't seem to want to answer my questions, why do you expect me to answer yours?"

"Sorry. I think that Chef Clethyn disliked Claire MacDonagh intensely and since he disappeared the same day she died; I'm checking into it."

"And why is one of the nuns from Gwenafwy Abbey doing the checking? Why not Constable Barnes or Parker Clough?"

"Let's just say, I'm working in association with them."

"Then let's just say, Chef didn't really like Claire. But you wouldn't either if she had done to you what she did to him."

"What did she do?"

"Side-lined his career. Her review in *Modern Cuisine* sent him reeling. Not just professionally, but personally. He lost confidence and eventually his job. And now he's at the Hotel Pryderi. A little restaurant in a little village in North Wales."

"That's where you are too."

"And that's another story for another time." He started to stand.

"No, wait. Sorry, again. Just a few more questions."

He sat down with a small sigh. "So much for my morning tea."

"How did he react when he heard that Claire MacDonagh was in Pryderi?"

Nickolas sighed and leaned back in the pew. He gazed up at the cathedral ceiling for a moment. "Let's just say there wasn't a chopping block safe in the whole kitchen."

"Really? Why? Did he say anything?"

Nickolas stood and buttoned his coat. "He did. But it's nothing I would ever repeat to a nun."

She watched as Nickolas hurried down the street past the Buttered Crust towards the hotel. She felt bad that she had made him miss his tea. She wrapped her scarf around her neck and headed towards Church Lane. She stepped onto the little foot-bridge over the River Pwy.

Peter MacDonagh and Owen Wiley stood next to the yew tree on the other side of the bridge. She stopped, trying to look incon-spicuous, although neither man appeared to notice her. She couldn't make out their conversation but for once, body language said it all. The usually laid-back Peter jabbed his index finger into Owen' chest and even though he was taller than Peter, Owen cowered under Peter's obvious anger. She watched in amazement as Peter shoved Owen back a step. Owen jerked away pulling himself up to his full height. Peter turned on his heel and strode off in the opposite direction from Sister Agatha. Owen turned and walked towards her on the footpath. He crossed the bridge, brushing past her without a word, his head down.

She started on the footpath towards Church Lane. Had she completely underestimated Peter? He had seemed like such a nice person. Claire's cousin, a horse man who helped Bartimaeus. But who was he really? And he seemed to know Owen Wiley. How was that possible? Both were strangers to Pryderi. What was the chance that they had known each other before and ended up here together? She climbed the hill barely noticing the wind. She had better get to her notebook soon or it would be impossible to ever catch up.

CHAPTER 30

Sister Agatha hung her coat on the coat rack. When Ansel offered her the *snug* room at the back of Saints and Sinners pub, she had explained to him why the little backroom was called a 'snug'. In 19th-century Wales, it was unseemly for women to drink in public. So pubs created hidden rooms for groups of ladies to gather and labelled them "snugs". Ansel had shrugged as he wiped down the table in the snug. "Okay. Whatever. It's yours for the evening."

"I hope Reverend Mother doesn't realize we've slipped out and down the hill to the Saints and Sinners," Sister Gwenydd said as she followed her in. "I believe she thinks I'm in the kitchen setting the breakfast rolls to rise and I'm sure that she thinks you're in the library."

"Deceiving Reverend Mother, are we?" Father Selwyn said, stepping into the snug and unwinding his muffler. "Does this make me an accomplice?" Arranging his coat on the back of his chair, he sat down and picked up a menu. "Are we eating or just drinking?"

"Drinking," Sister Gwenydd said. "If I'm going to sneak out this late at night, I'm at least having a pint."

"Not me. I'm on duty," Parker Clough said, as he entered the snug, shrugging off his coat. He hung it neatly on the coat rack in the corner and then squeezed into a chair at the small round table. "But I am definitely eating. I'm famished."

Sister Agatha pulled shut the door of the snug and the boisterous background noise of the pub faded. She took a satisfied survey of the table. Three of her favorite people. Father Selwyn, Sister Gwenydd, and Parker Clough. She would need all of them if this killer were to be found. The evidence and clues were piling up in the most disorganized manner and she could no longer determine what connected to what, and what needed to be studied further, or thrown out, or ignored. She stood. "I call to order this..." The door to the snug bumped open.

"Shorthanded tonight," Ansel said, his notepad out. "Ready?" He took everyone's drink order while Parker stared at his menu. Ansel tapped him on the shoulder with his pen.

"I'll have the beef brisket with the Perl Las cheese, smoked streaky bacon, beetroot and horseradish chutney, brioche bun, triple cooked chips, pickle and gherkin skewer." He closed his menu. "And a cherry plum soda."

"To be young again," Father Selwyn said, in an awed voice.

"I said I was starving." Parker Clough looked around the table.

Sister Agatha cleared her voice. "Ahem. Now that Parker is no longer in danger of perishing, then I call to order this meeting of the Gwenafwy Abbey Murder Club." A squawk of protest went up.

"Please no. Don't call us that. Sister, I am a member of law enforcement and the rest of you are church people. You couldn't come up with a better name?"

"Or how about no name at all?" Father Selwyn said. "Can't we just be concerned friends gathering somewhat in private to discuss murder?" He paused. "Oh. I see your point. Maybe we are the Murder Club after all."

The door bumped open again and Ansel slid two baskets of

crisps on the table and left again.

"Isn't that from a book by.... a book by...No! Netflix Originals. No... It was on....it was on....Hulu...." Sister Gwenydd's brow crinkled as she dug into the crisps. "Amazon Movies. I'm sure of it."

"It's James Patterson. While not my favorite author, he did do a solid job with the *Women's Murder Club*." Sister Agatha said, selecting a crisp the other basket.

"Why 'Murder Club'?" Father Selwyn asked. "I rather think of us like the characters in that show with the two women who garden so splendidly. Oh what is it called?"

"*Rosemary & Thyme*," Ansel said as he pushed into the snug again. He placed three pints and a bottle of cherry plum soda on the table and was gone in a flash.

"We are the Gwenafwy Abbey Murder Club and that's final." Sister Agatha took a sip from her pint and after putting it down, continued. "I have gathered us together tonight because Claire's murderer is now 72 hours out and as talented and hard-working as Officer Clough is...." She turned to the young man who could only raise his eyebrows and nod, his mouth was full of crisps. "The details of the investigation are getting away from us. I have decided that we must gather as a team if we are to make any progress."

"Fair enough," Father Selwyn said. He took a thoughtful sip of Guinness. "Where are we at?"

"I think we all know about the scarf in the picture?" Nods around the table. "And we agree that it incriminates someone-- we just don't know who."

"Well, knowing 'who' would pretty much solve it all, right?" Sister Gwenydd asked. "Because one thing is clear-- whoever was with her on the cliff that evening, the person wearing the scarf, has to be the one who pushed her."

"Not necessarily." Parker said.

The door bumped open again and Ansel entered backwards with a tray of food. He placed two steaming plates in front of

Parker. "Careful, the brisket's hot." Ansel looked around the table. "Everyone all set?" Before they could answer, he was out the door.

"They could have been a bystander," Parker said, picking up his fork. "Although, they saw her fall and did nothing which indicates malice."

"What was she doing out there, anyway?" Sister Gwenydd asked. "Late afternoon, the sun setting. Who would just go for a walk?"

"You mean someone took her there?" Sister Agatha asked, scribbling furiously in her notebook.

"Or arranged to meet her there." Sister Gwenydd reached over and with a smile, took a triple-cooked chip off Parker's plate.

"The real question, at the end of the day, is who wanted Claire MacDonagh dead?"

Father Selwyn said.

"And why?" Parker added.

The group sat for a moment, sipping their drinks and watching Parker eat. "How do you pack it away like that and stay so thin?" Sister Gwenydd asked, the disgust in her voice barely concealed. "I eat as healthy as possible and do Pilates every day and I could never eat like that. I don't know when I had brisket at eight o'clock in the evening."

Parker chewed and then swallowed. "Nerves. I work for Constable Barnes, don't forget." He bit a pickle off the gherkin skewer.

"Sister Agatha," Father Selwyn said, dragging his eyes off Parker. "Take us through your list of suspects from the beginning to the end. Just so we are all on the same page."

She began at the top: Sister Samantha, Sister Juniper, Reverend Mother-- here she had to wait while a gasp from Sister Gwenydd died down. She then moved on to her concerns about the boyfriend, Bickford Chadwick. She summarized his drunken night after having proposed to a woman named Kate. The group erupted into conversation about who Kate might be. Father

Selwyn knew two Kates in Pryderi who were about the right age, although each seemed a little unlikely in his opinion. She finally moved them off the topic of the failed proposal and how it might have affected Claire, had she known about it.

Next she explained her fears about Chef Clethyn. On this one, Parker raised his eyebrows. Fortunately for her, his mouth was full again, having made a brave start on the beetroot chutney. She quickly described the caustic article in *Modern Cuisine* and the unspoken comment overheard by the sous chef. Finally, Owen Wiley, a stranger comes to town; and Peter MacDonagh, who, although he seemed perfectly nice at first, then had been condescending about her involvement in the investigation, and finally aggressive with a homeless old man. This also led to a long discussion during which another round of pints was ordered. Finally, she told them about Peter's concern that Claire had taken her own life. A long silence followed.

"How do you know that she didn't die by suicide?" Father Selwyn asked. "Isn't it possible? A tragedy, but not out of the question."

"People can appear very happy and carefree, when they are actually really struggling." Sister Gwenydd said. "Maybe we should consider that more seriously. As much as I hate the thought."

"Yes, but someone was on that cliff with her," Parker said.

"Don't get me wrong," Father Selwyn said. "But are we absolutely certain that the scarf was worn by someone else. I mean, what if it *was* hers?"

Sister Agatha tossed her fountain pen on the table and blew out her breath. Her back ached and that second pint hadn't been the best idea. "Look, this whole case revolves around the scarf demonstrating that Claire was not alone that night." She stood and did the new yoga stretch Father Selwyn taught her. "And now we're just going to throw it out?"

Sister Gwenydd drained the last of her pint. "I say we pull back for a moment and look at our physical evidence. It might bring something to light that we're not seeing."

Sister Agatha took her seat and opened her carryall. They watched in silence as she rummaged around for a moment and then pulled out the enlarged photo of the selfie. "Here's the photo. You can see the label on the scarf that indicates it was knitted by Sister Winifred. And as anyone can see, Claire is not wearing the scarf herself, rather it's blowing towards her from someone else." With a fierce look, she slid it into the middle of the table.

Next, she placed a copy of the bible verse in the middle of the table and next to it, a page with nothing but "TL64". She told them about Peter saying it was the grandfather's birthday and initials. And also his explanation about a scavenger hunt. Finally, on top of it all, she placed the key for the dovecote, minus the frosting.

"Why would the birth date be on a flash drive that is hidden?" Sister Gwenydd asked. "And Claire doesn't seem like the scavenger hunt, type."

"I can almost see why you mistrust the cousin, Sister Agatha. But what if he is right? Two very simple, straightforward explanations." Father Selwyn looked up from the printout.

"But in her sock drawer?" Sister Gwenydd plucked a gherkin off Parker's plate.

Sister Agatha pulled the sheaf of articles out of the carryall. "Take a look at these. Especially the top one with the red line through Claire's name."

They passed them around and read in silence.

"That's rather ominous," Father Selwyn said.

"Do you think he crossed out her name because he...you know...crossed her out?" Sister Gwenydd said, no longer interested in eating off Parker's plate.

Parker tossed his napkin on the table. "I've been out of line here. As an officer of the law. I should never have involved any of you. This is dangerous. Someone out there has murdered Claire. And maybe they are right here among us in Pryderi."

"Excuse me?" Sister Agatha gave him an affronted look. "You're kicking me to the curb? After all I have done to move this investigation along?"

"I'm sorry Sister. You have certainly proved your prowess. It's just that I'm no further with solving this murder than I was the day Constable Barnes left on his vacation. And for all we know, it's getting dangerous." Parker picked up his fork and ran it around the empty plate in front of him as if to secure the last remaining crumbs. He put the fork in his mouth and finished off whatever might have been found on his barren plate. They all watched as he neatly centered the fork above his plate. "I just hate to tell him that I don't know anything."

"Don't give up yet," Father Selwyn said. Sister Gwenydd and Sister Agatha nodded, and both looked at Parker who sat staring at the pile of evidence in the middle of the table. "Why don't we divide and conquer? I will dig deep on the bible verse. Who knows where that might lead? I don't buy the scavenger hunt story either."

"What about Claire herself?" Sister Gwenydd said. "I found her a bit of a mystery. I'll see what I can uncover. If we knew more about her, we might figure out why someone wanted her dead."

"I could pull in Peter MacDonagh. And Scotland Yard is looking for Chadwick." Parker Clough looked up. "Sister Agatha, you keep pushing on the Chef Clethyn angle. But please be careful. Stick to the Internet—his social media posts might be revealing. Do not confront him in person."

"Very well then. We all have our homework to do. And there will be no calling Constable Barnes, right Parker?" She glanced at him.

"For the moment, anyway."

"All right then. The Gwenafwy Abbey Murder Club will gather again, two nights from now. Same time, same place. Meeting adjourned!"

CHAPTER 31

Sister Agatha raced across Grenfell Castle Square where she could see the gray Welsh transit, the five o'clock bus back to Pryderi, lumbering towards the bench right in front of one of her favorite used bookstores, Bus Stop Books. If she hurried, she could catch it, and then arrive back at the Abbey just in time for dinner. On a less hectic day, she might have spent a satisfying hour browsing the shelves for a used book, but not today. She had already lingered too long at St. Mary's chatting and drinking tea with the fashionable young Reverend Macie Cadwalader.

Macie was a favorite among the sisters at Gwenafwy Abbey since a few years ago, when the bishop had sent her to the small and declining parish in Grenfell. Congregational life had hit a near coma, under the leadership of Reverend Albert Jones. A beloved vicar, Reverend Jones was legendary in the parish for falling asleep during one of his own sermons. He had long passed the age of retirement, but the tiny parish didn't have the heart to let him go. Finally, after he died peacefully in his sleep one night, the bishop assigned Macie to St. Mary's. He assumed that she would close the dwindling parish. Instead, she jumped in with youthful enthusiasm and Grenfell St. Mary's transformed into a vibrant center of local mission and social justice. Of course, the congregation still didn't have any members under the age of 70, but the seniors were bringing it in with soup kitchens, coat drives, and after-school programs.

Reverend Mother had sent Sister Agatha to meet with Macie and interview her on how to start their own community meal. Now that they had all the added enthusiasm and workforce of the new nuns, it was time to step up their community outreach. Sister Agatha did indeed discover all the details on how Macie and her crew ran the soup kitchen, but she discovered the details of something else even more interesting. The Reverend Macie Cadwalader had a boyfriend.

All she would tell Sister Agatha was that his name was Thomas and according to Macie, he was handsome, intelligent and loved her church. Well, Sister Agatha was happy for her. And she would have stayed longer to hear more tales of the fabulous Thomas, but she glanced at her phone and realized that she would have to make a run for it, if she was to catch the transit home. Promising to return in two nights to attend the St. Mary's Community Meal, she raced out the door and down the street.

Just as she rounded the corner, she heard the hissing sound of the bus brakes as the air compressors filled. She grabbed her habit skirts and broke into a full sprint. But the bus heaved forward and out of the bus stop without her.

She stopped and caught her breath. The next bus wasn't for an hour. Perhaps Sister Gwenydd would save her a plate. She smoothed the front of her apron and unzipped her anorak. No reason to hurry now, she strolled along the sidewalk looking into shop windows. Perhaps a cup of tea followed by a browse at the used bookstore.

A cup of tea, a scone, and a nearly new paperback of Anne Cleeves' *Red Bones*, she settled onto the bench at the bus stop. As the sun dropped, so did the temperature. She stood and walked a few paces down the street just to keep her blood circulating. She passed the bookstore, a tattoo parlor, a jewelry store, and then the opening to a narrow alley. She glanced down the alley and stopped short. *Hubert Clethyn.* He turned just as she looked at him. The alley was dark, and she wasn't sure. She had only met Hubert a few times. But his unruly brown hair was distinctive. She remembered that. He hadn't seemed like the hair net type.

He stood at a heavy metal door that led into the side of a tall brick building, an abandoned factory common in these old mill towns. At his feet was a long, rectangular wooden box. He bent double and grabbing the end of it with both hands, dragged it up to the door. A round object, the size of a human skull, stuck out at the end of the box. She shuddered. Their eyes met for a split second as he opened the door. He gave the box a violent push and disappeared behind the door.

Had the person really been Hubert? She was almost positive he had been and took one step towards the spot where he had stood. Perhaps the door was unlocked or there was another passage in through the main building? Just then she heard the hissing of the bus's brakes and ran to the bus stop. With a single backwards glance, she jumped onto the bus to Pryderi.

CHAPTER 32

"Why would Reverend Mother want the silver tea set polished? We never use it. She thinks it is too extravagant for a convent where all the members have taken a vow of poverty and I have to agree with her." Sister Agatha picked up a tiny silver spoon and began to vigorously rub it.

"Stop," Sister Gwenydd said firmly, taking the spoon away. "There is a process to polishing silver and if you're going to help me, you have to do what I say."

Sister Agatha snorted, but sat up to watch. "We never did a lot of silver polishing when I was growing up. Since I lived on a sheep croft."

"That must have been a splendid place to be a child. I grew up in Kensington." She paused, thoughtfully. "Which had its good moments as well." Sister Gwenydd had spread the pieces of the silver tea set across the oilcloth which covered the farm table. "This set is lovely though. My grandmother has a set like it, and it will probably be mine someday. If my family ever gets on board with the fact that I'm now a nun."

"Your family's still cross about it, are they?" Sister Agatha said, picking up a large tea pot. "What is this exactly?"

"A spirit-kettle. Well, they are Church of England, but that doesn't mean they wanted their daughter to be a nun."

"Nice. The kettle that is, not your family. You'd think they'd be proud."

"They found cooking school difficult to accept, so you can imagine that a convent has them completely undone." She opened a large bottle of silver cleaner. "The pieces are spirit kettle, teapot, coffee pot, cream jug, and sugar bowl," she said pointing to each one. "Plus the spoons. I wonder how old this set is. Sterling silver. Probably worth a lot."

"Which might be why Reverend Mother is having us polish it."

"You don't mean she'd sell it, do you?"

"I do. Cheese sales are holding steady, but expenses are going up. At least that's what Sister Elfrida tells me."

While Sister Gwenydd dabbed a bit of cleaner on a soft cloth and began gently rubbing the sugar bowl, Sister Agatha updated her on Hubert Clethyn in Grenfell, including the suspicious looking box.

"But was it really Chef Clethyn that you saw?"

"That's just it. I am pretty confident that it was. But I'm not completely confident. That's why I haven't taken it to Parker Clough yet."

"Also, Parker told you to find Hubert on the Internet. Not a dark alley."

"Well, it's not like I went looking for him."

"Why would Chef Clethyn be in Grenfell?"

"Exactly. Why? I'm going back tomorrow night to work at the St. Mary's soup kitchen, and I plan to scout around."

"Do be careful. What if he is the one who killed Claire? And I don't like that box he had. You don't think it was a …?" She paused her polishing and looked directly at Sister Agatha. "Be careful, for once."

Sister Agatha picked up a cloth and dipped it into the silver cleaner. "I'm always careful."

"Yeah right," Sister Gwenydd took the cloth out of her hand. "Watch me. You rub the silver in a straight-line. Like this." Sister Gwenydd made back-and-forth motions on the coffee pot. "You're not supposed to scrub. You want to let the polish do the job." She watched as Sister Agatha carefully wiped the sugar bowl with silver polish. "Then we rinse with cold water. And finally, you must completely dry it. Make sure you're using a clean cloth. And it has to be soft cloth."

"Goodness. Reverend Mother picked the right person for this job."

"I love silver tea sets for some reason. They look delicate, but they are not. They're sturdy, resilient and like this set, will last forever with just a little care."

"Like a good Shetland pony! They look delicate-- small and have tiny hooves and short legs, but they are tough as nails."

The inside kitchen door swung open and a voice with an Irish brogue rang out. "Comparing Shetlands to fine silver, are we? Well, I'd have to agree." Peter stepped into the kitchen with a swoosh of cold air. "A good Shetland is indeed both beautiful and sturdy. All in one." He pulled off his anorak and woolly hat. "I hope I'm not interrupting?" He eyed the two women draped in heavy aprons and the tea set on the table.

"We're trying to work here," Sister Agatha said coolly. She had not forgiven Peter for saying that she should back out of the investigation. Especially after she had trusted him with her murder book. "Is there something we can help you with?"

"How about if I join you?" he said, hanging his hat and coat on the coat rack in the corner and then pulling out a chair at the table.

"It looks as if you already have," Sister Agatha sniffed and focused on the silver milk pitcher in her hands.

"Of course you can join us," Sister Gwenydd shot Sister Agatha a piercing glance. "It's just that we have a lot to accomplish this morning. Is there something you particularly wanted?"

Instead of answering, Peter picked up the silver teapot and turned it over, looking at the bottom. He then flipped it back over, opened the lid and peered inside.

"There's no tea in there if that's what you're hoping for," Sister Agatha said. "But if you want to make yourself useful, you could put the kettle on."

"Frank M. Whiting & Company. Sterling Silver. Five pieces. Very nice. It would be worth more if you left it tarnished. But then maybe you're not planning on selling it. Is the Reverend Mother planning a big tea? Perhaps the Queen is stopping by Gwenafwy on her way to Balmoral this year?" He sprang to his feet and in two steps was standing at the sink. "I'll just fill the kettle and show you how we do tea in Ireland."

Sister Gwenydd and Sister Agatha gave each other a simultaneous eyeroll. Why was he here and what did he want? She had liked Peter when they first met. He had dug her out of the cake boxes without a single snicker and acted as if one fell into a pyramid of cakes every day. He had presented himself as self-effacing, kind, generous of spirit. And then when he helped with Bartimaeus, she could have hugged him. But in her last few encounters, he had grown more and more arrogant. Was that possible? And a better question, why? She wondered if Parker had run a check on him yet.

"What's with all this Glengettie and Welsh Brew?" He stood over the tea caddy that Sister Gwenydd kept on the countertop. "You ladies need to start drinking real tea. *Assam or Ceylon.* When I get back to Dublin, I'll send you a box of Thompson's *Punjana.* You'll never drink Welsh Brew again."

Sister Gwenydd's eyes widened as she looked down at the silver creamer. Those were fighting words with Sister Agatha who practically thought of Welsh Brew as sacrament.

"Mr. MacDonagh," Sister Agatha said, tossing her cloth onto the table, "aside from an education on the virtues of Irish tea, what have you come to see us about? If you want to discuss arrangements for your cousin, Reverend Mother would be a better resource."

Peter slowly took a seat at the table and gazed again at the silver teapot. Sister Agatha's throat tightened. She realized she had just snapped at a man who was trying to deal with the death of a loved one. So what if he was being a bit obnoxious? Grief was different for everyone. "I'm sorry. Let me rephrase that. What can we do to help you this morning?"

The tea kettle began to whistle, and he stood again. "No, no. It's me. I can be abrupt. Apologies. Let me make the tea and I'll tell you why I am here." He walked over to the counter and clicked off the electric tea kettle. "Although," he twisted around. "You should get that silver appraised. But then, that's none of my business."

"What is none of your business?" Sister Gwenydd asked.

"That the Abbey could probably use the money."

"And what do you know of Abbey finances?" she asked.

"Nothing. Nothing, of course. Just an educated guess."

Sister Agatha found her momentary sympathy dissipating.

"As you know," he began, as he poured a cup of tea for each of them. "I am stuck here in Pryderi until the autopsy is complete which is not something that seems to move quickly in this part of the world. And more than anything, I need to reach Claire's parents. I want to talk to them before I have her body sent back to Dublin."

The three sat in silence for a long moment. Sister Gwenydd grabbed a tissue and dabbed her eyes and Sister Agatha was glad she had a cup of tea to quickly take a sip.

Peter cleared his throat. "I know Sister Agatha that you are investigating her death-- along with the constable's office-- and that I may have offended you when I told you to stay out of it." He gave her a boyish smile. "That was out of line and I apologize."

Sister Agatha nodded. He seemed to offend easily and apologize just as easily.

"And I appreciate that local law enforcement does not want to share sensitive information with just anybody."

Sister Gwenydd spoke up. "In other words, Parker Clough won't give you any information and you are hoping we will. Especially if you make nice to Sister Agatha. Am I right?"

He continued as though she hadn't spoken. "But this was my cousin. I just need to know what was going on here before she died. And somehow, it would just help me if I could hear from the people who were with her during the last few days..." He cleared his voice again. "Her last few days on this earth." He looked at both women. "Do you mind, if I just ask you a few questions?"

"Ask away." Sister Gwenydd said.

"Were either of you with her the day she died?"

"Yes," Sister Agatha said. "She and I went to the former Archbishop's apartment."

"Why?" Peter set his teacup down in the saucer.

"She wanted to get a quote about organized religion and its support of religious orders, such as the one here at Gwenafwy Abbey. For her article."

"Did anything happen when you were visiting the Archbishop?"

"Well, first, he's not actually the Archbishop he is the former Archbishop and his name is Reggie Thurston. All that happened at his small apartment is that we had tea and cake and he showed us his miniature Cathedral."

"Miniature Cathedral?"

Peter's voice lifted very slightly when he said the word *miniature*. She took a hard look at him. But if he had been at all perturbed, he had recovered quickly. "Yes, the Archbishop likes to make miniature cathedrals-- models of real cathedrals. The one in his flat is a model of St. Asaph."

"And Claire was interested in it?"

"She took several photos so I would say that indicates some interest."

"With her phone?"

"How else does a millennial take a photo?"

"Do you have the phone?"

"No, Officer Clough has it. The mobile and everything on it is evidence in the investigation."

"I would love to see the photos on her mobile."

"Why?" This from Sister Gwenydd.

"Because they are some of the activities that my cousin experienced the day before she died. And I would like to know all about that last day. I would like to...." Peter stuttered. "I would like to experience the day. You know, as part of my grieving process."

"I doubt Parker Clough would release them. But you could ask."

Sister Gwenydd handed Sister Agatha a dry cloth. "Time to start drying and then we can pack them up again." She gave Peter an impish grin. "That is until the Queen passes through on her way to Balmoral."

CHAPTER 33

Sister Agatha hurried down main street towards St. Mary's, telling herself that this time, she would not miss the bus back to Pryderi. The fellowship hall at St. Mary's was already bustling with activity when she got there. She waved across the room at Macie who came smiling towards her.

"Just in time," Macie said. The Reverend Macie Cadwalader was the most fashionable priest Sister Agatha had ever met. Even the Reverend Suzanne Bainton, Bishop of St. Asaph, who was tall and thin and rumored to have chosen between a career as a runway model for Chanel or as a priest for the Church of Wales, couldn't hold a candle to Macie. Macie wore black clericals with white leather fashion boots, a stunning pair of pearl earrings, and a pearl brocade on her tab collar. Her luxurious strawberry blond hair gave the impression of being simultaneously windblown and perfectly styled. "I need someone to take charge of the green beans."

The next thing she knew, Sister Agatha found herself wrapped in a plastic apron, sporting a blue hairnet and wearing latex gloves as she spooned servings of green beans with pickled shallots and breadcrumbs onto plastic plates. Having not had dinner herself, her stomach growled. Her mouth began to water as another plastic-swathed worker replaced the nearly empty pan next to Sister Agatha with one of roast lamb with laver sauce. She had arrived with the stereotypical image of a soup kitchen--beans and franks, crisps. Not lamb, roasted potatoes, fennel and radishes with lemon brown butter sauce.

She glanced across the room. All sorts of people gathered around the tables-- young and old. She didn't know what she had expected there either. A free meal these days was different than when she was young. Now, there was an entire group of people termed "the working poor." In other words, individuals who worked hard and, in this economy, still didn't have enough to make ends meet. A meal every Friday night was just the thing to see them through. She shook her head. What had the world come to when hard work wasn't enough to put food on the table?

She hadn't forgotten her goal of finding some time to slip out and scout around, looking for a sighting of Hubert Clethyn. Of course, she knew that the chance of seeing him again was remote. She hoped to return to the alley way to see if she could spot him. Maybe he was living in the old factory building? Hiding there after the murder of Claire MacDonagh. But why would anyone commit murder and choose to hide in Grenfell? Maybe he was hiding in plain sight. *Hiding in plain sight.* She felt like she was about to remember something. Sister Agatha's spoon stayed poised over the fragrant tray of green beans until the young man waiting with an empty plate, politely cleared his throat. "Here you are," she said, plopping an extra-large helping of green beans. "Sorry about that. Enjoy your meal!" And the thought was gone.

The meal ended, and the large room began to slowly clear out. Chairs were stacked, tables wiped down, large push brooms crisscrossed the floor. Macie seemed to inspire a hoard of volunteers. Sister Agatha found the energetic and cheerful atmosphere encouraging. She dished out her last serving of green beans, untied her apron and stepped out of the way as a young woman with jet black hair, a tank top, and multiple tattoos grabbed the empty tray. "Sorry, Sister," she said as she nearly bumped into Sister Agatha.

"No, my fault. It looks like clean-up is serious business."

The girl smiled and rushed the tray back to the kitchen which blasted Beyoncé, telling the kitchen crew that "if they liked it, they should've put a ring on it." Which reminded her that Macie had told her that she would meet Thomas tonight, the new beau. Not that a ring had been mentioned at all, of course. Sister Gwenydd had asked that she get full details on the young man. She smoothed out her habit skirts and tried to fluff her hair to repair it from the hair net.

She left her post and made her way back into the crowded kitchen. Macie had spent the supper hour working the crowd like the warm-up act for Oprah, but she had disappeared about ten minutes earlier. She wanted to meet this Thomas gentleman, give her thank-you's for a great evening. She spotted Macie, leaning with her back against the kitchen counter, facing Sister Agatha but talking to a heavy set man who had his back to her. Now there is someone who needs a hair net, she thought. The man had a wild mop of curly brown hair. Macie caught her eye across the noisy room. She waved and grinned then pointed, mouthing the word 'Thomas.' Sister Agatha stood glued to the spot on the linoleum floor. Curly brown hair. A chef. A bit overweight. He turned around smiling. *Hubert T. Clethyn. The T. must be for Thomas.* Macie's new boyfriend. The missing Chef Clethyn.

CHAPTER 34

"And he is in love with...wait for it...*the Reverend Macie Cadwalader*," she said with a flourish. Father Selwyn leaned forward in the club chair across from her and simultaneously brushed crumbs off the front of his black cassock. Were there McVitie's chocolate digestives to be offered? She wasn't sure she wanted McVitie's having not quite recovered from her embarrassing Jaffa cakes debacle. Although, she reminded herself, anyone can lose their balance and plummet into a tower of cakes. A fire burned in the fireplace grate between them while faint notes from the St. Anselm organ, a Casavant Frères and the pride of the congregation, drifted down from the organ loft.

"In love? With our Macie? What do you mean?"

"What do you think 'in love' means? He snuck away from the Hotel Pryderi and spent three days with Macie. In addition to that, he now does all the cooking for the St. Mary Soup Kitchen."

"Macie Cadwalader and Hubert Clethyn," Father Selwyn said slowly. "It seems so unlikely. He's always abrupt and angry and she's perpetually gracious and happy. Well, this calls for baked goods. Digestive biscuits or Jaffa Cake? Oh right, I forgot. Biscuits it is, then."

"I guess when he's not in the kitchen being a chef, he's a decent person. He says that in the kitchen he emulates that guy on that show...Oh, you know..." Sister Agatha's brow furrowed as she accepted a cookie. "The Hell's Kitchen guy."

"Gordon Ramsay." Father Selwyn kept up on all the cooking shows.

"Which is why everyone hates him."

"I can imagine. So it was Hubert who you saw-- the other night in Grenfell."

"Yes. And that box with the skull?"

Father Selwyn, his mouth full of Jaffa cake, raised his eyebrows in question.

"Cabbages. A donation for the soup kitchen."

"Makes sense."

"Indeed. And he goes by the name Thomas-- his middle name-- when he's not channeling Gordon Ramsay. Apparently he hates the name Hubert. He's also spent a lot of years hating Claire. He admitted that."

"Alibi?"

"He was with Macie."

"The whole time?"

"So they say. And I think we can trust the words of clergy."

"Well. Where is Hubert now?"

"Back at Hotel Pryderi."

"I wonder why he feels the need to be Gordon Ramsay when his staff would probably enjoy the real Hubert?"

Sister Agatha shook her head. "A lot of people these days seem to act one way when they are really another."

"Such as?" Father Selwyn took another Jaffa cake out of the box and offered her another cookie.

"Peter MacDonagh was sweet and kind when I first met him. Now he's coming on like a, like a, well excuse my language, but like a complete 'twpsyn' *idiot*."

"Strong language indeed." Father Selwyn smiled into his

teacup. "What do you mean? I thought he dug you out of the Jaffa cakes. And that he saved Bartimaeus?"

"He did. But then other times he practically interrogates me and for some reason, he doesn't take me seriously as an investigator."

Father Selwyn was quiet for a long moment. "Don't take this the wrong way, but..." Before he could finish, the door opened, and Bevan Penrose stepped in.

"Father, I'm about to leave for the day. But I wanted you to know that the old gentleman, Owen Wiley, has been around again. Asking for money. I offered a food card, but he wanted cash."

Father Selwyn frowned.

"He got a bit cross and I had to ask him to leave," Bevan said.

Father Selwyn sat up, pulling in his long legs. "If he comes back, send him directly to me. And if I am not here, do not hesitate to call Parker Clough."

Bevan stepped across the room and laid several files on Father Selwyn's desk. "Call the Constable? I think I can handle an old man who wants a few pounds."

"I'm serious. If you have any doubt, call Parker."

They watched Bevan close the door behind him and then sat in silence for a long moment.

"You have concerns about Owen Wiley?"

"Erring on the side of caution."

Sister Agatha pulled out her murder book and made a note. *Owen Wiley. What is his motive? Why is he in town?* She flipped back a few pages, scanning. "Have you made any progress on the bible verse?"

"Not yet, actually," Father Selwyn said.

"A verse about all secrets being out in the open? That must be a clue, don't you think?"

Father Selwyn shook his head. "Sometimes a bible verse is just a bible verse."

Sister Agatha sat for a moment, thinking. "All secrets being out in the open...." It was like the moment when she was serving green beans at the soup kitchen. There was a thought just about to hit her and then it was gone. "Well, bring it to the next meeting of the Gwenafwy Abbey Murder Club."

"Do you really think that is the best name?"

"It's spot on." She stood. "Thanks for the tea. I have a library meeting that I must get to. And then if I can do it, without missing lunch, I'm going to drop by the constabulary and give Parker an update."

"I think we might need to know more about Owen Wiley."

"Agreed." She squished her woolly hat over her short gray hair. "In fact, I think I feel a stake-out coming on."

CHAPTER 35

Shouting reached her ears as soon she stepped into the constable's office. She looked with wide eyes, at Porter Bivens, who sat at the dispatcher's station.

"Bora da, Sister," Porter said, raising his voice. "How can I help you?"

"I was hoping to see Officer Clough, but it sounds like he's occupied. Who's in there with him?"

"That cousin of the poor girl who died."

"Peter MacDonagh?"

Porter nodded and cast a glance at the closed door.

He reshuffled some papers on his desk. "I don't believe I've ever known Officer Clough to raise his voice."

"It does seem out of character," she said. They stared at the door. "Can you tell me what's going on?" Porter could always be counted on for a bit of gossip.

"Well, not that I am listening in."

"Of course not."

"But if you are going to shout, you can hardly expect privacy."

"True."

"It appears that Mr. MacDonagh wants the girl's mobile

handed over to him as next of kin, and Officer Clough isn't having it."

"Well, of course not. It's an ongoing murder investigation." She pulled off her woolly hat and smoothed her hair. "I'm going in."

"You can't. Officer Clough wouldn't like that."

"If asked, I will say that you tried bravely to stop me."

Porter grinned. "Well then, once more unto the breach, Sister."

Deciding not to knock, Sister Agatha pushed the door open and stepped in. Both men looked up in surprise. Parker stood, red-faced, leaning forward with both hands on his desk. Peter, sitting in the chair in front of the desk, twisted around. He gave Sister Agatha a long glance and then let out a laugh. Obviously, Peter was in *twpsyn* mode at the moment.

"Sister Agatha, could you wait outside?" Parker Clough said. "I am afraid this is private."

"I'm afraid it's not," she said. "You can be clearly heard on the sidewalk."

"Oh let her stay," Peter sighed. "I have a feeling there's nothing she doesn't know anyway."

"How can I help you, Sister Agatha?" Parker asked, sitting down heavily. She took the empty chair next to Peter.

"You know," she said, turning to him. "You might get people to give you information if you weren't such a *twpsyn* half the time."

Peter laughed again, but this time his laugh sounded genuine. "A *twpsyn* am I, now?"

"I am sorry to use such language, but it seems appropriate." She noticed that Parker's mouth was twitching, and his face had returned to its usual shade of pink.

"I apologize, Sister. For my ungentlemanly and *twpsyn*-like behavior," Peter said, standing and making a slight bow from the waist. "But the deputy here isn't even going to let me look at Claire's phone."

"I didn't say that," Parker said, his voice both annoyed and sullen.

"Then could I go to your Evidence Unit and under the watchful eye of you or the Sister here, take a look at her phone?"

Parker leaned back in his chair. "Tell me why again? Why do you want to see what's on her phone?"

Sister Agatha thought she saw a slight hesitation on Peter's part, but then it passed.

"It's just that the photos Claire took in the past few days of her life, are important to me. Almost a window into her last days. Into her...her...soul." Peter stopped and cleared his throat. When he looked up, his eyes were bright with tears. Sister Agatha handed him a tissue.

"Alright. Alright. Never let it be said that I kept someone from seeing into their loved one's 'soul'," Parker unlocked the side drawer to his desk. "Our 'evidence unit' is right here. My right-hand drawer, where we also keep the crossing guard flags and the food cards from Tesco. I will click through myself and find for you what you want. You say you want to look at the last few days of her life." Parker removed the phone from the drawer. "Although, I'll warn you. There's not a lot to see. There are a total of less than twenty photos on this phone. Most Millennials that I know have thousands on their phone. Even my mother has at least 500."

"I believe Claire got a new phone right before she left for Gwenafwy Abbey. I suppose she didn't have time to transfer all her photos."

"You know that, do you?"

"Know what, Officer?"

"That your cousin Claire just got a new phone? I thought that you were on a walking tour of Snowdonia?"

"That doesn't mean we weren't texting. Join the modern world, Officer Clough, people text all the time. Even while hiking through a National Park."

Back to twpsyn mode, she thought.

"But there aren't any texts about a new phone, are there?"

"I said 'perhaps she got a new phone.' I don't pretend to follow her every movement."

"Are you certain you don't? Because here is an interesting text." Parker looked at Sister Agatha who sat barely breathing.

"*Peter, all set. I have everything I need for my next big story!*" Parker looked hard at him. "And you texted back, '*Can't wait to see you. Where should we meet?*' Then she said,

I'll text tomorrow. Enjoy your hike in Snowdonia!"

"Tomorrow never came though, did it?" The room sat in a long silence with Parker Clough staring down Peter. Parker looked back at the screen. "And here is the text that Claire sent where she quotes the bible. Which you have explained is due to her love of scavenger hunts?"

Peter smiled and shrugged.

"And then you sent several texts over the next two days asking about meeting up."

"I kept sending texts because I thought she was ghosting me or something. When Claire got really focused on a story, she forgot everything else. Including her family."

"Then you showed up in Pryderi. And you were first seen in The Fatted Calf where I believe you met Sister Agatha."

"And?" Peter said.

"Your family does a lot of hiking," Parker said.

"Indeed. Is that a suspicious act now, Officer?"

"No, but it's curious. You're on a walking tour of Snowdonia. Her parents are hiking in the Himalayas."

"What is your concern, Officer Clough? Share it with me and I will try to set your mind at ease."

Parker squeezed the stress ball on his desk and glared at Peter. Sister Agatha got the feeling that he was about to close in on something big, but what it was, she couldn't figure out. And then she realized he couldn't figure it out either. Parker tossed the phone to Peter who caught it deftly. "There are the photos that your cousin took the day before she died."

Sister Agatha leaned over Peter as he looked at the screen. Sister Agatha cringed at the selfie of Claire and herself. Did her hair really look like that all the time?

"Thank you, Officer Clough. You've no idea how much it helps me to have a glimpse into the last days of her life." Peter cleared his throat. "Could I have a copy of the photos to keep and maybe share with her parents?"

CHAPTER 36

"Reverend Mother isn't going to notice that we took the mini-van?" Sister Gwenydd hiked her habit skirts up and sat cross-legged in the front seat.

Sister Agatha looked with envy on the young woman's flexibility. Criss-cross-applesauce again. When had she stopped being able to sit like that? She couldn't remember. "As long as we are back by vespers, no one will notice. It's tough to have to squeeze a stake-out in between dinner and prayer. But here we are." She had parked the mini-van across the street from Saints and Sinners Pub, a few car lengths behind a beat-up Ford Fiesta. She thought she remembered Owen Wiley telling them, that day in Father Selwyn's office, that he drove a Fiesta.

"Too bad we can't go in and have a pint," Sister Gwenydd said. "I mean why not? We could keep an eye on him in there and then follow him out. It's chilly in this van."

"We couldn't follow him out. Think of it. A guy leaves and two nuns in habits jump up and rush after him. Then we pile into the van, rev the engine and peel out after his car." Sister Agatha looked in the rear view mirror. "Not exactly the kind of cover recommended by Inspector Rupert McFarland."

"Your inspector is Scottish. I bet he'd be going in for a pint about now." Sister Gwenydd yanked her luxurious brown hair back into a ponytail. A sure sign that she was either going to assist Sister Agatha on an investigation or bake a difficult cake.

"We need to sit tight and see if he comes out."

"What if it's time for vespers and he's still in there?"

"We leave for vespers."

As they sat in the van sipping tea from a thermos, Sister Gwenydd gave Sister Agatha an update on her research into Claire. "She did a lot of journalism work that was top notch. I mean seriously good. She won a couple of awards in Dublin. But then it just ended."

"What do you mean?"

"I mean that about four years ago, nothing. Her Linked-In account says she's only been at *The Church Times* a year. So what happened for three years? I mean, where was she? And why *The Church Times*? Someone with her talent should be writing for *The London Telegraph* or the *Huffington Post*. Not some church paper. Did she have a period of depression, like Peter said. And wasn't able to be productive?"

"It's possible. Depression can be debilitating."

"Maybe her career got stalled, and doing this story on Gwenafwy Abbey was her way back? Which makes what happened even more sad." Sister Gwenydd turned away, staring out the side window. Sister Agatha wondered if she was thinking of her own stalled, and then restarted, career.

The sun sank completely behind Pryderi Castle and the warm lights in Saints and Sinners came on. They did seem to beckon and just when Sister Agatha had almost convinced herself that going inside for one pint wouldn't hurt anything, Owen Wiley stepped out the door. He stood for a moment in the light of the stoop, just long enough for Sister Gwenydd to exclaim quietly, "That's him, isn't it?"

"It is, indeed." She turned the key and gripped the steering wheel.

Sister Gwenydd sat up straight, uncrossed her long legs, and clicked on her seat belt.

They waited until he got into Ford Fiesta and listened as the engine in the rusted old car chugged and finally turned over. "Well, that's lucky," Sister Agatha said. "A stake-out isn't very productive if all you do is watch your perp wait on the motor club."

"My first car was a Ford Fiesta," Sister Gwenydd said, leaning forward and peering out of the windscreen. "Loved it. Built like a Sherman tank."

Sister Agatha pulled out slowly, careful to stay a few car lengths behind Owen.

"I wish you would let me drive. You drive like a poky old woman."

"I am an old woman," Sister Agatha said as she tapped the accelerator, her eyes trained on the rusted green Ford. "But I am anything but poky."

Sister Gwenydd snorted. "At least it's dark. It's hard to go undercover in a white van with 'Heavenly Gouda: Sisters at Gwenafwy Abbey' scrawled across both sides."

"Don't forget our website and phone number are on there also. It wasn't my idea to paint the van," Sister Agatha said, her eyes not leaving Owen for a minute. "Although, Sister Harriet did do a spectacular job. Especially the cartoon figure of Reverend Mother holding up a piece of cheese with a halo hovering above it."

"Over the top, if you ask me."

The green Ford had a broken turn signal and so when Owen turned right, it was a surprise to Sister Agatha. She swerved at the last minute and Sister Gwenydd grabbed the dash. "You're like a slow motion Father Selwyn," she said, sitting back up and straightening her habit. Father Selwyn was notoriously reckless in his 1968 BMW Mini.

Owen turned again and this time into the Castle View Retirement complex.

"Reggie," Sister Agatha said, not taking her eyes off the old car.

"I thought they had had a row and Reggie told him he couldn't stay with him?"

"Something like that."

"So what's he doing here now?" Sister Gwenydd scrunched down in the seat as Sister Agatha parked across from Reggie's apartment. They watched as Owen walked up the flagstones and rang the bell. Light flooded the small stoop as the door opened, Owen stepped in, and then darkness again as the door shut.

"He just let him in. Like he was expecting him. I don't like that."

"Why?"

"Reggie is getting frail and forgetful. Remember how he took that fall, last week? And went to the hospital. Well, according to Father Selwyn, he doesn't even remember why he fell. I don't feel good about a guy like Owen visiting him late at night."

"Is Owen that bad?"

"Father Selwyn told Bevan to call the constable if Owen came by the church again."

"You're kidding. That doesn't sound like Father Selwyn."

"That's what I'm talking about. We know nothing about him including where he was the night Claire died."

"And now he's in there alone with the Archbishop." Sister Gwenydd rolled down the window and leaned out. "I want to listen." She sat back. "Why don't we call Parker?"

"We might have to. But first, I'm going to get closer." Sister Agatha started the van and pulled up right in front of the apartment. The front window was less than five meters from where they sat.

"What will you say if they notice us?"

"I'll make something up. Reverend Mother sent us with an

order of cheese. Or we're inviting him to dinner after church on Sunday."

Sister Gwenydd snorted. "Let's just hope we're not noticed."

Just as she was rolling up the van window, they heard shouting and then the sound of glass shattering. The second time in one day that Sister Agatha had listened in on another persons' row.

"Do you think Reggie's okay?"

"I'm going in." Sister Agatha jumped out of the van and with Sister Gwenydd on her heels, grabbed her habit skirts and ran up the short sidewalk to the apartment door. Both women stood for a moment. Sister Agatha knocked. "Reggie? Reggie? Are you alright in there? It's Sister Agatha and Sister Gwenydd."

She didn't wait another moment. She flung open the door and burst in. Both men looked up at her in surprise. Owen was seated on the love seat, balancing a teacup and saucer on his knee while Reggie stood in the middle of the room, the tiffany lamp in shards around him.

"Sister Agatha and Sister Gwenydd. What a delightful surprise. Jolly good of you to stop by." He beamed at them.

"How did the lamp break?" Sister Agatha asked, looking from one man to the other.

"Frightfully clumsy of me," Reggie said. "I was about to pour the tea, and I lost my balance. Crashed into the table. Getting old is not for sissies, isn't that what they say?" He smiled warmly. "Would you like to join us? I don't often get two such lovely visitors in the evening."

"We heard shouting?" Sister Gwenydd said.

"I expect you did," Owen said, nodding towards the radio. "Before Reggie took his dive into the table, we were listening to the match. *Six Nations Rugby*. Wales is stomping England."

"Oh so you were cheering on the Welsh team?" Sister Gwenydd said.

"You think we'd cheer for anybody else?" Owen said.

"Can we help you clean up? I'll get the dustbin," Sister Agatha offered.

"Oh goodness no," Reggie replied. "We're right as rain here, aren't we, old chap?" He looked at Owen.

Owen beamed back. She thought it might have been the first time she had ever seen the old man smile.

"Well then," Sister Agatha said. "We'll leave you to your tea."

"Who drinks tea when they watch rugby is what I want to know," Sister Gwenydd said, clicking her seatbelt.

"I have a better question," Sister Agatha said, as she swung the van out of the drive to the Retirement Complex.

Sister Gwenydd blew on her hands. "Like why the heater in this van doesn't ever work?"

"No. Where was the miniature cathedral? It wasn't in the front room where he keeps it."

"Maybe he moved it."

"Maybe. But where? It's both large and delicate. And the apartment is small. Where else would you put it? I should have asked him, but honestly, I was a little rattled by the whole situation."

"Why does it matter?"

"Because whenever you investigate murder, you notice things. And I feel like that was a big thing that I didn't even notice until it was too late."

CHAPTER 37

"I call to order the second meeting of the Murder Club of Gwenafwy Abbey," Sister Agatha said, standing at the head of the table in the Saints and Sinners snug room.

"It's not that I have anything against the name," Father Selwyn said, taking a long drink from his Guinness. "But it makes it sound as if we're all from the Abbey. As if we were all nuns. When in fact, only half of our group has taken vows."

"And if I'm going to be a nun who chases down murderers," Parker said, pausing to take a long sip on his pint. "Then I would like to claim a little more success. Constable Barnes is back any day now and I'm no closer to solving this murder that I was the day he left."

Sister Agatha tapped her silver fountain pen on the table. "Please, everyone. Focus. The last time we met we decided that each of us would complete a detective task and then come back and report on it." She looked around the table. No one spoke. "All right, I'll start." She opened her murder book. "As you know, Hubert Clethyn was a primary suspect. And, I will admit, I liked him for the murder." She looked around the table for encouragement but finding none, continued. "He harbored animosity towards our victim which he voiced clearly and demonstrated that he had an anger management problem. So naturally, I needed to find out what he was up to." She paused.

"I thought you were going after him online," Parker said.

"Let's just say opportunity knocked, and I answered."

Parker rolled his eyes.

"Anyway," Sister Agatha went on, ignoring him. "It appears that during the time of the murder, the suspect was working at a soup kitchen while pursuing a romance with, well, with an acquaintance of ours."

"Who?" Parker asked.

"Macie Cadwaladr."

"The priest? At St. Mary's in Grenfell?" Parker asked.

"Yes. And Hubert has an airtight alibi. He was with Macie the night of the murder and she can corroborate his whereabouts. In fact, the entire soup kitchen at Grenfell St. Mary's can corroborate it, which is about a hundred people." Sister Agatha picked up her fountain pen and drew a heavy blue line through Hubert's name in her murder book.

The group sat in silence for a few moments. "I'm getting fish and chips," Parker finally said.

"Could we focus on murder tonight and not get so obsessed with the menu," Sister Agatha said. She felt deflated at the group's underwhelming reaction to her discovery about Hubert Clethyn.

Sister Gwenydd snorted.

Sister Agatha turned to her. "Yes, Sister? Do you have something you want to add?"

"You are forever eating, Sister Agatha. I can't believe you're telling Parker he can't have fish and chips."

"I never said he couldn't have fish and chips. I just said I wanted us to focus tonight."

"Fish and chips sounds good," Father Selwyn said. "Did Ansel leave any menus?"

Sister Gwenydd reached around behind her and grabbed a pile

of menus from a chair pushed against the wall. She plopped them in the middle of the table. "I think it should be in our bylaws. The Murder Club of Gwenafwy Abbey opens each meeting with a perusal of the menu."

"Order food. Order drinks. I don't care. But let's at least keep moving." Sister Agatha forced herself not to glance at the menu. "You're up, Father Selwyn. Sister Gwenydd you're on deck."

"Well, I'm sorry to say it, but I've got nothing on the bible verse." He leaned over, pushed open the door to the snug and looked out into the restaurant. "Where has Ansel gotten to?"

"You don't think it has special meaning?" Parker asked.

"I first thought that it must be a special message to Peter. Since it was a text message to him. With some sort of hidden meaning. But the fact that he doesn't seem to think it means anything is interesting. Except his scavenger hunt idea. I think that if we chase the verse too far, we'll find ourselves down the rabbit hole. And that will throw us off. If it has anything to do with Claire's death, it's way beyond my pay grade."

The door to the snug bumped open and Ansel poked his head in. "Well?"

"Fish and chips all around." Father Selwyn said. "On me."

Sister Agatha picked up her silver fountain pen. "Okay. So far, we have determined that the Bible verse is a dead end. I don't like admitting defeat, but ...." She drew a solid blue line through the words *Matthew 10:26*.

"Well, I do have something to add," Parker said. "I ran a check on Peter. I wanted to see if he had anything in his background that might make it clear why he came to Pryderi. Other than just to visit Claire. I must admit, there was a part of me that wondered if he really was who he said he was." Parker pulled his black vinyl notebook out of his breast pocket, opened it, and flipped through several pages. "'Peter MacDonagh described himself as a scholar of medieval literature, and that he came to Pryderi to visit Claire while he was taking a walking tour of Snowdonia.' First, one must ask, why would anybody take a walking tour of Snowdonia in January? However, I called the park station and found out that winter hiking is a thing and very popular with a certain crowd. Next, I googled him just to see what might pop up and I'm a little concerned that he doesn't have a very big Internet presence. But maybe that's not unusual for a medievalist. He has published a few scholarly articles listed on his Linked-In page. Graduated from National University in Galway. Teaches at University College Dublin. He has absolutely no priors, not even a parking violation. I can't say that I like the guy and maybe I still think he's worth keeping an eye on, but I don't have any reason to suspect him."

"Disappointing," Sister Gwenydd said. "I had a bad feeling about him that I thought was spot-on."

"Sorry," Parker said.

"Can't you bring him in for questioning?" Sister Agatha asked.

"On what grounds? Too law-abiding? Too uninteresting?" Parker said.

"Well, I've often thought that *uninteresting* should be a crime," Sister Agatha said. She drew a blue line through *Peter, cousin.*

The door pushed open and Ansel came in balancing a tray stacked with platters of fish and chips.

"We can eat while we work," Sister Agatha said. "We only have until Vespers so let's keep moving."

"Well, I'm up," Sister Gwenydd said. "And unlike the rest of you, I really have something." She pulled her thick brown hair back into a ponytail and opened a spiral notebook. Sister Agatha thought for a moment that she should help Sister Gwenydd get fitted out with a better detective's notebook, but on the other hand, spiral was a perfectly decent way to begin. "Okay, you know how Claire took those photos of the miniature cathedral? Well, her interest in the cathedral struck me as important." She slid copies of the photos in front of them. "As you can see, one photo features the outside of the Cathedral; and one photo is a selfie with the cathedral. And this photo is the tiny bible, inside the cathedral."

Sister Agatha had to admit that she had not even had time to take a close look at these photos. That was the problem of being a nun and a detective, you just never had enough time to do everything.

"Pay attention to this one." She held up the photo of the tiny bible. "Look closely. What do you see?" She waited a few moments. "It's not a bible! At least not a whole bible."

"Ah yes," Father Selwyn said.

"What is it?" Parker asked.

"It's the Gospel of Matthew."

"The mysterious bible verse is from Matthew." Sister Gwenydd looked at them, her eyes gleaming. "That can't be a coincidence."

No one said anything for a long moment.

"Well, aren't there a lot of verses in the book of Matthew? I mean, how is that not a coincidence?" Parker said, biting into a chip.

Sister Gwenydd yanked out her ponytail and stared at them. "Darn. You're right."

"Now wait a minute. It could make perfect sense. We know that Claire had expressed interest in writing an article on the cathedral." Father Selwyn picked a bite of fish off his plate with his fingers and popped it in his mouth. They waited while he chewed and swallowed. "The bible that Reggie put in the cathedral was the book of Matthew. Claire grabbed an intriguing verse from Matthew to use in the article."

"Like any good writer she was looking for a hook to grab the attention of the reader," Sister Agatha added.

"Which means it had nothing to do with the murder at all. Just notes she was taking for the article?" Sister Gwenydd looked crestfallen. And annoyed.

"Still better than Peter's scavenger hunt idea," Sister Agatha said as she drew a thick blue line through the words *tiny bible*.

CHAPTER 38

Sister Agatha's heart still trilled from the effects of Vespers as she climbed the stairs to the attic. Reverend Mother had given one of her most moving and powerful homilies ever. All about the song *Men of Harlech*. A mighty battle song that could inspire the most faint-hearted person to stand up and do what needed to be done. She hummed the tune as she climbed the steps.

Sister Agatha had not known this story until tonight when Reverend Mother recounted it for them. During the tragedy of 9-11 in New York City, the Chief of Security in the trade center had worked heroically to get people out of the burning building. Interestingly, he was a Welshman who had lived most of his life in Wales andnd like all good Welshmen, he knew how and when to sing. As he moved the hundreds of terrified people down the long flights of stairs, he sang to them to keep their spirits up. He sang over and over, the rousing and inspiring battle song, *Men of Harlech*. Finally, after saving countless lives, he entered the building one last time, never to come out again. And they say that as he went in, he was singing *Men of Harlech*.

. . .

She settled into her writing desk and gazed out the dormer window. Her mind turned to Bartimaeus. He had tossed his head and stomped his front hoof, just like his younger days, this afternoon when she took him his magnesium tablet slipped inside an apple. She wished she could ask Peter to come and look at him, but now she had such mixed feelings about Peter. Was he basically a good person with an abrasive personality? Or should he be at the top of her suspect list even though she had nothing on him except a gut feeling of distrust?

She opened her murder book and then closed it again, staring out the window at the moonless night. The murder club had been helpful, but only because it had ruled out so many potential suspects. Nothing new had come to light. Sister Agatha stood and did the newest yoga stretch from Father Selwyn. *Mountain pose.* Supposedly it awakened one's inner strength. She sat back down. If only there were a yoga pose to awaken one's inner brain cells.

The investigation seemed at a standstill and she had run out of ideas.

Her mobile pinged. A text from Father Selwyn.

Just talked to Parker. Owen Wiley went over an embankment on the A55 and flipped his car. He was dead when the paramedics found him. I'm on my way to tell Reggie.

She caught her breath and said a quiet prayer. She had not liked Owen especially. Though he did seem very down on his luck and he certainly didn't deserve to die like this. She entered a quick note in her murder book and closed it. She will find out more tomorrow.

"I'm looking for Reggie Thurston," Parker Clough said. He stepped into the pony barn looking, as Sister Callwen might say, like something the cat dragged in. His usually neat black hair was disheveled, eyes red and bleak, and his ruddy face pale and drawn.

"Well he's not in the pony barn," Sister Agatha said. "Sit down before you fall down and take a sip of that tea from my thermos." She gestured to the thermos sitting on an overturned crate. "What's going on?" She pulled a curry comb slowly over the curve of the pony's dusty back.

Parker didn't move to sit down or to open the thermos of tea. "Reggie isn't in his flat and I can't find him anywhere in the village."

"That's because he's in the greenhouse with Sister Matilda and will most likely be there all morning since I heard that he's staying for lunch. But take a breath and tell me what's going on. I know about Owen. Father Selwyn texted me last night."

Parker stepped to the other side of the pony and stroked his fetlock. "Why are the smells of a barn so comforting? You'd think things like manure and moldering straw wouldn't make such a great combination." He leaned both elbows on the pony's back as if he were the farm table in the Abbey kitchen. "It wasn't a car accident."

Sister Agatha's eyebrows shot up. Her brush stopped mid stroke. Bartimaeus twisted his head around and pushed at her apron pocket. Absentmindedly, she dug out a sugar cube for him.

"The preliminary autopsy showed signs of poisoning." Parker pulled out his phone and tapped the screen and then read aloud. "Gastrointestinal hemorrhage and excessive myoglobin in the urine." He looked up. "Also, he had vomited in the car and Dr. Beese thinks there is evidence that he was having convulsions which made him drive off the embankment." Parker looked up from his phone.

"Complete tox report?"

"Those take forever. But Dr. Beese is guessing that he ingested some sort of poison, maybe arsenic or antimony."

"*Murder is Easy*," Sister Agatha said, going back to brushing Bartimaeus.

"Excuse me?"

"The first book in which Agatha Christie used arsenic to kill her victim. In fact, she used arsenic in four novels and four short stories. I've read them all-- many times. I'll put money on the fact that it was arsenic not antimony. The question is, who gave it to him? And why?"

"It isn't just that," he said. He took the curry comb from her and ran it over Bartimaeus's flank. The pony threw his head back and nickered. Parker gave a slight smile and brushed him again. He handed the brush back to Sister Agatha. "If you'll give me that metal comb, I'll work on his mane."

She handed him the comb and watched in silence as he fought against the tangles in the pony's mane. Bartimaeus nickered and tossed his head like the old days.

Parker's eyebrows furrowed as he doubled-down on the final tangle in Bart's mane. "There," he said. "Now give me that soft brush and let me work it through."

"When did you become so good with brushing and styling?"

"I have three younger sisters. It was all about hair at our house, believe me. You just have to take out the tangles and then it's nothing till you're done." He stopped, one hand resting on Bartimaeus's back and one holding the brush. "We found Claire's green rucksack in Owen's car. It was rolled up and stuck inside the rim of the spare tire in the boot."

"So Owen was there the night Claire died?" Sister Agatha said, both a question and a statement. "Did Owen kill Claire? And why? I would have thought they didn't even know each other."

"I have a bigger question." Parker gave Bartimaeus's mane a final brush stroke and then stepped out of the stall. He peered over the half door at Sister Agatha. "If Owen killed Claire. Then who killed Owen?"

"Does the rucksack in his car's boot really prove that he killed her?"

"No. But it doesn't look good."

"Why are you in such a hurry to talk to Reggie?" Sister Agatha didn't like the defensiveness in her voice. What could a somewhat doddering old bishop have to do with it all? Owen Wiley must have had plenty of enemies who wouldn't mind giving him a pint of Guinness with a dose of arsenic in it. "You don't suspect him, do you? You can't think it's the Archbishop. I've known him for years. He's....well, he's a legend in the parish. In all of Wales." Sister Agatha caught her breath. Reggie had always been a sort of hero to the sisters at Gwenafwy.

"I'm sorry," he said. "I really am sorry. But Reggie's fingerprints are all over the rucksack."

"I'm surprised that you felt like planting flowers with Sister Matilda so soon after hearing about your friend's death," Sister Agatha said, as they settled into chairs in Reverend Mother's office. Reverend Mother sat directly across from Reggie at her desk. Parker stood, leaning against the wall off to one side and Sister Agatha took the love seat to the right of the desk. Parker thought questioning him in Reverend Mother's office would be more conducive to getting information than hauling him down to the police station.

"I suspect that does seem strange," Reggie answered, giving her a weak smile. "I suppose I find comfort here at the Abbey, especially among the plants in the greenhouse. And the company of the lovely Sister Matilda, of course. I guess I simply needed to be in a safe place with good people on a morning like this." Reggie wrapped his frayed cardigan around him as if he felt a chill.

"Of course," Reverend Mother said. "I think Sister Agatha was just surprised is all."

Reggie took a deep breath. "By the time you're my age," he said. "You know that during moments of sadness and tragedy, the best thing you can do is surround yourself with friends." He looked around the room with a small smile. "And although I am deeply saddened, I am not surprised at Owen's death. It is almost as if I have been preparing for...for...." His voice broke and he cleared his throat, he continued. "For his death all along."

"What do you mean?" Parker asked.

"I mean that he lived a life outside of healthy, safe boundaries. He loved risky behavior. He made terrible choices." Reggie shook his head. "Very sad, indeed."

"Where were you yesterday evening?" Parker asked, looking directly at Reggie.

"Yesterday evening?" Reggie said, his eyebrows up. "In my flat. Surely you don't think I had something to do with this, do you, young man?"

"And when was the last time you saw Owen Wiley?" Parker asked.

"Last night," Reggie said, nodding toward Sister Agatha. "With Sister Agatha and Sister Gwenydd."

"Oh?" Reverend mother said, leaning forward in her desk chair.

"Yes." Sister Agatha said quickly. She shot Parker and Reverend Mother both an apologetic look. "It was long before the accident, though. I was at the Archbishop's flat with Sister Gwenydd. We were driving by and we overheard shouting and a crash, and we felt like we should investigate." *Could she possibly tell this story without using the word "stake-out?* "And so we went in to see if the Archbishop was okay. And he was," she added.

"And you're just telling me this now?" Parker said. He looked at her incredulously.

"Honestly, Parker. I apologize, but when we were talking earlier in the barn, I didn't even think of it." Sister Agatha gave him the most appealing look that she could. "And Reverend Mother, it was just, you know, Sister Gwenydd and I were in the village and we happened to drive past the flat, and we heard this loud noise and shouting. And so we went in. I was concerned over the safety of the Archbishop. And he and Owen were there. Having tea and listening to rugby."

"Okay. Let's back up for a minute." Parker said, his voice tight. "What time were you and Sister Gwenydd at the apartment where you saw Owen and Reggie together?"

Sister Agatha could feel heat prickling at her palms. "We were there right between dinner and vespers so probably that would be about eight o'clock."

"And tell me again what you were doing there?" Reverend Mother asked.

"We were passing by and we heard, as I said, shouting. And a crash. Glass shattering actually." Sister Agatha took a breath. "So we stopped the minivan and we went in to see that everybody was okay."

"And what did you see when you got inside?" Parker asked, tapping his pen on his notebook.

"Well, we saw Owen sitting on the couch drinking tea. And we saw Reggie picking up glass shards off the carpet. The Tiffany lamp in his front room had fallen." Sister Agatha was desperately wishing that she had thought to tell Parker about this when they were standing in the barn. But with all the talk about death and poison, it had truly slipped her mind. A terrible turn of events because Parker had trusted her with so much information, and now he was going to think she was holding back on him. She gave him a glance, eyes wide in hopes of communicating all of this to him. By the look on his face, her communication failed.

"What was the shouting and broken lamp about?" Parker asked, looking to Reggie.

"We were shouting about the rugby match on the radio," Reggie said. "And I knocked the lamp to the floor as I was pouring tea. My balance is not what it once was. I'm not a young man anymore." He shook his head ruefully. "Sister Agatha and Sister Gwenydd were kind enough to inquire about my health and when they saw that I was just fine and enjoying a good rugby match, they took their leave."

"Tell me again what time you left?" Parker asked.

Sister Agatha repeated the time and she noticed that as he wrote into his notebook, he pressed down very hard with his black pen.

"And when you saw Owen drinking tea?" Parker asked, his eyebrows raised.

Sister Agatha nodded. She couldn't meet Reverend Mother's gaze. They hadn't lied about taking the minivan, but you really were supposed to check it out when you took it. Not just slip off into the night.

"What happened after they left?" His eyes bored into Reggie.

"Nothing of consequence. The rugby game ended in a fine finish and then Owen left."

Reverend Mother tapped her fingers on her desk. "I thought that you and Owen were not the best of friends? Yet, he was at your flat enjoying rugby and drinking tea with you?" she asked.

"As always, Reverend Mother, you are very astute," he said with a sigh. "Owen was not my favorite person. May he rest in peace. We had some frightful ups and downs over the years. But I felt as if I should make amends and somehow be a friend to him. He has had a terrible time lately. I don't know if you know this, but he struggles with addiction and is always falling off the wagon." Reggie rested his head in his hand for a moment and then slowly sat up. "I hate to say it, but I did give him money. I know you're not supposed to give cash, and it's just enabling unhealthy behavior. But he pulled at my heart strings. I felt so bad for him. So I sent him off with a few pounds sterling and a promise of more if he got his life together." Reggie smiled. "I've always believed 'that which you do for the least of these, you do for me.'"

Everyone sat in silence for a moment.

"So you didn't see or hear from him again last night at all?" Parker said. Sister Agatha wasn't sure when she'd ever seen him look quite so annoyed.

"No. I said goodbye to him at the door. I did my evening devotions and went to bed. Imagine my shock when Father Selwyn showed up at my door at midnight to tell me that he had been in a terrible car accident and had died."

"Reverend Thurston, I am going to ask you a direct question and I want a truthful answer," Parker said, fixing him with a steely gaze.

Reggie sat up straight in his chair and looked directly back at Parker. "I make it my habit to always tell the truth, young man. You don't have to put in a special request for it."

Sister Agatha noticed that his shaky voice had grown strong again and he sounded once more like the Archbishop that they had all known and loved. The one who'd stood in the pulpit and inspired them all to go out and live as better, more courageous people. He even looked a bit like the old Reggie, sitting up straight, speaking directly.

"Did Owen Wiley have anything to do with the death of Claire MacDonagh?"

"Not that I know of," he said slowly. "It's just that...."

"What, Reggie?" Reverend Mother asked.

"I feel compelled to reveal to you...." He hesitated, and then continued. "That there was a time when I thought he might have had something to do with that poor girl's demise. He needed money desperately and I thought maybe he thought she had money. I didn't know. It kept me awake at night. So I finally asked him directly." He leaned forward towards Reverend Mother. "And that's where our relationship took a terrible dive. He not only denied it adamantly, he was truly offended that I would doubt him to that level." He paused again. "It's why I wanted to talk to him last night. So that I could tell him I believed he had nothing to do with it and that I was wrong to suspect him."

"Were you wrong to suspect him?" Parker asked.

"Owen was not a particularly good person and he could certainly rub one the wrong way, but he was not a person who could, or would, kill. I've known him for almost 50 years, and I'm sure he wouldn't do a thing like that."

"But you thought for a while that he had, correct?"

"And I was wrong. Wrong to even think it."

Again the room stayed silent. Sister Agatha heard the bells calling everyone to lunch. Reverend Mother didn't move so she didn't either.

"My deputies found Claire's green rucksack in Owen's car."

"My goodness. I...I... don't know what to say. I was so certain that he had ...that he had nothing to do with this awful business."

"Archbishop, would you be surprised if I told you that your fingerprints were found on the green rucksack?" Parker asked.

Reggie paused for a moment, looking thoughtful. "No," he said, shaking his head. "I wouldn't be surprised at all."

"And why is that?"

"Because I handled the green bag recently." He turned to Sister Agatha. "Remember? When you and Claire were at my house and Esmeralda sat on the rucksack?" He waited for Sister Agatha. She hated to suddenly remember this after having forgotten it so entirely. She was not having a great day.

"Yes," she said, turning to Parker. "Claire left her bag at Reggie's. The day that we visited, and his cat fell asleep on top of it. And Reggie went back in to get it for her." She thought again for a moment. "He moved the cat off and then picked up the rucksack and brought it outside to Claire."

"So you see, young man, my prints would definitely be on the rucksack," Reggie said. "And quite a quantity of cat hair as well."

CHAPTER 39

"It was brutal," Sister Agatha said as she swiveled her desk chair around to face Sister Gwenydd. "To know that both Reverend Mother and Parker Clough were cross with me. My world crashed in. But I think I might have straightened it out. I really and truly forgot about our visit to Reggie last night in the light of the death of Owen and I would have told Parker all about it under normal circumstances--which I explained to him. In the end, he accepted my apology."

"I don't care about you and Parker. What about Reverend Mother? She knows I was with you, right?" Sister Gwenydd pulled her hair back into a ponytail and yanked it out again.

"No worries," Sister Agatha poured tea from a thermos into two cups. "I told her it was all my idea-- which it was-- and she isn't blaming you at all. But she did accuse me of leading you down the primrose path."

"Ha! There is nothing 'primrose' about you, Sister Agatha. But thanks for saying it was your idea. I owe you."

"In the end, Reverend Mother did seem to understand the importance of the stake-out and she understood why we felt we had to go in and check on Reggie. But no more secreting out of the mini-van."

"I can't believe she was so understanding."

"We're lucky. Not all Reverend Mothers have half her sense of adventure."

The village clock tower chimed three times and the bright afternoon sun poured through the attic's west window.

"I have to get back to cataloging Thomas Merton." She gestured to a stack of used books on her worktable. *The Journals of Thomas Merton: A Seven Book Series.* "But I have a little time. Fill me in on what you found out about the miniature gospel." Sister Gwenydd had left the last Murder Club determined to find out more about the little gospel.

"I'll tell you my research and then I have something to show you. But considering the fiasco that the stake-out turned out to be, you can't tell Reverend Mother. Or Parker."

"I'm not good at lying. Whenever I lie, my scalp tingles."

"Well, whatever." Sister Gwenydd pulled her hair into a pony-tail and sat across from Sister Agatha who sat up and opened her murder book. A ponytail re-do. She must have found something very interesting.

"The burning question," Sister Gwenydd began. "Is why did Claire take a photo of the miniature gospel? She snapped three photos that day-- a selfie with the cathedral, a picture of the entire miniature cathedral, and one of the little gospel. Now why was she so interested in it? There were lots of other detailed pieces of the cathedral that are more interesting and displayed far more craftsmanship than the little book on the altar. So why not snap photos of those things?"

Sister Agatha shrugged. "Come to think of it, she did talk about it on the walk home."

"What did she say?"

Sister Agatha thought for a moment. "She wanted to know how he made the colors so authentic."

"Ha! A question we should all be asking." She stopped to write for a moment in her spiral notebook. "Alright then. Some quick background. Did you know that little individual gospels like this were all the rage in the Middle Ages? They were mostly made for monks who carried them around tucked in the pockets of their robes."

"Interesting. Like Sister Callwen and her pocket-sized prayer bible." Sister Agatha thought for a minute. "I am suddenly getting inspired to downsize my Murder Book. I wonder if Smythson's on Bond Street carries miniatures?"

"Sister, focus. So anyway, these little gospels are extremely valuable. Especially if the tiny volume was an *incunabulum*."

"A what?"

Sister Gwenydd looked down at her notes. "Remember, you're talking to someone who barely passed their A-levels. All I wanted to do was go to cooking school." She read for a moment. "Okay. Here it is. An incunable, or sometimes incunabulum, is a book, a pamphlet, or broadside..." she looked up. "Not sure what a broadside is."

"It's what we would call a flyer."

"Anyway, these incunabula were printed in Europe before the 16th century-- before 1501." She looked up. "You know what happened in 1501?"

"Well, I would imagine lots of things. But most notably, the printing press."

"I'm guessing you passed your A-levels?"

"I did. But all I wanted to be was a nun at Gwenafwy Abbey. So we both got our dream."

"We did. But listen. 'Incunabulum' is a term that refers to books produced *early* in the development of the printing press. In other words, books printed before the year 1501. Incunabulum is Latin for 'swaddling clothes'. In other words, a book that was produced when the art of printing was still in its infancy." Sister

Gwenydd sat back, her eyes gleaming. "I believe that Reggie's little gospel is an incunabulum."

"How can you tell?"

"In all incunabula, the first letter of the first word of each chapter is larger than the other letters and it is always in red ink." She pointed to the photo. "See. It's obvious in this one. The letter is faded, but you can tell it's red."

"But all he did was make a book that *looks* like a...a... what do you call it."

"A miniature incunabulum."

"Right. He could have done that with parchment, glue, and a high quality print out from Google images."

"He *could* have. And if all we had was this one photo that Claire took, then we could conclude that he was just very clever." Sister Gwenydd took a deep breath and slowly removed her ponytail holder. She shook out her thick hair. But she didn't put it back in. She sat and looked hard at Sister Agatha.

"What?"

"I broke into his house this morning when he was at the Buttered Crust Teashop."

"You didn't."

"I did. I just had to see that little bible up close. And he left his back door unlocked." They sat and stared at each other for a moment. Sister Gwenydd finally broke the silence. "Am I a terrible person?"

"Yes. And I'm a terrible person too. Because I am so annoyed that I didn't get to go along."

"In that case, do you want to see what I have?"

"You didn't steal the little bible?"

"Of course not. I took photos." Sister Gwenydd spread ten photos on the worktable arranging them in sequence in which she had taken them.

"You took it out and handled it?"

"Well, at first I wasn't going to, but then, I heard Sister Callwen's voice in my head 'in for a penny, in for a pound' and I did. But what I discovered will change everything-- at least about what we think of the Archbishop."

"I don't know if I want to know."

"Why?"

"I think so highly of him. I mean, Reggie Thurston was Archbishop of Wales. He's almost a legend. He's like Father Selwyn only.... well, no one is Father Selwyn. Alright, alright, tell me."

"He stole it. From a museum or somewhere. It's an original and he lies all the time about it as if he has something to hide. Which he does, actually."

"No." Sister Agatha sat back and gaped at Sister Gwenydd. "I can't believe it."

"I held the thing in my hands, turned the pages. It's extremely delicate. Reggie did not make that little bible, no matter what he says. Some monk printed it on one of the first printing presses."

"You're calling the former Archbishop of Wales a liar?"

"I'm calling him a liar *and* a thief."

They sat in another long silence.

"Of course it's delicate," Sister Agatha finally said. "He made it years ago and he probably fashioned it so that it would appear delicate."

Sister Gwenydd shook her head. "It's way too authentic for some old guy with a glue stick and pasteboard from the Tesco."

"Maybe it's a reproduction? Like all those reproductions of Lichtenstein's and Matisse and Picasso's that were sold as real, but they were fakes? Maybe he picked it up at sale somewhere?"

"Then why does he tell everyone he made it himself?" Sister Gwenydd's voice had lost a bit of its bluster.

"Maybe he's vain. Just because he was Archbishop doesn't mean he's perfect." She studied the photos on the table. She had to admit, Reggie didn't create this. The print and scroll work were elegant. "I think it's a reproduction of what are you calling it? An incunabulum."

"I hadn't thought of that. A reproduction." She let out a long sigh and stuffed her ponytail holder into the pocket of her habit. "But that still doesn't answer why Claire took a photo of it?"

"Maybe she just saw it as an interesting human interest story. With some sort of history angle."

Sister Gwenydd sat back, deflated. "Of course, he purchased a cheap reproduction somewhere. Probably a museum gift shop. And reproductions always look super real." She sat staring at the photos spread out on the table. "I broke into his house and everything."

"Which I entirely admire. Just bring me with you next time! You know I suffer from fear-of-missing-out."

Sister Gwenydd gave a weak smile and gathered up her pages. "Not sure you missed out on much. I need to get back to the kitchen."

CHAPTER 40

Sister Agatha glanced at the stack of books on her worktable. *The Journals of Thomas Merton: A Seven Book Series* still stared back at her. Interesting, if not riveting, and donated by the Women's Institute in gratitude for all the work Gwenafwy Abbey had done at their last fundraiser. Sister Callwen would be up here clamoring for them soon enough and yet, there they sat-- still uncatalogued, hours after she and Sister Gwenydd had put away the photos of the little bible.

She tapped her silver fountain pen on the top of the writing desk and gazed out the attic window. *The little bible.* Not exactly. *The little Gospel of Matthew.* A miniature incunabulum. The photos from Sister Gwenydd's breaking and entering showed an intricate, beautiful work of art as well as a printed manuscript. The tiny words of the Gospel lined up in two columns, the small narrow margins filled in with delicate scrolls and drawings. The entire thing about four times the size of a decent postage stamp. Was it a reproduction that Reggie had picked up at a sale somewhere? Of course. It had to be. Then why not just say that? Why did Reggie lie about having created it?

She tossed her pen down and stood up and did another one of the yoga stretches that Father Selwyn taught her. Not mountain pose. Sunrise pose? Sun salutation? Good Morning Sunshine? She began to pace the room.

The bigger question was, why did it even matter? Two people were dead and ruminating about a miniature gospel wasn't going to bring them back. She paced from one end of the long room to the other, west dormer window to east dormer window. With every lap of the room, she passed Thomas Merton stacked on the table. Now he really was staring up accusingly. Recently, Sister Callwen had suggested that her detective work and her fiction writing were taking priority over her contribution to the Abbey. She hoped that wasn't true. Reverend Mother encouraged her writing. And there were even times when she encouraged her detective work. She stopped pacing long enough to place the slim volumes of Merton in a box under the desk. She closed the lid to the box.

She went over all the strange things that had happened since Claire arrived at Gwenafwy Abbey leading up to her death and then Owen's, ticking them off with every step across the brown carpet: the image of Claire snapping photos in Reggie's flat, a selfie that wasn't a selfie, a Sister Winifred scarf, mysterious figures at the dovecote door, a flash drive containing only a file labeled TL64, a king's cake with a key, a little bible that looked convincingly medieval. An Archbishop caught in a lie. A harmless lie, but still a lie.

She fell into her chair and her eye caught the picture of Agatha Christie. She envied her. Agatha Christie had entered crime writing with a very useful professional skill—assistant alchemist. A pharmacist, in today's language. And she knew her pharmaceuticals. Well, she knew her poisons. A much more useful skill than being a nun.

What would Christie say about Owen? *Killed by arsenic.* If not killed by the poison itself, at least his fatal car crash was the result of the effects of arsenic. Convulsions and vomiting, then going off the road and over an embankment. Whoever gave him the arsenic, must have known that he would soon be driving. She couldn't shake the picture of Owen sitting on the love seat at Reggie's, drinking tea. Or Sister Gwenydd's remark 'who watches rugby and drinks tea?' No. Not Reggie. Not the former Archbishop.

She flipped through the photos again that Sister Gwenydd had given her of the little Gospel. She had to admit, for a fake it looked awfully real. But then isn't that the way it works with reproductions? They do look real. That's how even the most astute art dealers can get swindled.

She didn't believe that Reggie would poison anyone. But then she wouldn't have ever thought that he would lie about making the little bible. If he lies so smoothly about that, what else would he lie about? But she *liked* Reggie. And so did everyone else at the Abbey. But didn't Inspector Rupert McFarland always say, 'never let your personal feelings get in the way of a case'? She could almost hear his Scottish inflection. She was allowing her admiration for Wales' former Archbishop to interfere with her detective's need to think logically.

She stood up and did another yoga stretch. Hello Sunshine? Here Comes the Sun? Keep on the Sunny Side?

She would follow a logical pattern of questioning until the end. Means and motive. What were the means to Owen's murder? In other words, where could Reggie get arsenic to begin with? She Googled "arsenic in the UK" and found out that only one online company sold it and they were in Asia. An online order of arsenic would take up two weeks to arrive. It would mean that as soon as Owen arrived in Pryderi, Reggie would have gone online for arsenic. Unlikely. Or did he keep a supply on hand? Sister Agatha shivered. She pushed the thought of Reggie keeping a bottle of

arsenic in his medicine cabinet next to his aspirin and deconges-
tant, out of her mind.

Motive was even less clear. Why would Reggie want to poison
Owen? He had admitted that his relationship with Owen had
often been rocky, but that he had reached out to him in friendship. And sent him on his way with money.

Tea. He had been drinking tea. She thought hard. Reggie hadn't
been drinking tea. Only Owen. She glanced absently at the photo
in front of her of the little book. Created before the year 1500.
Medieval. She sat up straight. *Arsenic and Old Books. The lecture at
the Pryderi Library.* What had that guest speaker said about
medieval manuscripts and poison? She opened her laptop. She
quickly located the power point slides that the speaker had sent
out after his lecture and scrolled through. "The 15th-century book
bindings as well as their front covers were often decorated with a
green paint, rich in arsenic. Several books with traces of arsenic
have been identified in England and Ireland, as well as Italy and
Denmark." She flipped through the slides. "Gloves and masks are
recommended when handling any medieval book, especially with
green paint."

She picked up one of Sister Gwenydd's photos and held it to
the light. *Green.* Faded, but definitely green. In the bottom right
corner however, the green pigment ended, and several square
centimeters were light brown. It looked as if the color had been
removed. Scraped off. Nor did the light brown part didn't look as
aged as the rest. Or did it? She really needed to see the book itself.
Had the green paint, possibly rich in arsenic, had been scraped
off? And when? And by whom? Worse yet, why?

She put the photo down and absently stared out the window.
Scraped off. Her pulse fluttered. Reggie had been at that library
lecture. He had raised his hand during the Q and A and asked if
the arsenic wasn't too old to harm anyone. The speaker had been
adamant. The chemical was still active and that's why he was
advising caution for any librarian handling old books.

If Reggie poisoned Owen with paint scrapings from the little bible, that proved that the tiny gospel was indeed from the 15th century, but it also implicated Reggie in Owen's death. Sister Gwenydd was right. Reggie was a liar and a thief. She sat back in her chair. A murderer too? If Reggie killed Owen, did he kill Claire MacDonagh? And why?

CHAPTER 41

"I've invited Reverend Mother to this meeting of the Murder Club because she has suggested I engage in a practice of... better transparency. The details of which I will explain later," Sister Agatha said, standing at the head of the long farm table in the Abbey kitchen.

"If I had known it would rouse me from my bed in the middle of the night," Reverend Mother said leaning into Father Selwyn sitting next to her. "I might not have been so insistent."

"But how often can you attend a gathering called 'The Murder Club' where they also have tea and lemon cake?"

"Good point," Reverend Mother said.

"Sister Agatha, I am assuming that you have some extremely compelling new information, or you wouldn't have called us all together so late," Parker said in a formal, crisp voice. Sister Agatha wondered if his tone meant that he was still upset with her, or that he hadn't slept in a week.

"Just my good faith effort to report to you everything that happens. As soon as it happens," she said.

He yawned and poured a cup of tea. "I'm with you Reverend Mother, I should never have been so insistent."

"We do have some startling new information," Sister Agatha added.

Parker raised his teacup in salute. "Well you certainly have our undivided attention."

"I'll make everyone a midnight snack," Sister Gwenydd said, standing. "I hate to tell you, but this is going to be a long night. Sister Agatha and I have made quite the discovery."

Parker got to his feet. "Sit down, Sister Gwenydd. You're always cooking. I'll whip something up."

The group watched with interest as he opened the larder and peered in.

"You cook?" Father Selwyn asked. "How refreshing. A deputy constable who knows his way around a kitchen." Father Selwyn depended on Bevan Penrose and the Buttered Crust Teashop for most of his meals.

"It's therapeutic," Parker said. "And I've learned a lot by watching cooking shows."

"Do you like Gordon Ramsay?" Father Selwyn shot Sister Agatha a knowing look.

"I'm more of a Great British Bake Off person myself," Parker replied. He removed a carton of eggs from the larder.

"Good man," Father Selwyn said.

"Is that your entire flour supply, Sister Gwenydd?" He pried the top off a large tin of flour and set it aside and then pulled a large saucepan off the rack above his head.

"That's five kilos of gluten-free, organic flour from Doves Farm. How much more do you need?"

"Not sure. But I do need an apron," he said looking around. "I don't plan to get flour on my uniform. Constable Barnes may be out of town, but he's a stickler for a neat uniform."

"When is he getting back?" Reverend Mother asked.

"Early tomorrow morning or late tonight. He was fuzzy on the details." Parker Clough replied. He slid his arms into a long habit apron and waited as Sister Gwenydd tied the back. The apron was decorated with rows of dancing cornflowers.

"Sorry, it's the only one I have," she said. "But at least it's long enough." The apron touched the tops of his perfectly polished shoes.

"I believe that one is mine," Reverend Mother said. "I like a long apron that covers my habit. So I can get creative when I cook."

"Is that what you get, Reverend Mother?" Sister Gwenydd gave her a wicked grin. "Creative?"

"Everyone. Please. We are not here to talk about aprons and cooking shows," Sister Agatha said. She once again wished she had a gavel. "We have a lot of ground to cover. And..." she looked around the table. "What you hear tonight might not be...." She turned to Father Selwyn and said in a softer voice. "Something that you want to hear." She took her seat. "Sister Gwenydd, why don't you begin with an explanation of 'miniature incunabulum'."

Sister Gwenydd walked everyone through what an "incunabulum" was, but when she began to lecture on the rise of the printing press Sister Agatha broke in. "Sister Gwenydd, get to the point."

"Please, this is intriguing." Father Selwyn said. "The printing press changed the course of Western Christendom. One really can't underestimate its influence."

Sister Gwenydd continued, finishing her recitation with the bombshell announcement that the little bible in Reggie's cathedral was a real one, from the 15th century or earlier.

"Now wait a moment," Reverend Mother said. She and Father Selwyn were staring at the printouts. "How do you know this isn't a reproduction?"

"We didn't, at first. In fact, Sister Agatha and I had all but decided it was a reproduction-- and a very good one." Sister

Gwenydd said, casting an eye behind her. "By the way, Parker, are you making *Crempog Las?*"

"I am indeed." He slid a fragrant, steaming *crempog* in front of them. Rivulets of butter slid off the golden brown pancake. "Just wait, I'll cut it into pieces. There should be more than enough for everyone."

"But how do you know," Father Selwyn asked as he took a large piece of the crempog off the platter. "That the little bible is authentic?"

"Because Reggie used it to poison Owen."

The room went silent, forks frozen in place. Parker slowly wiped his hands on his habit apron with the dancing cornflowers and took a seat at the table. "Talk to me," he said.

"In the middle ages," she went on. "The paint used to decorate manuscripts was made with arsenic. It was so toxic, that even today, if you handle books from that period, you have to be very cautious." She slid the photo of the book's front cover to Parker. "See how the paint is removed from the bottom right of the cover in this photo. But in this photo, taken several days earlier, the paint is untouched."

Reverend Mother slid her spectacles on and leaned over the photos. "I see it. The paint has been removed from the little book in this photo but not in the earlier photo."

"Not just removed. Removed and stirred into Owen's tea."

"Tea and rugby! Now I get it," Sister Gwenydd said almost to herself.

"Now wait a minute," Father Selwyn said, sitting up very straight. "I've known Reggie Thurston most of my life. He was my bishop in St. Asaph when I was right out of seminary. We've worked side-by-side in the parish all these years. He is a kind, decent, honorable man." He stood, pushing his chair back. Sister Agatha sometimes forgot how commanding Father Selwyn could be when he used his pulpit voice. "Reggie Thurston may be vain. And he might have lied about making the little bible--though I certainly couldn't tell you why. *But he would not kill anyone.* Much less give them a cup of tea laced with arsenic!" Sister Agatha had never seen him this passionate. For one second, she was ready to believe him.

Before anyone could respond, there was a knock at the door, and they turned at the sound of a man's voice. "Hello? May I come in?" Without waiting for an answer, Peter pushed in. "A cup of tea laced with arsenic? And I thought nothing exciting ever happened in a convent."

Later, Sister Agatha blamed everything that transpired next on the fact that Parker had neglected to turn the range off after he served the *crempog*. If he had turned off the range, the kitchen wouldn't have been so hot and if the kitchen hadn't been so hot, Peter would have left on his wool jumper. As it was, he stood there smiling at them-- Father Selwyn still red faced and standing. Reverend Mother half seated and half standing, looking at Father Selwyn, Parker still wearing the long apron with the blue corn-flowers.

Peter pulled his heavy gray jumper over his head. And that's when she saw it. The tiny gleam of metal in his waistband that revealed, for an instant, the gun.

"He has a gun!" she shouted, pointing at Peter. "A gun!" And then the melee began--a series of cascading actions that were discussed for weeks to come. Sister Agatha, jumping to her feet, hiked up her habit skirts, put her head down, and rugby-tackled Peter. Even before Peter hit the floor, Parker sprang into action. Unfortunately, he forgot he was wearing a long apron and as he lunged toward Sister Agatha and Peter, the toes of his polished shoes caught the apron's hem and he fell headlong across the tile floor. Sister Gwenydd, always a quick thinker, picked up the flour tin in both hands, rushed over and dumped it on top of Peter's head managing to cover not just Peter but also Parker, Sister

Agatha, Father Selwyn and herself with gluten-free, organic flour direct from Dove's Farm.

Sister Agatha, rolled deftly off Peter, got to her feet, shook out her habit skirt in a cloud of flour, and said in a calm but fierce voice, more powerful and chilling than anyone had ever heard her use, "Don't move. I've got you covered."

Everyone froze.

She stood like a rock, her arms outstretched, both hands on the gun, its barrel pointed at Peter who lay on his back under a mound of flour. His eyes on Sister Agatha, he slowly swooped his hands above his head. Later Sister Gwenydd would say it was like watching a person make a snow angel but with flour, and on a tile floor, and terrified.

Parker, got half-way to his feet, then crashed again still tangled in his apron, and with no other way to ambulate, began to crawl on all fours across the floor. "Wait," he said. But they never learned what he was going to say next because his voice dissolved into great hacking coughs. Each cough accompanied by a puff of flour.

"Sister," Father Selwyn said in a quiet voice from where he stood two feet behind her. "I believe that gun might be loaded."

"You bet it's loaded," she replied smoothly, her eyes trained on Peter. "You don't pack a Walther P99 with a...." She flipped the gun around and peered at it more closely, to the gasp of Reverend Mother. She flipped it back. "With a 14-round magazine and interchangeable 3-dot notch sights if you don't plan to use it. Naturally, it's loaded."

No one could have predicted what might have happened next if the kitchen door hadn't banged open and the imposing figure of Constable Barnes filled the door frame. Even in the stress of the moment, Sister Agatha noticed that he glowed with a healthy tan and possibly the tail of a Hawaiian shirt stuck out from under his navy blue regulation constable's jumper. With one sweeping glance, he took in the room, his eyes coming to rest on Parker.

Still on all fours, Parker had gotten his coughing under control. His nun's apron with rows of dancing cornflowers hung crookedly off one shoulder, his jet black hair caked with flour, and his face red and smudged. He looked up from the floor but seemed unable to speak.

"I gave you one job!" Constable Barnes bellowed. "One job!" He reached across Peter who was still lying snow-angeled on the floor and took the Walther P99 out of Sister Agatha's hands. He slid the magazine out and into his pocket. "One job! Keep Sister Agatha under control. That's it! Nothing else!"

During late nights, over cups of tea, when the sisters and Father Selwyn discussed the events of that night, Sister Gwenydd would always claim that what happened next was what she found the most surprising.

Constable Barnes seemed to suddenly realize that there was a man on the floor. He stared at Peter for a long moment and then threw back his head and rocked with laughter. "Well, if it isn't Special Agent Dougan Hennessey! And how are you, laddie? Not so good, I would say. Although maybe better than that night in the pub at the Policeman's Conference." He leaned down and offered his hand to Peter, pulling him to his feet. Constable Barnes' laughter exploded again, and Peter gave a weak smile as he brushed flour off his clothes. Constable Barnes had to lean against the kitchen wall to catch his breath. "Gave up your weapon to a nun, did you? Tell me how exactly Sister Agatha took you hostage in the kitchen of Gwenafwy Abbey! Now what will they say to that on Harcourt Street?" He went into more convulsive laughter.

"Special Agent? Harcourt Street?" Sister Agatha looked from Peter to Constable Barnes. "Are you talking about the *Garda*? Headquarters in Dublin?"

"Is there another?" Constable Barnes said, his breath coming in short gasps. He removed a handkerchief from his pocket and wiped his eyes.

"Are you saying that *Peter* is with the National Bureau of Criminal Investigation in Ireland?" Sister Agatha said.

"Indeed. And his name isn't Peter. It's Sergeant Dougan Hennessey, Special Agent in Charge of Arts and Antiques for the NBCI. Congratulations, Sister Agatha, you've just disarmed one of the most decorated officers of the *Garda Síochána*. Sorry to blow your cover, old boy," Constable Barnes said, slapping him on the back and raising a cloud of flour. "But then I'm not the one who gave up my weapon to a nun."

CHAPTER 42

"I wish you would stop repeating that he gave up his weapon to a nun, Constable Barnes. As if a nun couldn't disarm someone. Nuns are much more capable than you seem to think," Sister Agatha said.

Constable Barnes erupted into another spasm of laughter. Clearly, his vacation to Hawaii had relaxed him just as Mrs. Barnes had hoped. And he was indeed wearing a Hawaiian shirt under his navy blue constable's jumper, though no one had dared mention it.

If anyone had been complaining about being up in the middle of the night before, they weren't complaining now. They also weren't drinking tea. Reverend Mother had opened a bottle of red wine and everyone had a glass in front of them except Parker who had declined due to being on duty.

"Really, my boy?" Constable Barnes had said. "That's your biggest concern right now? Wine? How about the fact that you're dressed like a nun and sitting in a convent kitchen at midnight?"

"Don't bust his..." Dougan stopped and nodded to Reverend Mother. "I meant to say, don't give him a hard time. Officer Clough came the closest to seeing through my undercover identity as anyone has in a long time. He runs a tight ship, from what I observed."

"Well," Constable Barnes said, frowning.

"You ever want a job with the Garda, come see me," Dougan said to Parker who still looked a bit like a deer in the headlights.

"You can't have him," Constable Barnes said. "He's not half bad, when he stays away from Sister Agatha."

"Actually, she can have a job too. Where did you learn to tackle like that, Sister?"

"Four brothers. Rugby." She didn't mention that she might have dislocated her left shoulder.

"I want some questions answered," Reverend Mother said from her end of the table. "First of all, why were you pretending to be Claire's cousin?"

"And I want a final word," Father Selwyn interrupted. "Once and for all, regarding Reggie's involvement in Owen's death." Father Selwyn's voice was just bordering on pulpit. "He would never kill anyone!" Father Selwyn turned to Sister Agatha, his voice tense. "And a bit of paint supposedly scraped off a manuscript is a long way from stirring arsenic into someone's tea."

"Say what you like, Father, but Reggie Thurston is our primary suspect in the deaths of Kate Darcy and Owen Wiley based on the message we got from Kate, in addition to this information from Sister Agatha." He paused and looked at her, his eyebrows raised. "You really would have made a cracking Special Agent."

"You can't have her either," Reverend Mother said.

"Wait," Sister Gwenydd spoke up. "Who is Kate?"

"Special Agent Kate Darcy, known to you as a young reporter from Dublin, Claire MacDonagh. She was here undercover to investigate the stolen artifact, an incunabulum from the 15th century. We got a tip about a week ago that the miniature had been seen in a little village called Pryderi in North Wales. It's been missing from Trinity Library since 1964 and is worth 1.2 million pounds."

Sister Gwenydd let out a low whistle. "Claire was an undercover agent for the NBCI?

"And one of our finest." Dougan cleared his throat and his face took on a hard look. A look they had never seen when he was Peter, medieval studies professor on a walking tour.

"You sent an undercover agent into my convent without consulting me?" The room had gone frosty. An arctic chill blew into the Abbey kitchen.

"You might want your weapon back, old boy," Constable Barnes said quietly.

"Sorry Reverend Mother, but civilians cannot be informed of an undercover operation. For their own safety and the success of the operation. Entirely legal."

"Legal is not always ethical, Detective." Reverend Mother said in words that cut like a knife. She sat ramrod straight at the table, glaring at Dougan. Dougan shifted in his kitchen chair, cleared his voice, and took an exaggeratedly casual sip of wine.

"Hold on," Sister Gwenydd said. "I read articles by Claire MacDonagh written ten years ago. Cooking reviews."

"Kate was a journalism major in college and did a bit of freelance writing before joining the Garda. Her pen name was 'Claire MacDonagh'. We built on her past to construct her undercover identity."

"So no one is writing an article for *The Church Times* about the new nuns at Gwenafwy Abbey?" Reverend Mother asked.

"Afraid not," Dougan said.

Reverend Mother's sigh could have been heard halfway down Church Lane.

Dougan gestured to the photos on the table. "It's clear to us that Reggie possesses the artifact in question. Unless he's dumped it or, God help us, destroyed it, in the last 24 hours. We know that he was at Trinity in 1964, the year it disappeared, and our hypothesis is that he stole it. And has had it ever since."

"TL64!" Sister Agatha nearly shouted. "Trinity Library, 1964. It wasn't the grandfather's birthday. It *was* a secret code!" Sister Agatha tried not to look smug.

"I could tell you weren't buying that story." Dougan scooped a piece of *las crogen* off the platter. "This is good. Who made it?"

Parker raised his hand a few inches off the table. Constable Barnes snorted.

"Preposterous," Father Selwyn said. "Why would the Archbishop of Wales steal a valuable manuscript?"

Dougan shrugged. "Maybe possessing it gave him a sense of power. Control. Sometimes people steal because they think they deserve the item, or they will take better care of it than the library or museum." Dougan scooped a morsel of the *las crogen* off the platter. "Tell me, when did Reggie start making those little churches, the model cathedrals?"

Father Selwyn thought for a moment. "Probably thirty years ago. I remember the first one he did. He had just been ordained bishop and he constructed the model of St. Asaph. And he's been making them ever since. Why?"

"When he finished each cathedral, what did he do with it?"

"He would give it as a gift to that particular parish. You know, the parish where that cathedral was located. People love them."

"And in each one, he constructed a miniature bible that always sat on a miniature pulpit, right? Everything to scale?"

"I guess so. Most pulpits have a bible on them."

"So he developed a hobby of making antique-looking miniature bibles and placing them in elaborately constructed models of local cathedrals?"

"Yes."

"Think of it. All his cathedrals had pulpits with medieval looking manuscripts of them. He places the miniature gospel from Trinity Library, the one worth 1.2 million pounds, in the cathedral that he keeps in his house. No one would question it. It looked like all the fakes he had created."

Father Selwyn let his breath out as if he had been holding it. "He hid it in plain sight, didn't he? All these years I just thought...." Father Selwyn's voice trailed off. He shook his head and closed his eyes, as if in prayer.

"He must have figured out that Kate was on to him, and since he couldn't be found out--after all these years-- he killed her." The room fell silent again and Dougan stared at the tabletop. "Did a good job of it too-- a millennial taking a selfie at the cliff and falling backward. Kudos to you, Sister Agatha, to notice that she wasn't alone on the cliff." He stuffed the last piece of pancake into his mouth. They watched while he chewed and swallowed. "Our sources told us that Kate's boyfriend, Chadwick, had followed her to Pryderi."

"He proposed to her at the cliff walk, but she turned him down."

He sat back and looked at Sister Agatha. "You were right to suspect him. We think that maybe Reggie followed them to the cliff and when Chadwick drove off, Reggie was waiting in the bushes. Maybe Owen was getting a piece of the action at this point. We'll never know exactly how it happened." He looked at Constable Barnes. "Unless he confesses."

Sister Agatha wondered why Constable Barnes gave Dougan such a dark look.

Dougan sighed. "Well anyway, my office informed me a few days ago that Owen was Reggie's roommate at Trinity. So maybe Owen knew that Reggie had stolen it and was threatening to blackmail him. They had to get rid of Kate and any information she might have collected."

"Tall and thin, short and plump," Sister Agatha blurted out. "At the dovecote door. Reggie and Owen."

"Reggie shoved Claire...I mean, Kate...over the cliffs." Father

Selwyn said slowly. He took a breath. "And then the two of them broke into her room, stole her computer and her rucksack."

"Something went wrong in their relationship. And since Reggie had already killed once to save himself, he killed again."

"With arsenic?" Father Selwyn said, his pulpit voice gone.

"I'm sorry, Selwyn." Reverend Mother reached out and took Father Selwyn's hand.

No one spoke for a long moment.

"What about the bible verse?" Father Selwyn asked. "'Fear them not therefore: for there is nothing covered, that shall not be revealed; and hid, that shall not be known.'"

"Kate's clever way of letting me know she had found the stolen artifact. We needed to text in a way that was undecipherable to anyone else."

"Did you know that Reggie had the little bible?" Reverend Mother asked.

"No, only that it was possibly in Pryderi. We placed Kate at Gwenafwy Abbey because we thought it would be safe. And since it was a religious place, on the off chance that one of you had it. I don't even know how Kate found it at Reggie's."

Reverend Mother shook her head and smiled. "She found it because she was good at her job. Her secret agent job, that is."

"And Kate was always lucky," Dougan said.

"Not so lucky this time," Father Selwyn turned to Reverend Mother. "If Reggie practiced such elaborate deception with us, what else did he do?"

"Selwyn," she said quietly.

"Can you imagine what this will do to the people of Wales? The beloved Reggie Thurston wanted for a double murder?" Father Selwyn said.

Dougan threw back the rest of his wine. "Look everyone, we haven't got a lot of time. Normally, I would never bring civilians into a situation, but I'm making an exception. We're running out of choices and time."

Constable Barnes leaned forward. "You'll not endanger any of my people, Dougan Hennessey. This isn't the Garda. We're a small village."

Dougan ignored him.

"The tricky part is, lads," Dougan said. "This isn't a drug bust. We can't storm the ramparts with guns and dogs. With a stolen artifact, the perp may destroy it rather than be caught with it. Or it gets destroyed or damaged in the process of an arrest. And equally necessary, is the preservation of evidence. All the photocopies, cups of arsenic tea, and scraped-off green ink in the world won't convince a jury that the former Archbishop of Wales killed two people."

"I don't like where you're going with this," Constable Barnes said shaking his head. "I don't like it at all."

"Why? Where's he going?" Sister Agatha asked.

"We need someone to go in wearing a wire. To get Reggie talking. To confess. It needs to be someone he trusts; someone he likes and would open up to."

"I'll do it," Father Selwyn's calm voice spoke up. "Reggie certainly trusts me. We've been friends for years." Father Selwyn caught Reverend Mother in his gaze. "I have to. I don't want anyone else.... you know.... Maybe Reggie would turn himself in and have some dignity about it." His voice broke. They all watched as he pushed back his chair and strode over to the window and stood with his back to them, looking out over the night.

"Sorry," Dougan twisted around in his chair and talked to Father Selwyn's back. "Won't work. First off, you're a man. People who steal like this often have huge egos. He'll never admit it to you. Second, wasn't he your boss, at one point? When he was bishop? He's not going to come clean to someone who was his inferior."

The room fell silent again. Constable Barnes cleared his voice and Sister Gwenydd drained her wine glass. "Oh just say it!" she exclaimed. "It's almost time for me to start breakfast. Who?"

"Sister Agatha."

"No." Reverend Mother said. "Not on my watch."

Whenever Reverend Mother used the phrase 'not on my watch' you might as well just pack up and go home. Dougan obviously wasn't aware of this universal truth.

"It has to be her," he said. "Reggie likes her. She's talkative. She's visited him before so dropping by now could be believable. And anyway, she's got moxie."

"This man has killed two people and so your best plan is to send in a defenseless woman?" Reverend Mother glared at him.

Dougan chortled. "Defenseless? I've been with the Garda for twenty-two years and no one's ever taken my weapon, knocked me to the ground, and covered me with flour." His laugh dried up in the silence of the room. He leaned forward. "We'll protect her. I promise."

No one spoke for so long that the bells in the village clock tower chimed four times and the sky outside the window began turning a grayish pink. In an hour they would all gather in the chapel for matins.

Finally, Reverend Mother turned to Sister Agatha. "I may regret this forever, but I leave the choice with you."

"Well," Sister Agatha said, pausing and turning to Dougan. "Will I get to carry a Walther P99?"

"No," he said.

"A Sig Sauer?"

"No."

"An M9?"

"No."

"An M11?"

"Sister, please." Reverend Mother broke in.

"No concealed weapons at all?"

"None."

"Oh well," she sighed. "Can't have everything. I'll do it."

CHAPTER 43

"We can't go inside and sit down? I was hoping we could have a cup of tea and maybe some of that wonderful almond cake your house-keeper bakes," Sister Agatha said to Reggie. They stood on the flag-stone walk that led up to his front door. Reggie was bundled up in a frayed coat and flapping flannel scarf. He had lost a bit of his pear shaped physique, and looked more like an old man, short, frail. "Your apartment is always so cozy on a winter day." She had walked into the village as usual. What wasn't *usual* was the tiny listening device sewn into the bottom hem of her habit. The day had turned warm for January and she nervously pulled off her woolly hat.

"Sorry, but the landlord is fumigating my flat right now." Reggie nodded towards the panel truck parked a few meters down the street. "They're doing all the Castle View flats this morning. We've been asked to vacate for the morning which I think is blasted inconvenient, but what can one do? I was just about to pop down to the Buttered Crust and then on to the library."

"I see," she said as cheerfully as possible.

"Come with me!" he said brightly.

"Well." Her mind raced. Reggie was hardly going to break down and confess to murder over tea and scones at the Buttered Crust.

"Come on, let's get out of this wind." Reggie walked over to a blue car parked on the side of the street.

"I didn't know you had a car. Or even drove. I always see you on your bicycle."

"Just bought it a few weeks ago. Pre-owned, of course. A Honda Jazz. Do you like it?"

"It's splendid."

"The arthritis in my knee is acting up today. I thought I'd drive to the Buttered Crust."

"Right. Of course. Drive to the Tea Shop. Why not?" She would just have to make this work. *No way out but through.* Maybe get him talking in the car.

He opened the passenger side door for her, and she slid in, watching nervously as he hurried around to the other side. He suddenly seemed agile for a man with acting-up arthritis. She wished she could spot Parker or Constable Barnes. She knew they were strategically placed around the flat. How would they manage if she and Reggie were at the Buttered Crust?

Reggie sat behind the wheel of the car and stared at the controls. "I don't drive often," he said. "I'm always a bit nervous behind the wheel."

"We can just sit here and talk then. If you want."

"My gracious, no. A scone and cup of tea will do us good." She watched as Reggie hesitantly pressed the ignition button and then tapped the accelerator. The engine came to life. He reached over and pressed another button on the dash, and she heard the simultaneous click of the door locks. She reached beside her on her door but felt only the smooth surface of the top of the door. "Oh did you lock my door too?" She asked.

"Safety locks. All the newer cars have them."

"But isn't that for the children?" Sister Agatha gave a thin laugh. "I mean, I prefer to lock and unlock my own door."

"And I prefer everyone in my car to be safe." Reggie pulled out in the street in front of his flat and after a momentary pause, took off with a squeal of tires.

Sister Agatha grabbed the dashboard, glad she had remembered to click her seatbelt. "Reggie, slow down. We're only going to the Buttered Crust, remember?"

He made a hard left at the end of his street.

"Hey." She spun around in the passenger side and looked behind them. "The Buttered Crust is on Main Street. Where are you going?"

"We're going for a ride, Sister Agatha." He careened down the street, turned hard again, and in less than a minute, they entered the A55.

The safe word that Dougan had given her was 'marigold'. She was to shout 'marigold' and Parker and Constable Barnes would swoop in and pull her out. She had protested that 'marigold' was a ridiculous word. How would she work 'marigold' into a conversation?

"It's not to be worked into conversation," Dougan had told her. "You say it when conversation is irrelevant, when all is lost, and you need out." She wanted desperately to crane her neck around and see if anyone was following them. This whole operation had been planned for Reggie's front room, sitting with a cup of tea. Not in a blue Honda Jazz with safety locks, speeding north on the A55. She willed herself to stay calm. Maybe he really was just taking her for a drive. "So where are we going? I was looking forward to the Buttered Crust."

"Don't you ever feel like getting out of Pryderi? So claustrophobic, right? Everyone seems to know everything about everyone else."

"Well, small villages are like that." Sister Agatha tried to keep her voice upbeat. She couldn't let him see how nervous she was.

"But where are we going? You know, to get out of Pryderi?" Even if Parker and Constable Barnes had started to follow the car, she at least wanted Dougan to hear their destination.

"Just driving."

"But driving where?" Brown, empty fields zipped past on either side. A few crofts with smoke coming out of their chimneys and some scattered sheep. Normally, Sister Agatha would have found this landscape heartening and pastoral. But now, trapped in a car with a man who had killed two people, the desolate landscape brought her to a near panic.

She grabbed the dashboard again as Reggie spun the steering wheel, taking them flying off the highway onto a dirt drive and then into the empty field. Reggie clutched the steering wheel as the car bumped across the frozen field towards a dense wood about thirty meters away. Behind the wood, a tall, rocky hill rose up, "Rydw Fynydd" *Mountain of the Lost*. During the heyday of slate mining in Wales, the hill had held eleven mines and a labyrinth of caves. Most of the passageways had been blocked for years but a few, that ended in cathedral-like open caverns, were now guided tours for hikers and tourists. Sister Agatha had explored *Rydw Fynydd* as a Girl Guide. She remembered a pleasant picnic lunch and a presentation on the flora and fauna of caves.

Reggie turned the wheel hard and started across the frozen ground towards an abandoned barn, its roof sagging. "Wait. Stop." She didn't want to yell marigold yet, for one thing not a single car seemed to be following. What would Reggie do to her if he figured out that she had a code word and he was being recorded. Reggie jerked the car in behind the croft and hit the brakes.

Sister Agatha slammed forward. "Humph. Ow! Reggie! I don't know what you're doing but...."

He unlocked the doors to the car and was out his door before she could get her seatbelt unfastened. He yanked open her car door and reached in to grab her. She threw herself away from him across the driver's side. She had no plan except to get away.

"Marigold!" she screamed. "Marigold!" She fell forward, landing headfirst the frozen ground. She felt Reggie grab her habit skirts from behind and heard a loud rip. She kicked hard and was free. "Marigold!" Marigold!" She scrambled to her feet as Reggie came around the car. The frail, arthritic old man was gone. He moved faster than she would ever have imagined. "Marigold!"

Reggie held up the ripped piece of fabric from the bottom of her habit. "What a curious word, Sister Agatha. I believe it isn't the season for marigolds, is it? We could ask the delightful Sister Matilda."

She watched as he ripped open the hem and the listening device shaped like a small black button dropped to the frozen ground. He ground it under his heel.

She reached into her jumper pocket and grabbed her mobile. In one instant, Reggie wrestled it from her but not before she kicked him in the shin. He took a small pistol out of his coat pocket. The handle appeared to be carved out of ivory and the tarnished barrel decorated with intricate designs. An antique perhaps, but she knew that even an antique gun can do damage. In a moment she heard a ping. He had turned her mobile off. He flung it into the middle of the field. Holding the gun in one hand, he grabbed her arm with the other and began to pull her into the wood.

"Ouch!" she yelped. "If you insist on dragging me, could you drag my other arm? I've hurt that shoulder. Better yet, don't drag me at all."

The steady whine of distant sirens grew louder and she twisted around for a glimpse at the highway. Her stomach sank. A trio of police cars flew past. They had missed the dirt drive turn off. Her heart leapt though when she saw that not far behind was the convent mini-van.

"Poor Marigold. Your knights in shining armor can't find you."

Surely, they would turn around soon but if she had disappeared into that thicket of trees and the car was hidden, how *would* they find her. She dug her heels into the ground. Reggie, who was surprisingly strong for a man who had seemed aged and frail, put the cold barrel of the gun against her neck and shoved her into the trees. She took one look back. With the car hidden behind the croft, the field they had crossed appeared as empty and peaceful as any meadow in winter. Not a mark on the frozen ground. Not a sign that anyone had ever been there.

Reggie shoved her again and she fell stumbling through the wood, scrambling over a forest floor thick with branches and vines. Branches kept snapping back and hitting her in the face and she turned her ankle painfully. She took a sidelong look at Reggie. He wasn't even breathing hard. In fact, he exuded energy. How had they underestimated him so completely?

She stopped and leaned against a tree. "So why don't you just shoot me? Get it over with?" She desperately wanted to keep him talking. Distract him. Maybe she could get the gun out of his hand.

"I have no desire to shoot you, Sister Agatha." He kept the gun aimed at her. "I would prefer not to shoot you." He grabbed her arm. "Keep moving."

She yelped again. "Just let go of my arm. It's not like I could make a run for it in these woods." She looked around. Could she run for it? He would start shooting, no doubt. But could she dodge the bullets? "Why not shoot me now. Out here in these woods. No one would find me." Could she knock the gun out of his hand?

"Which is exactly where you are wrong. Disposing of a dead body is almost impossible. People don't know that. But dead bodies are nearly always found. I prefer to get rid of the body while it's still alive." He gave her his warm bishop's smile.

She stopped and stared at him. The wood was dark, but enough sunlight filtered in to see his face--the same beatific face she had loved and trusted as her Archbishop.

"Let's go." He tried to grab her arm, but she pulled away.

"Is that why you shoved Claire over a cliff and poisoned Owen? So you could get rid of the body?"

"Clever, wasn't I? I have learned the hard way, however. Do you recall The Right Reverend Albert Jones, beloved vicar of St. Mary's in Grenfell?"

"Of course. Albert was a lovely old man. A bit dotty, but kind."

"He died peacefully in his sleep."

She felt her stomach rise.

"Remember, that there had been some rumor that he over-dosed on opioids? Addicted to them, following that botched back surgery?"

"Well, yes. So?"

"And my office stifled the rumor? Because I didn't want to destroy the memory of an old man." Reggie clucked his tongue. "I also started the rumor."

Sister Agatha stopped again and stared at him. "You officiated at Albert's funeral." Her mouth had gone dry.

"I know. A beautiful service. I always do the funeral of the one I kill. You can't believe the rush it gives you. I didn't know that at first, of course. Ah well, live and learn." He said all this cheerfully. As if they were discussing football or what to order for lunch.

"And do you remember that very annoying little organist who played for years at All Saints Chapel in Portmeirion?"

"Yes," she said slowly. "She fell out of the organ loft and broke her neck. It was frightful."

"The old girl liked to practice late at night. Dreadful organist. Played every hymn with the energy of a funeral dirge. Poor thing, blood alcohol through the roof. And a near-empty bottle of Penderyn whiskey stashed in the music cabinet."

"You killed her?"

He smiled modestly. "I don't kill. I help people gently die when their usefulness is ended."

"And you're the one who decides that their usefulness is ended?"

Reggie smiled again. The gentle warm smile that had once made Sister Agatha think all was right with the world.

They suddenly stopped. The trees had thinned out and they stood at the base of *Rydw fynydd*. Weeds grew through a crisscross of rusted bars that lay on the ground and a small wooden sign with the word DANGER rotted off to the side. Through a wall of brambles, she could see a small opening in the hill.

"No Reggie, I'm not going in there. I'll take my chances with that toy gun of yours before I go into a closed-off slate mine."

"I did consider tossing you in and letting you die in there. But I have bigger plans."

"You're a horrible person, you know that? Horrible. Father Selwyn believed in you. We all did." Sister Agatha spit her words. "And all the time you were a hideous, vicious person posing as a loving priest. You killed people just to protect your stolen book. Is that why you killed Father Albert and the organist? Did they start to figure out that you were hiding the miniature gospel?"

Reggie's eyes went wide and then he laughed. "The miniature gospel? The incunabulum? It's no wonder that you've never advanced beyond a simple nun all these years. That's why you think I killed people? To protect that little book? Why, I only held on to it for the amusement factor. Every time one of you church ladies came over for tea, you would exclaim over it. *However did you do it, Archbishop? Pasteboard and glue? You're so clever, Archbishop.*" He pulled the brambles back. "And all the time, only I knew it was a priceless work of art." He grabbed the shoulder of her red jumper and shoved. "In."

Sister Agatha shoved back with all the strength she had left, and they went down in a tumble in front of the opening. She remembered getting the gun from Dougan and told herself she could do it again. She clutched for the antique firearm, but he held it just out of reach. What she really needed was a tin of flour on his head. He rolled away from her and she got to her feet. Reggie stood breathing hard, his face red, waving the gun like a flag. She dodged left and then right and had just positioned herself to execute her best rugby-tackle, when her foot hit a small log. Her ankle rolled and she went backward into the brambles.

He stood above her with the gun pointed. "You see, even a toy gun, as you called it, ensures cooperation."

She struggled to her feet, bits of briars stuck to her red jumper, pain shot through her shoulder.

"Go feet first into the opening," he said, grabbing her by her red jumper. If memory serves me, there should be a slab of limestone right inside. Sit down on it and then push off with your hands to jump down. Unless I'm wrong, you'll land in sand."

She took a deep breath and crawled in, the briars stabbing her face and hands. Inside she found herself perched on the edge of a flat rock. Reggie pushed in right behind her. "Jump," he commanded.

"I'm not jumping into the dark. If it's so safe, you go first." The next thing she knew, she felt the shove of Reggie's boot in the middle of her back and she landed about two meters below on a sandy surface. She stood slowly, in the almost pitch dark. Reggie was still up on the slab trying to pull branches over the opening.

"Shine your torch around, I want to see where I am."

He flipped the torch up and down and then in a circular motion. A large, open cave room, about the size of the chapel at Gwenafwy Abbey. Not unlike the outing with the Girl Guides. Although this walk wouldn't be ending in a picnic lunch.

Off to the left, the torch illuminated what looked like an opening that led further in. She said a quick prayer that that wasn't where they were headed. "How do you know about this place?"

"I lived out here. On a sheep farm. This mine shaft leads into a series of caves. It had closed by the time I was a teen and so I explored it. I know every inch of these caves. I barely need this torch, in fact."

"You don't think it's changed in the last fifty years? You know, rockslides? Stuff like that?"

The moist air was warmer than outside. She remembered that caves have their own climate, independent from the outside. She pulled off her scarf and shoved it in her jumper pocket. Her fingertips touched her prayer book. She felt around: silver fountain pen, *Murder on the Orient Express*, an embroidered handkerchief on loan from Sister Callwen, her Girl Guides knife. Her Murder Book was in her carryall in the car. Reggie shoved her towards the opening in the wall. Then he stepped in front and shone the torch ahead of them. Sister Agatha leaned against the wall, closed her fingers around her prayer book and let it slide silently to the ground.

"This is the trail we want. I remember it like it was yesterday."

"I'll bet you do." She ducked her head and with her heart fluttering, plunged into the near-darkness. She found that she could walk standing up, however, and when she spread her arms wide, she could touch the walls on either side with her fingertips. The barrel of the gun on her neck made her jump. They followed a path that suddenly sloped steeply downward and she lost her balance on the loose stones, pain shooting up her ankle. "What's the plan here Reggie?" She struggled to regain her balance. Maybe he would wear out and she could get the gun. He was an old man after all-- no matter how perky he was acting.

"Keep moving."

Reggie was obviously far more calculating than she had ever realized. He was not the kind, old bishop who had made a youthful mistake of theft. He was a cold-blooded killer. A psychopath. And she was alone in a cave with him. She just had to stay alive until they found her. If they found her.

. . .

"Tired? Need to rest?"

"I'm fine."

"I bet you wish you'd gotten that pace-maker the doctor recommended."

The gun poked into her neck again. She put her hands in her jumper pockets as if she were cold, and then with her right hand, she slid the silver fountain pen up into the sleeve of her jumper. Pretending to stop and tie her shoe, she let it drop into a shadow.

"You know, Reggie, if you are so worried about getting rid of my body, why not kill me here in the cave and pitch my body off a ledge?"

"Have you seen any good ledges so far?"

"No." It took effort to keep her voice steady.

Reggie snorted. "Although that wasn't my original plan, it doesn't entirely lack merit. Keep your eyes open, my dear."

They walked on, following the twisting trail, passing the openings to other trails, some of them tall and cavernous, others even narrower than the one they were on. She realized with a sinking heart that the underground cave was a maze of trails. How could anyone find her? She had dropped her girl guide's knife and the Agatha Christie. She had tried to tear pages out of it, but the paper was too loud. When he stopped and bent over coughing, she dropped her red Sister Winifred scarf. There was nothing left except the handkerchief.

"Do you really know where you're going?"

"Of course, I do. I know these caves like..."

"Yes, I know. Like it was yesterday."

The trail narrowed suddenly, and Sister Agatha felt a rising panic. Soon they were walking hunched over. Her claustrophobia which she had been able to hold at bay, threatened to consume her. The path turned sharply and in a few crouching steps, the space opened. She stood up and stretched her arms out. "Oh thank God."

Reggie flashed the torch around. The torch barely cut through the darkness, but their voices echoed as if they were in a stadium. She stumbled over to a slab of limestone that stuck out from the wall and sank down. She leaned back and closed her eyes. Her throat burned with thirst and her legs and feet ached. How long had they walked? How long since they left Pryderi in Reggie's car?

Reggie sat down on a flat rock about six feet across from her. He put the torch in his lap but kept the gun in his right hand. "Don't try anything."

"I don't have it in me to try anything. Do you really know where you are? I mean have you been in this big room before?"

Reggie hesitated a second too long, "Of course. I know right where we are."

"No, you don't. I think you're lost. You're not just a monster. You're stupid."

"I'm stupid?" He smirked. "You're the one who got in my car with me. What was your plan? To get me to tell you all about my terrible sins. While the dear deputy listened in?"

She sat in silence for a while, exhausted. Finally she spoke. "Why'd you take it?"

"Take what?" Reggie looked up absently. He had been studying the antique gun with the torch.

"The tiny gospel, what else?"

"Oh. Well, I blame the library. They left it sitting out in a display. And it was so small. It was just begging to go into a pocket. So I figured, why shouldn't the pocket be mine? The better question is, why did I keep it? I should have sold it like my other little procurements."

"You stole other things?"

"Only from rich people's homes. A silver teaspoon here, a gold snuffbox there. Things one can slip into the pocket of a cassock. No one suspects the Archbishop."

"That's terrible."

"Is it? Or is it terrible that some people have everything, and others have nothing?"

"I wouldn't say you have nothing."

"There was a time when I had nothing." His voice had a bitter edge.

"When you were an orphan?"

"How do you know that?" His head snapped back.

"Father Selwyn."

Reggie snorted. "Selwyn."

"But you were adopted, right?"

"If you call *indentured servitude,* adoption. Then yes, I was adopted. I was taken in by a farming family who thought a ten year old boy would be the perfect work hand. They were brutal. Today they'd be thrown in jail."

"I'm sorry." To her surprise, she felt a tiny bit sorry for him. "What happened?"

His modest smile returned. "One night, the barn mysteriously caught fire and burned to the ground. No one could prove anything, but they sent me back to the orphanage anyway-- that's what we called it in those days. Not that my life improved. Draconian headmistress. Always a smile for visitors, but then for the children...." Reggie's voice broke. "Ah well," he cleared his throat. "Her cruelty came back to her in spades, you might say."

Sister Agatha was afraid to ask. "You burnt the dormitory down?"

"No. Interestingly, over time, the headmistress developed all sorts of dreadful ailments. Her hair fell out, poor thing. Her face got all puffy, bruises all over her neck and arms. Then one day, she cut herself, by accident. Bled to death on her kitchen floor."

"Rat poison?"

"How did you guess? Tiniest bit. Builds up in the system over time. You see, one of my jobs was to take the headmistress her tea tray every morning. My other job? Worked for the gardener and had a key to the garden shed." He shrugged and gave an apologetic smile.

. . .

"You don't feel guilty about any of this? Theft, murder, burning down people's barns?"

"Why should I? I only steal things that no one notices. And I only kill people no one notices." He paused and looked off into the darkness. "The barn and the headmistress-- the motivation for those actions must be obvious even to you. Now, old Albert, was a dreary curmudgeon whose endless sermons and weedy little voice was a drain on that lovely little church. Not only were they better off without him, they barely missed him! And the organist was atrocious. Deaf as a post! Everyone wanted her gone, but they didn't have the heart to sack her. I just did for them what they couldn't do for themselves."

"They didn't want her dead!"

Reggie continued as if she had not spoken. "And Owen. Good chap, back in the day. But he overstepped his bounds."

"You pretended to be his friend." She fought down a wave of sickness. To think she had held Reggie in such regard! Always hale-fellow-well-met. If she had trusted him and he betrayed her, who else was not to be trusted? "You gave him arsenic!"

"And kudos to you, Sister Agatha. How very clever the way you figured that out. Perhaps your finest moment. I did indeed mix green paint scrapings from the miniature gospel into his tea. We both were jolly brilliant there, wouldn't you say? Well done to us!" Reggie let the gun dangle from his hand as he gazed at her in silence for a long moment. "I can tell this revelation about me bothers you."

She cringed. He was using his warm, consoling vicar voice.

"Think of it this way, dear Sister. The people I kill are like the things I steal. No one was making any use of them to start with. I ask you, does Justin Welby need another gold and diamond encrusted tie clip?"

"You stole from the Archbishop of Canterbury?"

"A weekend at Lambeth Castle gets tedious. One looks for excitement where one can find it. To this day, I don't think he knows it's gone." Reggie shifted the gun to his other hand. "And like old Welby's tie clip, the individuals that I kill are rarely missed. They are expendable."

"What about Claire? She was in the prime of her life. She wasn't expendable."

Reggie sighed. "Claire was a mistake, I admit it. Arrogant girl. Barged into my flat demanding to see the little gospel. Wanted to write an article for that ridiculous paper, *The Church Times*. I put her off, but I could tell she was determined. Anyway, I saw her later at the cliffs. I take an evening constitutional every day and I try to mix it up as to where I walk. That day I chose the trail along the cliff. Came right up on her as she was taking one of those obnoxious selfies. Knock and the door will be opened. Seek and ye shall find. What can I say?"

"So it was your scarf that showed up on the selfie photo?"

"Indeed. My burgundy Sister Winifred scarf."

"You dropped it then, that evening at the cliff? After you pushed her?"

Reggie gave a sheepish grin. "Sister, I have something to tell you that you may not take kindly to."

"Oh really? Because the last few hours have been so enjoyable?" She forced her voice into its snarkiest tone. The forced sarcasm was giving her a tiny bit of strength. Anyway, it was either be cheeky or burst into tears.

"I have been, as the young people say, *messing* with you." He chortled and leaned back, stretching his short legs. "I've been dying to tell you everything. May I?"

Sister Agatha stared at him. "You mean you haven't killed all these people? You were making that all up to scare me?"

"Oh gracious, no. I killed everyone I told you about. And a few others. No, I noticed right away how earnest you were about solving Claire's murder. Which I thought quaint, if not curious.

And then I heard that you fancy yourself an amateur detective. Delightful! A nun who writes crime and solves crime. Or at least has convinced herself that she does. Splendid, I thought. So extraordinarily *BBC*. So *Father Brown*. What an amusing fantasy world to live in. I envy you for your delightful diversion."

"It's not a diversion. I am a writer. And I am an amateur detective. I figured out that you killed Owen." She hated the defensiveness that had crept into her voice.

"Brava!" He stood and with the gun still in one hand gave her a sweeping bow. "Sister Agatha cracks the case!"

She wondered if she could charge him and get the gun. He'd probably shoot her before she could tackle him.

"You see, I saw you spying on us that night when Owen and I let ourselves into the cottage. I thought that annoying girl might have started to write *The Church Times* article and so I wanted to remove anything that could connect her to me."

"You saw me that night?"

"Indeed. And you looked so charmingly furtive standing there in the shadows. Owen and I had quite a chuckle about it on the drive home. I will admit-- it was then that I hit upon the enchanting idea of providing you with a true mystery. So to amuse myself, I planted clues for you to discover. The scarf, the green rucksack in Owen's car. It was the most fun I've had in quite a while."

Sister Agatha stared at him.

"Oh my! I'm forgetting the best one!" Reggie sat up, leaning forward. "The key in the cake! Oh that one was rich. You should have seen your face. I had been in the kitchen talking to that pretty Sister Gwenydd, when I realized I still had the blasted key in my trouser pocket. She turned her back and I pushed it into the cake dough! Clever! *The Key in the Cake*. Now tell me, Sister, could anything be more *Nancy Drew* than that?" He threw his head back and laughed. "Oh, it's been fun. I shall miss watching you and that young deputy scurry around. Your late night meetings, your secret murder club, jotting things down in your little notebook!" Reggie took a breath and looked at her, his head cocked. "Alas though it's almost over, I have only one final amusing task left."

Sister Agatha thought that if she had not been so thirsty, exhausted, and aching, she might have been the tiniest bit embarrassed. *The Key in the Cake.* It even sounded like the title of a Nancy Drew book. "Last amusing thing? Kill me, perhaps?"

"Better. I am going to create one last final mystery, the kind you thrive on. Although it will have almost no good clues. Ask me the title of my mystery." He leaned forward again and grinned.

Was he more articulate than an hour ago? Giddy almost?

"Alright, I'll just tell you. Here's the title.... wait for it...The Death of Sister Agatha!" He sat up straight, still grinning. "Catchy, isn't it?"

She stared at him, unspeaking. She was done with his games.

"Here's the plot-- you and I are going to follow the trail we've been on for another 30 minutes or so. And guess where we will come out?" He waited. "Guess!

She sat in silence.

"You're not being any fun. We'll come out at an opening to the sea."

Her heart leapt. Were they really that close to the sea? "This isn't a sea cave, is it?"

He nodded, grinning.

She didn't know if she believed him or not. If the cave did open out to the water, she stood a chance of escaping. "But are you sure you know the way out? You didn't seem to expect to find this big cave room."

"I told you, I played in these mines as a youngster."

"I thought you were in the orphanage developing your skills as a thief and murderer?"

He stood and pointed the gun at her. "The Death of Sister Agatha!" he yelled. "Don't you want out how it ends? We'll follow the trail out and when we get to the opening, my yacht will be waiting for us."

"You don't have a yacht. How did you pay for it? Stolen tie clips?"

"I didn't just steal tie clips!" he said petulantly. "You know how everyone thought I was a lovely person, but bad with finances?"

"Yes."

"A brilliant ruse. I embezzled. And I invested. And now, I'm a wealthy man."

"You stole from the good people of the church?"

"I like to think of myself as an opportunist. Anyway, my yacht will pick us up. And we will head out to the Atlantic and when we get far enough out, you will take a little swim--while wrapped up in a body bag with a cement block or two. Once we bid each other good-bye, I will head to the Caribbean where I have several very healthy offshore accounts. And under my new alias, I plan to live happily ever after."

She could make her getaway while they boarded the yacht. She could jump into the water and swim. She would do *something* that did not involve a body bag and cement blocks.

"The Death of Sister Agatha will be the perfect mystery. *Sister Agatha disappears without a trace.* By the time deputy-dear figures out that you and I went down into the cave, if he figures it out at all, we will be out to sea. They will tear this entire cave apart. But they will never find you. Never! You see what I have constructed? I have written the perfect mystery." He looked up brightly. "I should have been a novelist."

Sister Agatha snorted. "Hardly. Anyway, you left something out."

"Oh? A missing plot point? Do tell."

"You killed Claire, right?"

"Yes." Reggie gave her a dark look. He reminded her of a toddler. Exuberant one minute, then tired and sulky the next.

"Well, I hate to burst your little ego-induced bubble, but there is no Claire." She paused for dramatic effect.

He looked at her, his head cocked, an inquisitive smile as if she had said, "there's no pudding with dinner."

"*Claire* was the undercover name of Special Agent Kate Darcy. A detective and officer of the *Garda Síochána*. She worked for the National Bureau of Criminal Investigation and she was investigating the theft of the little gospel from Trinity Library missing since 1964. And you killed her. You killed a member of the *Garda Síochána*. I may be a wanna-be detective with a delightful diversion, but you took down a member of the Irish Guard. And I think anyone would agree that those guys don't do well when one of their own is killed." Even in the dim light, she could see the color drain from Reggie's face. "Oh. And that guy, Peter? You know, absent-minded professor? Also undercover. Detective Sergeant Dougan Hennessey. He's in Pryderi to find the person who killed his fellow officer."

"Now wait just a minute, I..." Reggie stood. "I don't believe you." His voice peevish. "You're making this up to throw me off."

"You didn't kill some *expendable* person this time, Reggie." Sister Agatha rose to her feet, daggers of pain shot through her shoulder and her ankle, but she felt a modicum of strength coming back. "The Garda will search you out and they will find you. And may God have mercy on your soul when they do." And with that, she lunged forward and rugby-tackled Reggie.

CHAPTER 44

The strange thing was, when she had tackled Dougan the night before, she found herself lying on top of him. When she tackled Reggie, he vanished. Still lying on the cave floor, she heard two far away thumps and then a moment later, a distant splash. She grabbed the torch from where he dropped it and while still on her knees, she pointed it towards where he should have been lying. She screamed and went backwards on her knees as fast as she could and then crawled on all fours to the granite slab. Her heart pounded in her head. She knelt on the floor of the cave, clinging to the stone slab, her forehead pressed against the cool rock. They hadn't realized it in the pitch black, but they had been sitting next to a ledge with a harrowing drop off. She had been an inch away from going over herself. One false step, and she could have... she choked back a rise in her throat. When she finally could breathe properly, she crawled slowly towards the ledge and with the torch, peered over. The weak light shone on the surface of the water far below.

She pushed back several feet and lay on the floor, focused on breathing. Finally she sat up. "Reggie!" she called and waited. Nothing but her own voice echoing back to her. She called again and again. Finally, she said his name quietly, this time almost a question. She shone the torch around. She didn't see the gun. It must have gone over with him.

She crawled back to the slab bench. Reggie had said they were very close to the sea cave opening, but then he didn't seem to know the cave as well as he thought he did. Should she set out? She shone the light at the path at the far end. Was that the opening that led to the sea? What if she were only a short walk away? A short walk to the sea breeze touching her face. To the crash of waves. To the sun glinting off the water. Or what if she wasn't, and she became even more hopelessly lost--entangled in a web of trails? Then she would be lost forever. They always told you in Girl Guides that if you got lost, never leave the trail.

She clicked off the torch to conserve its battery and the pitch black fell over her like a heavy blanket. She leaned against the wall at her back and fought the urge to cry. She had never been so desperately alone in her life. Would she ever see the people she loved again? Father Selwyn, Reverend Mother, Sister Callwen, Sister Gwenydd? She took a shuddering breath and buried her head in her hands. As she huddled there in the dark, she remembered the story that Reverend Mother told them in chapel only two nights ago, the story of *Men of Harlech*. The bravery of the Welshman, Chief of Security, at the World Trade Center. He never gave up. He fought on and on and the whole time singing *Men of Harlech*. A song of valor, of courage, of Wales.

She began to hum the melody. And then, as the words came to her, she rose to her feet, her voice lifting into the darkness.

> *Men of Harlech,*
> *Hear the trumpet sounding*
> *Forward ever, backward never*
> *This proud foe astounding*

The marching beat and the inspiring verses echoed off the cave walls and they brought her a renewed spirit if only for a moment. She took a breath and sang on. Soon, with all the echoes upon echoes, it seemed as if the cave were singing with her. She paused. The cave *was* singing with her. And in parts! A bass, a tenor, another tenor! She stopped altogether and listened, tears falling down her face.

> *Fight for father, sister, mother*
> *Each is bound to each as brother*
> *With his faith in one another!*

"Sister Agatha! Sister Agatha!" came the voice of Constable Barnes. "Stay right where you are. We're coming!"

CHAPTER 45

The nuns, young and old, sat in stunned silence around the warming room fire, as Sister Agatha retold her long story of Reggie's secret life of theft and murder.

"I can barely believe it," Reverend Mother said. She sat on one side of Sister Agatha and would not let go of her hand.

"Believe it," Dougan said. "There was a boat waiting at the mouth of a sea cave about a mile north of where we found Sister Agatha. Not quite a yacht, I think our Reggie was prone to exaggeration, but it would have gotten you out to the Atlantic. Although, he might have been more lost in that cave than he thought he was. The captain gave it all up when Her Majesty's Coast Guard boarded him while a MH-65 Dolphin hovered above." Dougan paused. "The lads found a body bag, ropes, and cement blocks. Reggie had paid a couple of thugs to go out to sea with him and well...."

Reverend Mother shuddered. "I cannot believe I let you do this, Sister Agatha. I should resign my position as leader of this convent. I am not fit to serve."

"Nonsense," Sister Callwen said, placing a hand on Reverend Mother's shoulder. "Who would have ever thought this of our

Reggie? A man who could barely match his socks or remember what day it was? He fooled a lot more people than just you."

"I should have put a tracker on that listening device. I underestimated him shamefully. You're not to blame, Reverend Mother," Dougan said. He shook his head and exchanged a glance with Constable Barnes. "If anyone should resign, it's me."

"Don't be so hard on yourself, laddie," Constable Barnes said. "Mistakes were made. By all of us! No way around that. Although," he reached over and slapped Parker on the back. "If there is a hero in this story-- other than Sister Agatha, of course-- it's young Parker here. We flew past the place Reggie turned into the field and when we circled back it was as if you had vanished into thin air. I nearly panicked myself. If it hadn't been for Parker's quick thinking, we'd still be searching."

Parker nodded. "I had noticed that Reggie's Ford was leaking oil the other day and told him to fix it before he parked on the village streets again. So we looked for fresh oil on the highway, found a bit and then followed it into the field. We found the car in short order, but then spent an hour searching in that wood. It was nearly dark when we spotted the bramble bush full of red wool. We went into the cave on the double, only to find that it was a labyrinth." Parker paused and took a sip from his wine glass. "We were about to despair when I found the prayer book." The three men exchanged a glance. "You can't imagine what it felt like, to see that prayer book lying there."

This time, Constable Barnes didn't slap Parker on the back, he squeezed his shoulder. "Good lad," he rumbled and then took a very large handkerchief out of his shirt pocket and blew his nose.

Father Selwyn, as tired as Sister Agatha had ever seen him, stepped in from the kitchen. "I've been on the phone with Archbishop Davies. He's calling a meeting of bishops." He shook his head. "The fallout from this will be tremendous."

"Would everyone please stop being so gloomy," Sister Agatha said cheerfully as she shifted the ice bag on her shoulder. "I'm not in a cave! A murderer and thief has been stopped! And Sister Gwenydd tells me that you recovered the miniature gospel."

"We did," Dougan replied. "A representative from Trinity Library is arriving tomorrow to take it back."

A voice piped up. It was Sister Samantha. "Sister Agatha, I'm so glad you're okay." Grateful nods all around from the young nuns. "But could I ask you.... you suspected me at first, didn't you?"

Before she could answer, Sister Juniper's clear voice rang out, "And me?"

"Well," Sister Agatha started. Reverend Mother interrupted her. "Don't let it bother you, Sisters. She suspected me as well. Didn't you, Sister Agatha?"

"Oh dear," she said. "I was wrong all around. I couldn't have been more wrong. Although, Reverend Mother, you kept going for walks and not telling where you had been. You must admit, that is unlike you."

"I was checking on Bartimaeus. And I didn't want you to worry."

Sister Agatha felt her eyes fill. She blinked hard. "Well, to all those that I have ever offended with my sleuthing," She turned to Dougan. "Or my rugby tackles. I made a blanket apology."

"Sister, without your sleuthing and rugby tackles, a murderer would still be on the loose," Dougan said.

"Hear, Hear!" Father Selwyn said, raising his glass. They all raised their glasses. "Hear! Hear!" Everyone was laughing and congratulating Sister Agatha and Parker when the door opened and Ben Holden, just home from the Yorkshires, stood in the door frame without speaking. The room fell silent.

"Sister Agatha," he said. "You better come to the pony barn. I think it's about over for the old boy."

CHAPTER 46

She knelt in the straw next to Bartimaeus and stroked the silky fur around his ears. His sides heaved as he labored to breathe, and she noticed for the first time how his ribs now showed through. "Bartimaeus," she whispered, leaning down. His eyes flickered open and shut again.

Father Selwyn sat in the straw across from her, the pony between them. He pulled his prayer book out of his cassock pocket and waited.

"Dougan," she said without looking up.

"Right here, my friend," he answered. He and Constable Barnes and Parker had followed her out to the pony barn along with Reverend Mother, Sister Gwenydd, and Sister Callwen. "Are you really a horse man, or was that just part of your undercover identity?"

"I really am a horse man. My family has raised horses in Ireland for generations. And I truly do believe that Shetlands are the grandest of the ponies."

"What do you think, then? Do you think...the end is here? He's not just having a lie-down." Her voice caught and tears dripped onto the pony's mane. Sister Callwen passed a handkerchief down to her. Sister Agatha wiped her eyes and twisted around so she could see Dougan.

"No, Sister. He's not just having a lie-down," Dougan answered.

Sister Gwenydd began to sob and leaned against Reverend Mother who put her arms around her. Sister Callwen held her hand to her mouth, but kept her eyes, filled with tears, on Sister Agatha.

"Is he suffering?"

"I'm afraid he is," Dougan answered, his voice quiet.

Ben Holden spoke up. "I called Tupper a half hour ago and he's been waiting in his truck. I'll go and bring him. If you want me to."

She nodded, unable to speak.

The crowd in the pony barn made a path and Tupper Ross came forward and knelt next to Sister Agatha. "This first injection will make him relax and all of his pain will go away. Then with the second one, he'll pass."

Sister Agatha choked with sobs. She leaned forward and buried her face in the pony's mane. Father Selwyn put one hand on her shoulder and wiped his eyes with the sleeve of his cassock.

With the first injection Bartimaeus's harsh breathing became slow and gentle. In fact, for a moment, she thought he seemed a bit like he could be the old Bartimaeus again, as if he could still trot over to the fence and toss his head in the morning breeze.

Tupper reached into his bag.

"Wait, don't give him the last one just yet," she managed to say. She cleared her throat, took a deep breath, and placed her hand on the pony's head. "Bartimaeus, you were never anything but strong and courageous and glorious your entire life. You were truly everything that God wants all of us to be. And now...and now...you shall return to the One who created you." She stroked the silky fur around his ears one last time and then nodded to Tupper.

In a few moments, Father Selwyn began the prayers of the dead.

As she sat back, listening to the ancient words from the Anglican Prayer book, she gazed around the barn. Such good friends, she thought. Such very good friends, indeed.

Father Selwyn closed the prayer book and from the back arose Constable Barnes's rumbling bass soon joined by Parker's tenor and Sister Callwen's soprano. Then Sister Gwenydd caught the tune with her wandering contralto. And as Reverend Mother stepped forward, smiling through her tears, she helped Sister Agatha to her feet. Clasping hands, they joined in.

Hold Thou Thy cross before my closing eyes
Shine through the gloom and point me to the skies
Heaven's morning breaks, and earth's vain shadows flee
In life, in death, O Lord, abide with me.

ACKNOWLEDGMENTS

I'm enormously grateful for the encouragement of my agent, Stephany Evans, who has always believed in me, my writing, and Sister Agatha. Stephany, thank you from the bottom of my writer's heart.

Barbara Melosh, my writing partner and colleague in ministry who read the whole thing more than once and helped solve every problem from punctuation to plot. And thank you for being such a good person to laugh with.

Jane Gardner, my first writing partner in life and always available to tell me to keep going when I feel like quitting and that includes more than writing. I can't wait to see what your writing future holds.

Dr. Anne Nafziger, who was always ready to discuss poison, drowning, heart attacks, and anything else that might mean murder.

Eric Huard, invaluable expert on British cars.

Jerri Williams, retired FBI agent, the murder would never have been solved without you.

Kayla Lighter and Keri Barnum, you are an amazing team.

A huge thanks to Ayesha Pande Literary for making this book possible.

Finally, my deepest thanks of all to my husband Don, the source of all magic in my life. And when I told him that I was emptying the walk-in closet so I could turn it a writing space, he painted the walls, carried in my desk, and found a new place for his shoes. Thank you, Don.

ABOUT THE AUTHOR

Jane Willan is the author of the heartwarming yet murderous Sister Agatha and Father Selwyn Mystery series. Writing clerical mysteries comes naturally to Jane since she is the pastor of a white steepled church in a small New England town and divides her time between composing sermons and dreaming up murder—seldom letting the two overlap. She does her best writing in a converted walk-in closet at the church parsonage with just enough room for one desk, two dogs, and a Royal Manual typewriter. Jane likes to transport her readers to the rural countryside of North Wales where lush fields are dotted with sheep, church bells chime the hour, and the tea is always ready to pour.

Learn more about Jane and her writing life at www.janewillan.com. While you are there, be sure to sign up for Jane's newsletter and she will send you the recipe for Sister Gwenydd's delicious King's Cake featured in *Abide With Me!*

Made in the USA
Middletown, DE
29 November 2020